The Lost History of Redwyn

William Jay

Lancaster Books

Publisher's Cataloging in Publication

Jay, William, 1956-
    The lost history of Redwyn / William Jay
    p. cm.
    1-881271-50-1

    1. Romances, English--Fiction. 2. Adventure and adventurers--Fiction.   I. Title.

    PS3560.A37J3 1992   [Fic]
                            QBI92-434

            92-071456
    Library of Congress Catalog Card Number.

Printed in the United States of America

First Edition

1 2 3 4 5 6 7 8 9 10

EDITED BY MARY ST. JAMES
BOOK DESIGN BY DEBRA LEE SKORA

FOR SMALL BEAR

THE LOST HISTORY OF REDWYN
Contents

Legend holds that after the fall of King Arthur, around 500 A.D., Merlin recovered the powerful sword *Excaliber*. One version of the legend tells that the sword was given back to the Lady of the Lake. Another says Merlin hid *Excaliber* in an enchanted forest, within the interior of a tree.

"...I the Lord build the ruined places, and plant that that was desolate:" - Ezekiel

BOOK I

The Autumn Prince

Chapter 1
Roads

The early evening sun was orange over the faraway hills of Cumberland, and from the fork at Grinmere the pilgrim's path split off and ran ahead like a pale ribbon through the olive hills and brown pastures of August. An old road ran straight through the forest, Grinmere, the place where the Roman conquests had stopped. But legends of the forest's wild inhabitants and the bloody battles they had fought with the Romans had left the old road untraveled, its arbored portals, dim and green, deepening into a blackness that no one dared enter.

Earlier in the day the road that avoided the forest had flowed as if it were a river, bearing small bands of pilgrims upon the yellow earth of its meandering course. From the clearing at Grinmere it was possible to watch them for a long time after they passed by, moving off into the distance, shrinking to dark clusters raising tiny clouds of dust, vanishing and reappearing again as the road meandered between the hillsides, until they shrank away to nothing and were gone.

But now the road was vacant beyond the clearing, running emptily beneath the tinted sun. Now it was too late to go on and reach an inn or the town of Solway before dusk. So weary bands of pilgrims, their faces red from the sun, were leaving the road to overnight at the Grinmere fork.

The first campfires burned in the cool green shade near the river, and the pilgrims' voices carried notes of excitement in spite of a long dusty day spent in travel. For this was the last overnight before the fair at Solway, and for weeks now while travelling on the roads and at night around the campfires, veterans of the fair had told of the exquisite goods to be found there. They spoke of cloths in rich reds, blues, deep greens, and pale lavenders; of cloth from Spain, studded with jewels of colored glass. They told of pearls, silver and leather goods, and fine wines. Some spoke of practical things, such as wool from the highlands of Scotland, oil, tar, and black-smiths to do work. Even for nobles or the wealthiest of merchants there would be things to buy, they said— spices and silks from the farthest eastern corners of the world.

The veterans told of great bargains that had been struck, of goods brought back to villages and peddled lucratively. A few peasants had bought their freedom this way. Others had become rich merchants or made profits enough to buy a wagon or a flock of sheep. Tonight especially the pilgrims would sit around the fires and their eyes would glow and they would listen. For although the stories were by now familiar, on the eve of arrival at the fair they took on a note of prophecy, tempting the weary travellers to dream of new and brighter days.

So the pilgrims of commerce made camps, built fires, cooked salted meats on the ends of long sticks, and murmurs of anticipation stirred the air. Water was hauled up from the river in animal skins, and two women paused with their dripping vessels to discuss in deep seriousness some aspect of the coming day. More pilgrims arrived; acquaintances made on the road were renewed. For on this, the last night before the fair, bread was broken freely and wine shared with a generous and comfortable ease.

Their shadows stretched behind them, a few late-arrivals

limped into camp with the half-step characteristic of blistered feet. They were welcomed by raucous cheers and raised wine skins and beckoning to sit at a host of different fires. With the approaching sunset the last sorties struck into the surroundings for firewood and foraged along the riverbanks and in the dismal tangle of cedar trees that grew around the dangerous bog. The wood gatherers gleaned from the shallow hardwoods that bordered Grinmere, and a few brave souls even ventured to the forest's edge, to peer for a moment into its enchanted depths. An unnatural sound or an owl gliding between the ancient trees was enough to send them hastening back to the clearing, perhaps to tell of the adventure under the calming influence of some other pilgrim's wine.

The last handful of stragglers arrived: a woman limping on a crutch with an adolescent boy beside her, a fat man carrying a reluctant goat. Three old wives in a donkey cart showed signs of relief as they spotted the camp, for it was close upon the dusk now and well known that there were dangers on the road after dark. Not only were there wood demons and wolves as always, but highwaymen, who had made a pilgrimage of their own, to spend their days in the taverns and bathhouses and their nights practicing the vile art of waylay with their swords.

At the day's end the sunlight blazed into the deep ruby that is so characteristic of sunsets in the northern climes, then failed to violet, and the trees began to melt into their shadows. As the camp settled, a few children found each other and ran hurry-scurry between the campfires, and the high, hollow fluting of a minstrel band lent fabric to the air, into which the stories of the evening could be woven.

And it was then, at dusk, that a large yellow wagon creaked into camp. It skirted along the border of the clearing and then turned toward the river. There were alchemist's symbols painted sloppily on the planked sides of its box-like enclosure, and the dark horse pulling it was lathered and foaming at the mouth.

A matronly woman pointed and remarked to her husband how lovely she thought the wagon's horse was. The husband paid no attention to her remark, but a big monk overheard and looked to see where she was pointing. Even in the twilight it was obvious to him, the monk, that the horse was no draft animal, but rather a stallion, costly and bred for speed. The monk's black eyes widened beneath his thick eyebrows, and he followed the wagon's progress until it disappeared behind some trees.

Chapter 2
Nymph

The wagon's driver had chosen this time to enter, for he knew that as the dusk fell the pilgrims would avoid the riverbanks and stay close to the security of their fires. Belief in water sprites– lonely goddesses who lured men to drowning so as to have the amorous company of their souls– would keep the pilgrims from the river. His thin, muscular face smiled. Because of certain difficulties in his past he had done much swimming at night, but the amorous company had always come before the water, not after it.

That was Venice, he thought; and he remembered that almost no one had been concerned with phantasms or wood elves there. Venetians were busy with commerce and shipping ventures, travels, courtly pleasures, and the intrigues of love. But now on a wooded trail darkening into the purple translucence of a Scottish nightfall, his mind involuntarily went back to Edinburgh, to the superstitions that all the people held there and the bond it made between them, and he remembered those he, too, had believed in when he had lived there as a little boy.

Near the end of the trail the driver's hands flexed back on the reins. But the horse had already sensed the river in front of it and refused the command, quickening its pace. The driver jerked hard on the reins and shouted for the horse to stop, but it started down the riverbank. He jumped down quickly and pulled the pin from the harness tongue. The horse kept walking and splashed into the river. The driver threw his back against the wagon to brake it from rolling further down the bank, wedged his shoulders tight, and stuck his legs out in front of him for leverage.

He was young, only five years past twenty, with the long powerful build of a good swimmer. Thick blond hair fell richly about his shoulders, and his shoulders were strong and hard against the wagon planks. His face was angular and handsome enough, eyes very pale green and seemingly hungry for whatever they fixed upon, their conspicuous lack of pigment lending a vacant, wolf-like intensity.

Unseen to him a young woman was bathing just below the rapids, upstream. She saw the horse sloshing toward her and moved out of its path. Then she saw the driver straining against the wagon and submerged enough to cover her naked breasts.

The driver grunted and shoved harder, moving the wagon a little up the steep bank. The young woman was submerged so that only her head remained above the water. Her eyes flashed luminous grey as she watched him and her black hair streamed in the dark current. The driver was panting, resting to be able to move the wagon again. As his eyes fell upon her– her lips thinned to an expression of indignant rage.

"Call your horse back!" she commanded.

"It should be obvious that he doesn't obey me."

"Then turn your head!"

He did so and the wagon slipped. He struggled to regain his footing, gravel loosening under his heel and falling into the river. Then he found solid ground again and looked down at her and said, "Please, come help me with this wagon."

"Swine!" she yelled, "You...swine!"

The horse came up in back of her, sniffing cautiously, and

then it snorted in the water just behind her head. She lurched forward into the current and was swept a few yards downstream. Her hand caught a partially submerged tree limb and, grasping it, she was able to raise her head above the water.

"Help me!" she cried.

"I cannot!" he called back.

"Swine!" she cried, her voice half-drowned by the current's wash. "Mongrel swine!"

He groaned and with a single effort pushed the wagon half-way up the riverbank.

The young woman began pulling herself toward shore along the tree limb. "Are your eyes shut?" she called, nearly to the shore, floating on her stomach, white buttocks awash above the surface like smooth river stones.

"Yes!" he shouted.

"I am going to leave now," she called.

"Yes, go," he yelled.

The wagon slipped a bit as he craned his neck to watch. She emerged from the water and pulled herself up the riverbank using grasses and exposed tree roots for anchors. She reached the top of the bank and stood erect, glowing white in the dusk, flipped the wet hair against her back then parted the foliage in front of her and disappeared.

He saw a rock sticking half-way out of the clay and pried it loose with his foot and kicked it under the wagon wheel. The horse was looking at him from the river. The driver looked toward the foliage for the naked girl but she was really gone now and he was glad that no one else had seen him.

He hitched the horse and backed the wagon up the river bank then climbed into the seat and drove into the woods, to stay out of sight until nightfall. He steered toward the camp but smelled smoke from the pilgrim's fires and turned further into the trees to skirt around the clearing. The woods grew dark and the trees were towering above him. The horse stopped in front of a big boulder that was laden with an emerald covering of moss.

He realized he must be at the edge of Grinmere, the ancient forest, and slapped the horse quickly with the reins and turned back toward the clearing. The wagon rolled silently over the soft forest floor, then hooves struck solid ground and he saw that he had crossed onto the Roman road. To his left the road tunnelled into the forest's depths. To his right, and much further than he thought it would be, the firelight from the clearing shown through the arbored portal and relieved him. He slapped the horse with the reins again, turned toward the clearing, and drove until he could distinguish individual pilgrims at their fires. He would wait here, he thought, stopped and climbed down. He would wait here until nightfall and then emerge from Grinmere to perform his magic show.

Chapter 3
Sorcery &
Damnation

He had changed into a long black robe that was embroidered with the same symbols of alchemy that were on the wagon, and now stood waiting alongside the horse.

It seemed the light was fading rapidly. Behind him the road disappeared only a few yards away. The campfires were burning more brightly in the clearing. He stood close to the stallion, patted it, then climbed onto the seat and looked around the wagon, behind him. He felt chilled and turned back toward the clearing quickly and fixed his eyes upon the campfires there. The horse started moving, and the driver whispered, "Yes," as if in agreement with it, and rattled the reins to go a little faster.

He watched the fires growing larger as he drove, the peasant's faces becoming more distinct, redder and less intelligent looking as they stared into the fires with blank expressions. Under the portal at the forest's edge the firelight reflected on the shiny oak leaves that were moving slightly in the breeze. The Magician slapped the horse hard with the reins and the wagon lurched forward from the forest into the firelight, pounding hoofbeats and creaking wood, and several pilgrims pointed to it and started from their seats.

The Magician turned right quickly and drove a little further, stopped, jumped down and tethered the horse. He hurried to the rear door of the wagon, opened it, and climbed in.

Inside, there were three lamps burning with low blue flames, and the rest of the apparatus glowed in front of him. It was a flame-throwing apparatus of his own design, consisting of a kettle of boiling lard connected to the base of a bellows by a thick tube; the bellows sat on the floor of the wagon and from its spout the lard would be pumped through two narrower, jointed tubes and pass over a pair of hand-held lamps.

His heart beat faster as he prepared. The pilgrims were assembling outside and he could hear them murmuring about Grinmere. Then someone recognized the symbols on the wagon and shouted, "Magician! He's a magician!" and the crowd responded with a loud, "Ahhh!"

He finished running the tubes through his robe sleeves, removed a conical hat from the shelf and put it on. He picked up the tiny igniter lamps, cupping them carefully with his hands, took a deep breath and pulled out a peg that released the side panel of the wagon. The panel fell down with a loud "crack!" The pilgrims jumped startledly away.

The Magician stood there with his conical hat, regarding them from the wagon with an aloof, supernatural gaze. A few came closer and stared with uncertain faces. Then he lifted his eyes and raised his arms slowly, becoming trance-like in aspect and, unseen to the pilgrims, began to pump the bellows of the apparatus with his feet.

For a moment it seemed as if he were simply entranced, but then suddenly his head snapped level. He shouted, "The flames of hell!" and two plumes of fire burst explosively from the robe sleeves of his outstretched arms.

The blue flames roared and billowed above the heads of the pilgrims. Women screamed and men cowered, shouting oaths to God as the fiery vapors hissed directly over them but then, just as suddenly, vanished into the night sky.

The whole crowd looked up, most of them crouching, and just as they started to raise themselves, the Magician yelled, "The flames of hell!" And the blue fires shot over their heads again, and curled and hissed. He heard screams from some of the audience, but kept pumping, making the fires dance, criss-crossing the streams in mid air, increasing the pressure to make the fire shoot twenty, thirty feet over the crowd, until at last he shouted, "Out!" and the flames just curled into the sky and disappeared.

Some burning oil had dribbled onto his cuff and in full view of the horrified crowd he flapped his arm theatrically against his side to extinguish it.

Then it was silent, uncertain. After a long moment one man started clapping. The whole crowd followed in loud applause.

The Magician raised his arms and protested, "Please do not applaud me, for I am a cursed man. I bear a burden which no mortal should bear. I have been charged with the very flames of hell!" And as he shouted "hell!" straightened his arms and the flames burst from his robe sleeves, but for an instant, curled up over their heads and disappeared.

Their eyes stayed fixed on him now as he lifted one arm slowly to remove his conical hat. He said, "It is a sad charge indeed." And as the crowd drew up nearer to listen, a shrill voice rang out:

"He's not old enough to know magic! He's a cheat!"

It was an old woman who said it. He found her in the crowd. She had a face like a withered squash, and he pointed down at her feet and said, "Old hag! if your feet were roasted by hell's fire, then would you believe!" The pilgrims made a loud, "Ooooh." Some of them were smiling at the remark.

The Old Woman pushed her way toward him. She squinted and leered and showed her rotten teeth. "Hell's fire, eh?" She spat. "There's my measure of it."

"This is trouble," the Magician thought; for he knew he

recognized her from somewhere.

Just then a hawknosed, emaciated man stepped up, shoved the old woman aside, and raised his hands to the Magician. He had prominent front teeth and a half-lidded expression that made him seem like he was talking in his sleep.

"Yes, hell's fire," he said, and turned to face the crowd.

The Magician watched in disbelief as his hard won audience shifted its attention to the man. He looked hopefully to the old woman to start a brawl, but she was barred from stepping forward by the forearm of a burly, leather-smocked tradesman who had heard enough of her.

The hawknosed man went on with feigned, evangelical solemnity, "Hell's fire awaits. And I ask now, who among you is without sin?" He began to pace along the forefront of the crowd. "The well dressed Merchant? grown fat by taking advantage of his fellow men? The Tradesman, here, whose guild allows him to charge four times what he is worth. Or the quarrelsome Old Woman, who spits out venom like the devil's snake." The crowd laughed. "And who among us knows when he will die?" The evangelist walked past a monk, a huge man whose flat black eyes, the Magician noticed, were set in a different direction from the crowd's. He looked in that direction, in time to see the girl from the river turning away to move back toward the fires.

The hawknosed man had stopped pacing and stood in front of the assemblage's center. The Magician heard him say, "Now I am a Pardoner..." And the crowd groaned.

The Magician looked back to the crowd, hopeful again. Some of the pilgrims, those the Pardoner had insulted, looked angry. The hawknosed man reached into a cloth bag that hung from a lanyard around his neck. He produced two good-sized bones and held them up with one hand, like a cross, and raised his voice.

"These are holy relics!"

The pilgrims quieted a little.

"The Bones of St. Peter The Martyr, himself!" The Pardoner went on indignantly. "Yes, holy relics with the power to absolve your sin!"

The Magician was squinting, trying to see the bones as the Pardoner waved them at the crowd. Suddenly he whirled around to the wagon's interior. He pulled the apparatus tubes from his robe then began to search hurriedly through the wagon's cupboards. He wrested a big over-ripe mutton joint from one of the shelves and came back to the opening as the Pardoner was finishing his pitch.

"And so I say to you– you who scoff– you with sin, *kiss these holy relics*, or burn! What say you, Merchant. Will you kiss the bones?"

The fat Merchant leaned backward, resisting. He looked fretfully at the bones shoved toward his face, his round cheeks shining in the firelight. "I'll wager there's a price attached to those bones," he said.

"Three silver shillings," answered the Pardoner quickly. "A small price, eh– for salvation."

The Pardoner waited for the answer, and The Magician, holding the stinking joint out away from him, said quietly, "So it's the bones of St. Peter, is it?"

The Pardoner turned and looked up.

"Kiss *my* bone!" The Magician said. And he hurled the meat with a whip action, and it struck the holy man's face with a loud "slap!" The Pardoner stumbled to the ground and the crowd erupted into laughter.

The Magician shouted from the wagon, "Sweet Christians, St. Peter must have walked on four legs! For if you look closely, the bones of my mutton joint are the same this charlatan would have you kiss in solemn tribute!"

There was a short pause, some inspection of the bones, then the Old Woman appeared again and began to kick the downed clergyman viciously. The crowd followed her example, and loud jeers and the thump of feet soon moved him out of the assembly.

With The Pardoner gone the crowd looked up to The

Magician again. He said to them, "Good travellers, hear my words. For I speak of magic now, and magic I know well. You all saw where I came from. Would anyone not well armed with the forces of necromancy dare to travel Grinmere wood?

The Magician stepped down from the wagon and closed the panel. The lamps still burned on the apparatus– he had forgotten to extinguish them– but now that could not be helped. He turned around and the crowd, a little afraid of him, moved back. He began to address them personally, singling out individuals with his wolfish eyes.

"My skills were taught me by a wizard, a sorcerer all powerful and known to all. From him I learned the ancient rules of alchemy and the grammar of the nether world. I learned of demons– of their conjuring, and how to send them back. So listen to me, good fellows, when I tell you that the world is not just as it seems. There are demons, the worst of them... close to us right now." The Magician gestured to Grinmere.

The crowd seemed receptive enough, a little frightened, most looking off toward the forest. The burly Tradesman had been listening with fascination. Wide-eyed, he shouted, "I've seen a demon! Sitting on the body of a dead man."

The Magician turned to him, "Aye, you've seen one, eh? And what d'you think you'd find in there– in Grinmere wood?"

The tradesman, who had a flat nose from brawling, just nervously shook his head.

"I'll tell you," said The Magician. "Headless men, with jaws where stomachs ought to be. Ghouls dragging corpses dug from unhallowed graves. Water Nymphs," he said thinking of the girl. "These things are common place. But once, on an excursion to gather the nectar of a rare flower that blooms only by the moon, I spent the night in there. It got late, a fatigue overcame me, and I sat against a hemlock tree and slept. Close to dawn, when the grey light is like a mist,

I woke, and before me, at the entrance to a cave three harpies sat. Women harpies are, witches, but with the skin and wings of bats. They sat, the three of them, in the bleak damp of waning night, clawing at each other and screeching with fangs curved like scimitars. Suddenly I heard the flap and whoosh of giant wings that scattered the fog upon the ground. I looked up and there, hovering above the cave, was the mother of the other three. Huge, she was. In her mouth she carried a human infant, and another in each claw. The others flew up and greedily snatched their prey and before I knew it, devoured them. They sat afterward, screeching, the skin of their bulging stomachs stretched shiny like black wax, and with the first true ray of dawn they scurried back into the darkness of the cave."

The crowd, especially the Merchant and Tradesman, seemed well taken by the tale. A child coughed and a woman spanked him and sent him back to the fires. The Merchant was sweating and he gestured nervously toward the forest and said, "Here now, Magician. If what you say is true, how is it you may travel these woods in safety?"

"If you say. Before your eyes I summoned the flames of hell. Yet you question me? It is a simple thing to ward off demons and ungodly beasts. I learned it as a child."

The Magician was standing in front of The Tradesman. He smiled and said, "Good Tradesman. You who have some knowledge of demons, stand forth and I shall demonstrate the spell."

"Spell, you say".

"Aye," answered the Magician matter-of-factly. "To protect you from all manner of demon and ghost."

Nervously, the Tradesman said, "Aye." and stepped forward, out of the crowd.

The Magician reached up to clasp the Tradesman's shoulders, but the man was so big that he only patted them and said, "Now brace yourself." Then to the crowd, "A single spell, cast only once, will protect him from the unnatural world." The Tradesman stiffened as if awaiting a strong wind.

The Magician crossed his wrists over his chest, his eyes rolled back, and he began to emit a humming, grumbling sound from deep within his chest. From this unnatural drone, he incanted, "Quid est animum volat!"

Whereupon the flat-nosed man's face exhibited the effects of a profound change being wrought inside of him. He grimaced, and his eyes bulged, and he grinned. The crowd responded to his transformations with astonished gasps, and only after several moments was he recovered enough to stand there steadily again. He blinked his eyes and said exultantly, "I can feel it! Like an armor, this spell!"

Applause and cries of "Here!" "Good Magician." "Magician!" could be heard.

The Merchant shoved his way forward through the others. He said, "Good Magician. I apologize for doubting you. Any one who controls the flames of hell– What say you, give me your benediction."

The Magician glanced down at the Merchant's purse. It was a fancy, glass-jewelled affair with ermine tails sewn onto it.

"A purse with ermine tails."

"Why– yes," The Merchant answered.

The Magician gestured casually toward Grinmere. "The Pardoner asked three silver shillings to kiss a sheep bone," he said. "I am not a merchant. Tell me, what is my magic worth?"

The Merchant considered the question anxiously, the rest of the crowd waiting, looking on. Finally The Tradesman shoved The Merchant's shoulder and said, "I've had the benediction. It's worth every bit of four."

"Yes, all right," said The Merchant, nodding quickly. "Let the price be four."

Immediately the crowd moved forward, but the Old Woman stepped up and tried to block them.

"He's a cheat!" she yapped.

A well dressed dame stepped around her, another pilgrim shouldered her aside as the whole crowd came forward to receive their benedictions. The Merchant asserted his place first in line. The Old Woman threw her arms down, made a throaty hiss and walked into the clearing. The Pardoner was there, still dusting himself from the scuffle.

"He's as much a bilker as you are!" She said to him.

The Pardoner pulled his cap down on his head. "Shut up, you hideous witch. What do you know about it."

"I know what I've seen," the Old Woman cackled. "And it was no hell that made those fires in his sleeves!"

The Pardoner put his hands on his hips and leered at the procession of donors giving coins to the robed Magician.

"How do you know?"

She shook a bony finger toward the wagon and said, "A fortnight last, this 'Sorcerer' was in Scarborough."

"So?"

"He left his wagon door open and I just happened to see somethin'."

The Pardoner was mildly interested. The Old Woman perceived his interest and lifted a purse that hung by two oversized leather thongs at her side. "It feels purty light," she said, bobbing the purse. The Pardoner took out a copper and thrust it impatiently into her hand.

"Well?"

She held the coin into the firelight, squinted to focus her old eyes, and crackled, "Stinking thief. I wouldn't tell you my name for this!"

"I wouldn't ask for it," said the Pardoner, and he went back into his purse and took out a silver coin. He held it up and the old woman snatched it. He said, "Now speak, hag, before I kick you into the bog."

She moved close to him and hissed out her words.

"He was boilin' lard, and had some kind'a lamp that he was pourin' it into!" The Pardoner reached to take back the coin, but the old woman slapped down his arm and croaked out the rest of her secret.

"He pumped the flames out'a' blacksmith's bellows on the floor!"

The Pardoner looked at the Old Woman quickly. After a moment he turned back toward the wagon and began to nod. "Fling mutton at me, eh? Very well, old witch, tell me all you know. But keep you back. Your foul mouth blows a stink like rotting mackerel."

As another coin dropped into the Magician's purse, he said, "Quid est animum volat!" and raised his right hand in a flourish. The weight of the pouch was growing, and he smiled, hefting it unobtrusively with his left hand.

"Dear Lady!" he exclaimed as the next pilgrim, a woman, stepped forward. But his voice faltered as she moved into the firelight, for she was late in years and used a crutch to support a lameness of her side. A young boy stood beside her, poorly clad and silent as she spoke.

"Please, Sir, I haven't any silver to contribute. But if you could bless us, my boy and I, we'd give you these four coppers." She turned and brought her son forward. He held out his hand to show four brown pennies in the dim light.

"You mustn't–" The Magician started, but checked himself. "Very well, Madam, if it is all you have." He lowered his arms to his sides and pronounced, "Quid est animum volat!" then reached over smoothly with his left hand and took the coppers from the boy who stood to his right. "Now go," he proclaimed, "And know that ye are secure of all demons!" The coins made a diminutive clink as he dropped them into the bag.

The woman nodded in appreciation and turned to leave, but the boy stood motionless. The Magician's voice grew soft. "Go boy," he said, "Go on with your mother." The boy looked down and opened his hand to see the four gold florens that now glimmered from the fire. He looked down at the coins, then back at the Magician, and the Magician's forehead was wrinkled.

"Go boy," he said.

The boy whispered, "I thank you," very softly, and turned away.

Just then there was a loud "crack!" and the whole crowd turned to look. The side of the wagon had fallen down and the Pardoner was inside of it holding one tube of the apparatus. The Magician shouted, "Thief! Do not touch a sorcerer's wares, lest you perish for your ignorance!"

But the Pardoner had found the bellows and saw one of the lamps that was connected. He nodded to himself and yelled, "He's no Magician! I can make the flames too!"

The Magician shook his fist desperately, "Leave it alone or you'll burn!" The crowd grew noisy and some repeated his words.

But the Pardoner held a tube and tiny lamp out in front of him and started to pump the bellows. A small blue flame spurted forth and he was frightened, but laughed nervously and yelled, "You see! He's a fake!"

The crowd grew quieter. The Pardoner pumped the bellows again, harder, and a large flame roared forward and vanished in a curl.

Now in the dead silence the Magician yelled, "Get out of there!" But the pilgrims turned toward him and someone spat, "Cheat!" They surrounded him and moved in, but he kept yelling at the Pardoner.

"You'll burn! The other tube! Get out of there!"

The Pardoner did not see the flames rising behind him in the wagon and shouted exuberantly, "Tear off his robe! Relieve the burden of his magic robe...Ha Ha Ha!" He was pumping the bellows as he shouted, holding out a single flame-spewing tube of the apparatus, as the other pumped flames into the wagon.

"Worship no false idols– or perish in the true hell of Satan!" he cried, and pumped the bellows harder and watched through the flames as the now snarling crowd grappled the robe from the Magician and hurled the tattered fragments into the air.

"Chastise him!" The Pardoner screamed, and the crowd obeyed like a trained animal and forced the Magician to the ground and began to kick him and to pound him with their fists.

With a shocking 'thud!' he saw a red flash and felt the pain shoot through his neck and shoulder. He rolled as the tree branch came down a second time and it landed on his side and he heard his ribs crack, the pain coming through him again sharp and unbelievable. He reached into his purse and hurled a handful of coins into the crowd. The branch was dropped near his head. He groaned, raised himself and reached for another handful, but someone snatched the purse away. Then a knee smashed his face and knocked him backward onto the ground. He was raising himself again when the lard pot exploded, "Voom!" and splitting wood. He rolled and saw a yellow ball of flame ascend churning into the night sky. The pilgrims were screaming, the timbers of the wagon crackling as it burned. The Pardoner was dead.

The Magician struggled to his feet and nearly swooned as a wave of heat scorched his beaten body. He turned and saw the bearded monk leading his horse away. Then he turned around again, and the pilgrims were coming back after him.

Their faces were angry and scared, all half illuminated as they moved toward him in the firelight. He looked for a direction in which to run, for a moment his mind went blank, and then the portal was like a door of blackness in the fire-brightened trees and he gasped, "Grinmere!"

He started toward the forest, half-staggering, saw a burning splinter on the ground in front of him. He came over the piece of plank and reached, but a hand snatched it away. He stood up with his fists clenched and saw the lame woman's boy holding the splinter out for him. The boy looked worried, and the Magician smiled at him and took the torch. Then he was limping again, the portal far ahead, heard their shouting behind, the thud of footsteps on the ground, scattered thudding at first, louder and then suddenly much, much louder, and he knew the whole mob had begun running after him.

He could feel the vibrations as they closed, their feet pounding, the sound like running horses. The pain was stunning as he struggled to overcome it and broke out running himself, the portal still perhaps sixty yards away. He strained to run faster, pressing, with pain shooting through him each time he filled his lungs. But they were still closing, and he could feel their presence behind, knew they were catching up, reaching for him, that any instant he would feel the hands grappling at his back to pull him down and beat the life out of him. And straining at the limits of his diminished strength, making noises from the pain with the portal looming nearer and the footsteps closing, the portal spreading wider but the footsteps upon him now, certainly upon him but at the last instant faltering in their rhythm, he felt a sudden chill and realized his torch was only an ember as he entered the void of blackness, the pure and sightless blackness that was Grinmere.

Outside the forest the pilgrims had halted, colliding into each other. They stood and watched as he made his escape, watched his form vanish quickly; then panting, standing together in mutual silence, stared on as the spark of the splinter came back into a tiny flame and moved off erratically, seeming to float into the darkness, getting smaller and farther away until it was gone entirely. And the pilgrims returned to the clearing, in silence, where a few children were searching through the scattered, still burning fragments of debris.

Chapter 4
The Foundling

Behind him the firelight shone through the arbored portal like an amber mist in the immense darkness of the woods. He held the torch out as he walked, and his breath curled thickly in its dim rays. Grinmere was cold and still. He was wheezing slightly. His footsteps padded softly on the solid ground.

A pale form appeared to his left, and the Magician thrust the torch over and raised his fist in readiness. The form glowed motionless and dim, and he moved closer and saw that it was only an outcropping of rock. His side throbbed, and he lifted his eyes and could see no stars but only the canopy of trees that seemed to smother him in unyielding blackness.

It was a half day's walk to the town of Solway, he knew, and the splinter would never last. He began searching the ground for small sticks and kindling, and near the outcropping of rock saw a bare patch on the forest floor, held the torch down, and found it was a path that connected to the road. He started along the path slowly, but the failing torch prompted a quickening of his pace.

He came into a small clearing where an ancient oak had

uprooted and lay dead upon the forest floor. The moon and stars shone through where once the great tree's canopy had been. It was lighter in the clearing, and the tangled skeleton of a withered dogwood stood solitarily in the moonlight.

He set his torch down on the great dead tree, then went over and began to dismantle the dogwood. The first armful of twigs he carried back and lay in a pile against the timber, then placed his torch carefully underneath, put a tuft of dried ground lichen on the tiny flame and fanned it gently with his hand. The twigs caught easily and the fire grew. He finished breaking up the dogwood and piled the remaining branches an arm's length from the fire.

A layer of mist was forming over the forest floor. It swirled about his feet as he walked toward a sapling pine at the clearing's edge. He could see the stars as he stripped the fragrant pine boughs, and he carried the boughs back and made a bed by criss-crossing them so that they formed a springy cushion beside the fire. Then the Magician eased himself slowly onto the soft needles that rendered an aromatic vapor as they warmed.

The heat caressed the stiffness of his wounds, and the pine vapor seemed to ease his labored breathing. He removed his waistcoat, bundling it for a pillow, and turned on his side and stared deep into the flames. His wagon was gone, as was his purse. His horse had been taken by a bearded monk in a black robe.

The Magician shut his eyes, his body heavy against the earth, and by the sound of the crackling twigs the image of the burning wagon became vivid in his mind. He opened his eyes. The glowing branches settled beneath the crush of their own weight, and he reached over to the pile and tossed a few more on the fire. The warmth had made his injuries more bearable, so he tried sitting upright but felt heavy down in the pit of his chest. He was hungry and sad and lay back again and looked up through the clearing of trees. A meteor streaked across the sky, and he thought to make a wish but then exhaled and began to speak, to the stars, in the stillness of Grinmere.

"No more wishes, no magic at all," he whispered. "There are no spells that can charm a burdened life."

He listened in the silent wood a moment, then said aloud, "What a soft bellied lout you are– to cheat honest peasants and then moan because they caught you! A rotten, unprincipled whelp, that's what you are– probably a bastard, though you cannot be sure, with no country, relatives, nor a single friend you can trust. And you are moaning again. If there were profits to be had from such a situation, then you have surely reaped them. You are rotten, eh? So do not be righteous. And if you stand on the summit of your years a cheat and beaten swindler– so be it. You are fortunate the midwife did not know your fate, or she would have left you for the rats and flies."

He turned back toward the fire to bring its warmth to bear upon his wounded shoulder and said, "Life is simple enough. For you it means being lost, because an orphan can never go home or ever find peace in his desire. So resign yourself to that. And know that the one profit to a drifting soul is that there is always somewhere else where you can go."

The fire hissed as the flames consumed the rotten timber, and his tears cast a reflection of the fire's glow.

"If only it meant something. I could stand the pain if only I had a reason. Yes, well there it is stars, there is my wish after all: *I want a reason.*"

Then he closed his eyes and slept. And for a time the forest seemed to hold him in a sympathy of calm. Only the fire made sounds as the flames rose higher and licked the big log that had begun to burn colorfully. The clearing grew brilliant as the lichens and moss burned at the fire's edges and colored flames rose in pillars of green and violet that reflected on the surrounding mist.

Then the center of the giant timber began to glow like the

bed of a forge. Steam issued as the sodden wood turned to vapor, the hiss of escaping steam growing as the pressure built inside. The Magician turned in his sleep, and the shattered rib sent a wave of pain that brought him to near-wakefulness. The firelight penetrated his eyelids. For a moment it seemed the sun had risen, but then the queer shriek of escaping steam caused him to struggle to his knees, to lurch to his feet in confusion.

He gasped and rubbed his eyes, trying to focus through the blear of exhaustion, and saw the flames, like pillars, rising from the center of the massive timber to fuse in a chest-high archway of fire. The log's core was white hot and radiant, and the steam screeched as it shot forth and billowed in the cool, still air.

He stepped back and mumbled something. As if by in-cantation the hissing stopped, the flames diminished some-what, and the thick plumes of vapor ceased to issue. There was a faint crunching, creaking sound from the log. He stood there blinking for a little while then lay down again, exhausted, on the pine boughs. The fire was big and hot, so he turned face down to expose his sore shoulder and had released himself to the seemingly inexorable gravity of sleep, when a sharp "bang!" as when a dry plank is snapped, again brought him convulsively to his knees.

A shower of sparks billowed outward from the embers, surrounding him, and he covered himself but the sparks rose harmlessly, orange and glimmering into the night sky.

The center of the great timber had exploded. At first his overtired eyes saw only the gash left in the tree. Then he saw something else that made him crawl upon his knees toward the fire; closer to be sure that it was real; closer, until his whole body glowed in the ember's light. The fire was nearly out, but there, shining like a hallucination, the object of his vision was a sword. Imbedded in the center of the timber and rimmed in crimson embers, it looked new, as if it had been forged that night in the fire.

He moved his hand out slowly, and almost touching the mirror-like blade there was no heat. But then he brushed the metal with his fingertips and the sudden burning stopped his breath and made him flinch backward in pain. A breeze came down into the clearing and the weapon seemed to glow from the reflection of the brightening coals. The Magician moved back and looked at its entire length. Long and slender, it had a bright gold handle and the head of a roaring lion at the butt. As the breeze ebbed the embers darkened again. The sword looked icy blue in the fainter light and he drew closer to study it. His deep red reflection moved in the polished metal. The log crackled and the weapon dropped into the ashes. He used a pine bough to pull it out.

He gathered the scattered coals into a mound and threw on a handful of twigs to give himself a small blaze to see by. The sword felt only warm but as he picked it up it was almost too hot to hold. He switched hands quickly and raised it into the air. It was burning but he wanted to hold it and at last had to let it drop onto the pine boughs and rubbed his hands vigorously on his arms.

After building up the fire again, the Magician lay down close beside his newfound possession and looked up through the clearing. Another star streaked across the August night. He shut his eyes and made the sign of the cross and whispered something. Then a moment later, drawing breath in deep sighs, he was sleep, and never saw the eyes that turned away, nor heard the footsteps that left the clearing and moved back whence they came, back into the depths of Grinmere.

Chapter 5
Nelrum

The Magician awakened to the sound of crows cawing high in the branches above. He raised onto his elbows and pushed himself to stand against the pain of his sore shoulder. The timber had burned completely through, charred ends still smoldering; and through the grogginess of sleep the memory of the sword came back to him like an event from a distant past. He picked it up from the pine boughs and walked into the clearing and sat down upon a white boulder in the sunshine.

"Well you belong to Redwyn now," he said. "In truth, you are the only thing that belongs to him." He turned the weapon over and sunlight flashed upon the polished metal– blinding him– so that as his sight returned an inscription gone unnoticed the night before seemed to resolve itself magically upon the blade.

"Ho! What's this!" he said.

The writing was not Greek or Latin, nor could he remember ever seeing the likes of it in any of the copyists' shops where he had worked for most of his life. He tried to sound the words out, "DREADOR– NAY– UL– NOM– PLOMBE– HORTRE." And just as he finished, a clear sharp voice from behind him said, "So Redwyn is your name!"

He turned and wrenched his battered shoulder.

Standing at the edge of the clearing, not twelve feet away, was a tall, white haired man in a grey robe. His face was smooth and clean, unwrinkled except for long creases around his eyes that extended to the hairline of his temples. His eyes were steady, unnervingly so, and bright blue and sad in the sunlight. A satchel was slung about his shoulder, and he had a plain walking stick in his right hand.

The Magician said, "Where have *you* come from?"

The white haired man cocked his head toward the path and answered, "The river fork."

"You mean the Grinmere fork?"

"The same."

The stranger raised his eyebrows as if surprised about something, came up to the boulder and sat down. The Magician stood uncomfortably as the old man removed a withered sandal and flicked a pebble from the sole of his foot.

"You must have followed me. If you want your money back I don't have any," the Magician said.

"I have not come for money," answered the visitor. Then, replacing the droopy sandal, "Only to be sure that you were safe."

"Why should you care for me, Old Man?"

"Perhaps I shouldn't. I have not yet decided that. But I was curious to know why a common swindler would give an old lame woman four florens of gold."

"You take risks," the Magician told him.

The visitor looked up with a smile that seemed to grant a measure of patience to the ignorant, and said, "I think not."

"No? Well, what if I chopped off your old white head with my sword?"

"My 'old head' would be of no use to you, if you cannot manage with your own."

"In truth, because it is a madman that you are!" said the Magician. "Out here what is to stop me, in a forest where no one comes, if I, say, gave you a quick chop and stole your satchel?"

"What, this?" The visitor unslung the leather bag and tossed it to the Magician's feet. "I packed some food for you."

"By the bones of Christ– who are you and what do you want!"

"I followed you last night after the crowd dispersed, saw your firelight in the treetops. When I came along the path you were amusing yourself with this sword."

"You haven't answered me."

"I felt sorry for you, I suppose. That was quite a good magic act last night– if only you hadn't tried to instill the fear of hell into those people. Otherwise good."

"But you called me a common swindler."

"And it's a swindler that you are!" the visitor said cheerily.

The Magician picked up the bag and tossed it back at him. "I don't want your satchel, old man. I wouldn't have hurt you, really. I never would. Go back to the fork now, go along your way."

"Oh, I *am* sorry. I have been alone, and I suppose my manners have become quite coarse. Forgive me, Redwyn, if that is your name. I only meant to say that your use of rhetoric and fear was quite unbecoming. Much like the church's own method of buggery."

"It's a blasphemer you are as well!" the Magician protested. But he grinned at the remark in spite of himself, and the old man's face lightened too.

"Now tell me why you gave the old lame woman four florens of gold."

The Magician shrugged. "It was the wages of sin."

"And yet the risks you took to get it were severe. When that club came down a second time I thought you were done in."

"Yes; I thought so too, old man." And faced with the memory of his burning wagon again the Magician's distrust of the visitor seemed suddenly less important. He sat down beside him on the rock.

"At least you have your sword."

"I didn't until last night."

"Truly?"

Redwyn lifted the weapon and could see the visitor peering over his shoulder in the polished blade. "Yes," he answered. "I built a fire underneath that log, yonder. It cracked apart and I'll be hanged if this wasn't inside. It is the strangest quirk of fortune."

"Most astonishing!"

"I thought so too."

The visitor stood, extended his hand and said, "My name is Nelrum."

"It is a strange name," answered Redwyn, clasping the hand in greeting.

"And yours, is it truly Redwyn?"

"No, I am an orphan. My true name is unknown to me."

"I like it," said the old man.

"It doesn't mean anything I know of," Redwyn told him, awkwardly rejecting a compliment with which he did not concur.

They both stood there a moment, staring at the ground. Then the old man said, "Well, come down to the river now. A cold bath will take the ache out of your wounds. And I'll give you some food. You are hungry, aren't you?"

"I am."

"Then come!" He started walking toward an opening in the brush. "I will give you a feast to put the fire back in your sleeves!"

They followed a path down to where the river was wide and languid. The water looked black in the shade of the forest, and where the sunlight struck the water glowed in patches of pale yellow. Redwyn undressed and slipped down the bank into a deep pool. It took only a moment for the cold to numb his entire body, and against the sluggish current he had only to wave his hands to stay abeam his clothing on the shore.

The old man looked odd, he thought, as he watched him remove the food from his satchel to set it on a fallen tree. For in spite of his white hair, his body was without the slightest defect of posture, his shoulders exceptionally broad and strong looking, and movements deft and sure. His eyes, too, were steadily intent upon his work, and there was not the faintest cast of milkiness veiling their deep azure. He had set out a veritable banquet upon the log.

"Did you really bring that food for me?"

"I never lie," the visitor said, his blue eyes flashing from the shade. "I am confused at times, but I never lie."

"Like your blasphemy of the church."

"The church? No, I have never been confused about them. Eat something now."

Redwyn climbed out and found a shower of sunlight to stand in while skimming the water from his body. Then he rolled on his breeches, put on his blouse and waistcoat, and came up and set his sword against the log where the food was.

"Bread, cheese, boiled apples– but where did all this come from?"

"I brought it for you."

"It is funny I don't remember seeing you at the clearing."

"I was back among the wagons mostly, making some travelling preparations for a lady friend."

"Oh." Redwyn was about to seat himself, but stopped and said, "Excuse me. It is your food. You first."

"That is quite a turn from, 'I'll lop off your old white head and steal the satchel.'"

"Forgive me that. I said I didn't mean it."

"Then eat, young man."

Redwyn sat down straddling the log and picked up a piece
of cheese. He was so hungry that the smell of food made
him dizzy, but before he could take a bite felt compelled to
ask, "How is it that you seem at ease here? Everyone else is
afraid of this place."

"There are many things in the world more frightening
than legends about an old forest."

"You should have made your presence known last night,"
Redwyn said matter-of-factly.

"Had there not been enough difficulty for one evening?"
asked the old man.

"Yes, I'm sorry. I had to ask."

"It isn't poisoned, if that is what you think." Whereupon
the visitor reached for some cheese. But Redwyn shook his
head No and smiled at him and started to eat.

"Last night did you see the man who took your horse?"

"Yes, a monk I believe. Think of it– a monk stealing my
horse. Still, he might have burned tied up to that wagon."

"That was no monk."

"Well, he was dressed like one."

The visitor used a wooden mug to dip some water from
the river. Then he came back and set it down on the log.
"We'll get started when you are finished."

"Where?" Redwyn asked.

"To Solway. I think I can show you where the horse is."

"I'm not so sure it is wise. After all there are pilgrims
who may recognize me."

"In a city of many thousands?" The visitor grinned in-
credulously.

"Yes, you're right, old man. And of course the mob
wouldn't be together now."

"Then finish up here and we'll get started. And perhaps if
I called you Redwyn, you would call me Nelrum. It is my
name."

Redwyn grinned. "All right. By Christ, I've known some
unholy monks in my time, but horse stealing is, well..." He

did not finish, and superstitiously tossed the last bit of cheese away. A big crow swooped down and plucked it from the forest floor, and they both watched as the bird flew back into the treetops, its oily feathers glistening in the sun.

"That was no monk," Nelrum corrected.

Chapter 6
The Plombe
Hortre

They walked through Grinmere on the old road the Romans had abandoned so many centuries before. Rays of sunlight shot down through the canopy of trees and glowed like celestial pillars throughout the forest. They were silent as they walked until when, passing the first milestone, Redwyn stopped and gestured to its inscription.

"How many years this must have been here."

Nelrum stopped too, and leaned on his staff. "Yes," he agreed, "how many years."

"This is a very old place, isn't it?"

"As old as any other; the legends only make it seem ancient."

"I suppose that is true."

They started to walk again.

"The stone seems old because of an inscription," Nelrum said. "But in the lifetime of a stone it might well have been put there yesterday. Still, this is an old place; old from the living and dying that has been here."

Redwyn said, "I read something about it once in an ancient manuscript of the Benedicts. There were great battles fought in these woods against the Romans, and later, when

King Arthur defended the realm."

"Go on."

"I don't remember much more. Except that legends still persist of a race of beings who lived here before the Romans or even the Barbarian hordes. I forget what they called themselves. They were a *pagan* race."

"They weren't legends," Nelrum told him. "You will soon see their artifacts in the forest ahead."

"Then you must have been here before."

"Many times. This is a shorter road to Solway. It follows the river almost the entire way. And even the brigands, at least most of them, are afraid to travel it."

Redwyn grinned at the obvious barb. "Aren't you at all afraid?"

"No. The ancient race of the Druids has long been extinct As I said, there are many more frightening things in the present world."

"It is true. Last night I preferred the legends to an angry mob. I remember now. The Druids. They were beast and tree worshippers. They worshipped anything. They were pagans." And again he said the word *pagan* with an air of dismissal.

"You have quite a superior knowledge of them, Redwyn. Is your history as polished as your Latin?"

"What do you mean?"

They stopped in the road and appraised each others faces. Nelrum pronounced with mock oratory, "*Quid est animum volat!*" Redwyn put his hands on his hips and grinned. Their eyes glistened with the unexpressed thought, and then they both burst out laughing in the still morning air.

"You weren't content to have their gold," Nelrum said chokingly. "Really! You had to tweak their noses too!"

Redwyn sputtered, "Stop now!" And they erupted into another series of bestial, high pitched wails.

After a while, Nelrum sniffed and said, "Come, we'd better get along, or we are not likely to find an inn at Solway."

"You laugh just like I do," Redwyn muttered, and they started to walk again down the ancient arbored path.

"It feels good to laugh," said Nelrum.

"It is best if your ribs aren't broken."

"Well, you deserved them."

"Perhaps. But in spite of what you heard last night I really do know Latin. That milestone read: 'All praise to the Emperor Hadrian,' and it told the distance to the wall."

"Most impressive."

And Redwyn felt a prick of annoyance at his newfound companion's incredulity.

"I know a lot of things, old man. I was a copyist's apprentice in Edinburgh. We had the business of all the nobles for two hundred miles. I have done a lot of copying of manuscripts. I have read more than all the simple minded students of Oxford and Edinburgh combined. The Benedicts, Capuchins, Trappists– All of them great scholars. And I have read their books."

"I am sure your mind is a virtual reliquary of information. But look here and I may add something..." They were approaching another milestone and Nelrum pointed to it with his staff.

"Once upon a time, five hundred or so years ago, two very good friends said goodbye here. One of them was a great and noble king. And the other, a religious man, pagan though you would call him, was a priest and, legends holds, mentor to the Christian king.

"They had met quite by accident, as best friends often do, and they discovered shared beliefs in many things. At first this disconcerted the King, for he was a godly an, a soldier of Christ, who had sworn himself to defend Christianity and honor. It was unsettling to him that a pagan should uphold lofty ideals too. But in time the virtue of the priest's beliefs seduced the King, and he grew torn between the Christian and Pagan faiths and came to practice them equally, but with a troubled heart.

"For twenty years their friendship lasted. By the King's rule the realm was a fine place to live. Hope lived in the good men of the land, and the King cultivated the hope and guarded it with a passion for righteousness. Even the peasants felt joy awakening in their tired hearts; for they owed their obedience not to a king, but to a king's honor.

"But men of power are never content with peaceful life and handsome children, nor to leave the soil unmixed with blood. The King's dukes conceived a plot of treachery, and his major-domo, a fraud and sycophant, complied. The church was bribed to accuse him of heresy, and men were forced to choose between God or Monarch. The horror of civil war was unleashed upon the land.

"Then one day near the end, the royal army– a handful of peasants and a few loyal knights– made ready for battle at the river fork. As it was their custom to meet on this particular day of each month, the King rode into the forest and found the Priest awaiting him at this milestone.

"They both knew it was their last meeting. The Priest was filled with remorse. He said his counsel had brought the downfall of his friend. But the King avowed that the pagan beliefs were truly his own, as were his Christian convictions. His greatest regret, he said, was that he had not reconciled church and conscience to a single end.

"The King rejoined his army and died in battle that day: not a battle really, more a gesture to pride. It was the end of a brief epoch of dignity."

"You speak of Arthur," Redwyn said.

"Yes."

"And the pagan priest?"

"Merlin."

"A wizard!"

"No. But a priest, a Druid high-priest."

"That is a story. And to think it happened at this milestone. Where did you read it, a Benedictine book?"

"No, no. Trappist."

"Ah, well, they are fine scholars too."

Redwyn was deep in contemplation of the tale, then he said solemnly, "The wrath of God."

"What did you say?"

"Don't you see? By practicing a pagan faith Arthur condemned himself. He obscured the vital light of God from his entire kingdom and, thus, it was undone."

"Oh yes," said Nelrum.

Redwyn was pleased with himself for having made the deduction. He said, "Stand here a moment," and removed the sword from his belt.

"I was thinking of this forest, that it is so old; and I thought that if the sword were in a tree, especially one of enormous girth, that it too must be old..." He extended the weapon flatly, so that the inscription could be easily read. "Well look," he said, holding it. "There is writing on the blade."

The old man took it and held it down the full length of his arms. "Yes, I see, he said. *'Dreador Nay ul Nom Plombe Hortre.'* Yes, this is a Druid sword."

"Aha! Now what does it mean?"

"I do not know. It is not an easy thing to translate." Nelrum gave the weapon back. "The Druid words are intricate and I am not an expert on them, only having read one book. It was a long time ago; there were many more important things, then..." His voice started to drone as if another story were forthcoming, but Redwyn interjected:

"Please! try to remember what it means."

"But those are pagan words."

"A lot that matters to you, blasphemer that you are! Tell me what the words mean!"

"I am not sure that my Druid is as good as your Latin, but I will try. May I see the weapon again?"

Redwyn drew it impatiently from his belt and placed it across the old man's outstretched hands.

"Well then, Dreador Nay ul Nom Plombe Hortre: Dreador

Nay ul means Without Shame or Fear; Nom Plombe Hortre: The Innocent Heart. So putting them together: Without Shame or Fear is The Innocent Heart. But this is not at all veritable."

"Why?"

"I told you these words are intricate. The first part is straightforward enough, but Nom Plombe Hortre is difficult to explain. It was the center of the Druid faith– just as God is the center of yours."

"Ours," Redwyn corrected.

"That is what I said."

"Nom Plum Hortay."

"No, no," and Nelrum sounded it out carefully: "Nahm, Plahm, Hor-treh"

"All right, but what is the purpose of saying it if I don't understand the meaning?"

"The Plombe Hortre or Innocent Heart was what the Druids meant by the soul," Nelrum explained. "Not the soul as you might think of it; theirs was a soul of all *mortal* life. They called it 'Innocent soul,' because all creatures, even the smallest ant and field mouse, seem to have it: the earth given soul, the will to survive. In the Christian faith the soul belongs to God and when life on earth is over there is eternity beyond. But the Druids dedicated themselves to this life. They felt a respect for all living things and set the highest purpose of man to preserve and extend life. They defined morality as the effort to increase the good in man. So their fundamental precept was that: *Before there can be good in man, man must exist; therefore human life is a requirement for human good and, thus, life is sacred above all things.*"

"Those are intricate words," Redwyn said softly. "But does this not forsake the divine God, and invite destruction upon mankind? There can be only one sacred-above-all thing. And even if man chooses life, to preserve it for himself and his fellow men, then he has defied the supremacy of his maker. It is sacrilege."

"Of course." The creases around Nelrum's eyes deepened. "And this was Arthur's dilemma."

"Nom Plombe Hortre," Redwyn said reverently. "I am sorry I called them beast worshipers now. But there is one other question: Why would the member of such a sect own a sword?"

"Why indeed?" Nelrum said. "Come, we had better quicken our step, or we are not likely to find an Inn at Solway."

So they walked on past the ancient milestones, between the columns of sunlight that came through the trees and tilted more with each passing hour. Redwyn paused at the wonders of a civilization long past. There were huge stone sundials, enormous thrones of solid rock, and alters covered by moss. There were faces in stone, hideous and grotesque, and he marvelled at their size and at the tools that must have cut them. Each time Nelrum knew their history, knew the purposes for them in their ancient world.

Then the last orange flecks of sunlight disappeared from the forest floor and Grinmere began to submerge back into the depths of its peculiar darkness. Redwyn took long powerful strides and was astonished at Nelrum's ability to keep pace. As the light faded the artifacts turned grey and disappeared slowly amid the trees. Nelrum tapped a milestone as they passed and said, "That is the last one. Grinmere's end is near."

The road ascended a steep hill and there was a light through the trees where the forest must have ended. They scaled to the summit, and Solway and the sea lay before them, the last rays of sunlight glancing over the open countryside.

Chapter 7
Friends

The road twisted down from the highlands of the forest and made a wide turn along the sea. Merchant ships bobbed in the docks outside the town. Each ship had a single mast flying a banner, and a carved figurehead at its bow. Across from the docks the fairground was settling into the purple twilight. Some of the merchants had built campfires near their tables. Others loaded wares into two-wheeled carts and led their donkeys toward town.

Through the gates of the city began the main street of Solway. On the left side, at the waterfront, were the merchant shops and taverns, and on the right side the houses that were all connected and rose higher than the shops to look out over the sea. Outside each doorway was a pile of reeds and filth. The lights fell dim yellow from the windows, and tiny black rats scurried through the lights, between the rotting piles, with the street getting dark and the outline of the rooftops showing black against the faintest shade of twilight in the western sky.

Noises echoed along the buildings from sources unseen in the darkness; the noises grew louder, then curses became distinct and a fire rose at the far end of the street. The flames illuminated the buildings that before could not be seen; and forms of men became visible with their shadows lengthening as the fire grew. There was shouting, a splash, then another, and the flames lowered and went out. Two more splashes came from the darkness and the voices diminished to a murmur.

A young boy was walking along the doorways. His voice made an unsteady chant and he swung his arms loosely as he walked. Two men were coming from the direction of the fire, opposite the boy, and as they passed one of the men grabbed him.

The boy had a startled look on his face as the man moved him into the light of a tavern doorway. Both men wore floppy hats, and the man who held the boy was very short and wore a merchant's coat of embroidered cloth, and pointed shoes. He was holding the boy by his linen shirt and made an expression of rage and roared into his face.

"Rarrrrh!"

As the men began laughing, the boy's look of terror faded and he began to smile with them. "Here's a wit for you!" said the short merchant, still holding him.

"A prince of the realm no doubt," said the other man.

"Are you a prince?" asked the Merchant.

The boy nodded and smiled.

"Prince Witling!" cried the Merchant, and he shook the boy vigorously. The other man bowed, then turned to show his buttocks and made a vulgar sound with his mouth.

The short merchant laughed and the boy raised his eyes to his laughing captor and smiled. "Look at the finery of dress," the short merchant said, and he put his hand through a hole in the front of the boy's linen blouse. "My Lord, in Venice we wear them a bit looser!" he said, and drawing his hand down through the hole, ripped the blouse wide open.

The other man bellowed with laughter, and the short one continued, "Do you approve, My Lord?" He smiled and nodded and the boy mimicked him. "Wait, you're not a prince! But rather a vandal, I'd say!"

The Merchant nodded again, but the boy did not return it.

"He confesses!"

"Vandal!" yelled the other man.

The Merchant shook the boy and turned him in the light. "It was *you* who started the fire, was it not?" He nodded but the boy did nothing.

The other man picked up a dead rat by its tail and moved toward them. "Perhaps if he had a meal he could think more clearly," he said.

The short merchant gripped the boy's chin and forehead and struggled to pry his mouth open. The other man dangled the dead rat and moved it slowly in front of the boy's face, then downward and toward his mouth. The child wriggled and squealed plaintively; his eyes widened with horror but then fixed on something that was behind his two attackers. Just then the flat of a sword blade flashed in the dim light. The rat was knocked away, and when the men jerked around Redwyn was there.

The man who had dangled the rat now clutched his smashed knuckles and groaned. Redwyn caught the short merchant by his embroidered coat and pulled him away from the boy. Redwyn was taller than either of the two men and stronger. His forearm was bared through the vent of his coat sleeve and his muscles flexed in the light as he tightened his grip around the Merchant's collar.

The short man wheezed, "Please, sir! I am no warrior. I'm a merchant, sir, come to sell my wares. I want no quarrel with you!"

Redwyn's eyes flashed and he twisted the collar until the man's face bulged. "What are you selling now?"

"Only garments, sir," the Merchant coughed. "The finest garments."

Redwyn let him go and raised his sword toward the floppy hat. The little man's eyes widened as the blade flashed menacingly close.

"You sell garments?"

"Yes, Lord."

"Then perhaps my young friend, here, would consent to exhibit some of your wares."

In a spasm of defiance the short man said, "I won't!" and flinched backward like a misbehaving child. Redwyn's sword flicked out deftly and snagged the floppy hat from the little man's head. Nelrum took it from the blade point, put it on the bewildered boy, and the short merchant winced and hastened to unhook the buttons of his coat.

"There will be a fee for these services," Redwyn said, turning to the other merchant who was holding his hand, badly swollen now, to his chest. "A floren would be sufficient. Two more will pay my fee as go-between."

The taller merchant looked at him in astonishment and Redwyn turned quickly back and jabbed his sword at the short merchant's legs. "The breeches too!" he snapped. "The shoes you keep; I will not have my friend wearing *pointed* shoes." The taller merchant produced his purse and hurried to render up the three gold coins.

A few moments later the boy was looking at his new clothes in nervous disbelief.

The short merchant was naked. He eyed his companion and they both started to back away. Redwyn knelt down to the boy, and the two men started running, one entirely bare except for his pointed shoes, the other clutching his smashed knuckles awkwardly to his chest. A gaggle of drunkards passed the runners in the street and barked obscenities after them and laughed.

Redwyn knelt on one knee and said, "Well, my friend, it is time for supper. And the garbage piles are no place for a fellow of your fine tailoring." The boy looked down at the coat sleeves that hung floppingly over his hands.

"Do you know what this is?" Redwyn asked. He held up a gold floren. The boy snatched it and ran into the tavern.

Redwyn saw him run to the barmaid and clutch the folds of her dress. In a few moments the little waif emerged again, with a meat pie and several shillings in change.

Nelrum counted the coins and said, "He was charged a fair price," and gave them back to the child who stuffed them greedily into his new waistcoat. He looked up and nodded, first to Redwyn, then to Nelrum, then turned and bolted into the darkness, his rapid footsteps growing fainter and then gone.

"He will fare well enough."

"I hope so," Redwyn answered. He put the sword through his belt and opened his hand to show the two gold coins that glowed dully in the light. He shook them and made them rattle.

"Shall we?"

Nelrum glanced into the tavern door. "I have something to do first."

"What is it? I'll come with you."

"No, no. It is nothing. You had best secure our beds. I will be back before long."

As the old man walked away Redwyn stood in the light of the doorway.

"And Redwyn?"

"Yes?"

"Stay out of trouble, won't you?"

"Don't worry," he called back; and he felt happy about Nelrum, in a strange way even close to him.

Chapter 8
A Night at
the Inn

Redwyn put his hand in the doorway and made a short leap into the tavern. The room was smoky and he could see that most of it came from the fireplace where a robust barmaid was putting green logs on the fire. She stopped when she spotted him, grinned and eyed him from head to toe. There were men sitting at long wooden tables. The room was crowded and very noisy. A dice game was being played in the corner, the players shouting after each roll.

Near the back of the tavern a short, portly man was tapping an oak barrel. As Redwyn approached, the man looked up and said, "Just a moment, sir, I'll have her started in a moment." Then he picked up a large wooden mallet and placed the spigot over the bung. He struck the spigot twice. "There she is: the finest liquor from Venice!" he said, and grabbed the barrel. Redwyn helped him lift it onto the shelf.

The man took two mugs down from hooks on the wall and held one under the spigot, the amber liquor tinkling metallically. "Not too much," he said. "One finger of this and you're warm for the evening; two and you sleep like a stone. A tankard and your head could drop right off!" He handed a mug to Redwyn and said, "Here you are, sir.

Warm for the evening."

Redwyn drank the liquor in one swallow. His eyes watered and he shook his head and coughed a little. The portly man laughed, "You see, sir? What did I tell you!"

Redwyn looked approvingly into the empty mug.

"Welcome to King Arthur's Inn, sir. I operate this noble house." The portly man outstretched his hand, and Redwyn clasped it.

"King Arthur's Inn, eh? Well, it is good to be here." He took a floren out and pointed to the empty tankards.

The Innkeeper nodded and dribbled two more draughts. "That's right, sir. It was this very ground that bore the King of Camelot! 'Course over five centuries ago. You've seen the fairgrounds? Well, the royal tournaments were held there."

Redwyn was about to lift one of the mugs but the Innkeeper pushed his arm down.

"The castle of our Baron? Why, it has some of the same stones that were used to build Camelot itself. You can see the ruined walls."

"That's fine."

"Well, thank you, sir." The Innkeeper bit his bottom lip as he raised a mug. Redwyn lifted the other tankard. They paused for a moment where a toast might have been, but only clinked the mugs together and then gulped the liquor down.

"Haaaaah," the Innkeeper exhaled. "Our poor Baron. God have mercy on us. Only He knows what is to become of us now."

Against his better judgement, Redwyn asked, "What now?"

And the little man rolled his eyes over him, as if seeing him for the first time. Apparently satisfied, he went on.

"The Baron of Solway and his family left the castle to attend the coronation of the Duke. That was last spring, in Edinburgh. Well, they never reached Edinburgh. They died, sir. Every last one of 'em."

Redwyn frowned, "But how?"

The Innkeeper wrinkled his high forehead, leaned close and whispered, "The plague!"

Redwyn swallowed hard.

The Innkeeper set down three stacks of shillings in change and then began to wipe the pie board perfunctorily with a piece of cloth. "That's right, sir. All dead except the Lady Lynn."

"The Lady Lynn?"

"Lynn," said the Innkeeper in an obvious tone.

"She survived," said Redwyn.

"Oh, she was in Venice at the time. Poor girl, with no place to go now, no family."

"But why doesn't she live in the castle?"

The little man looked up and twisted the wiping cloth in his hands. "That's the terrible thing, sir. She can't go back to the castle because of *them*."

"What?"

"The Robes."

Redwyn questioned with his eyes, and the Innkeeper nodded to the corner where three men clothed in long black robes were playing dice.

"Will that be all then, Master?"

"No," said Redwyn, turning back, "I need two beds for the evening."

"You will have my best. Through the back doorway and up the stairs. Oh, and don't forget to raise the latchstring, will you? With all the ruffians about these days I feel better sleeping behind a few inches of hard oak."

"I won't forget," he said and gave his host two more shillings and drew himself a half-mug of the liquor.

"You'd best have something to eat with that, sir."

"I am waiting for a friend," Redwyn told him. "We shall dine together."

He sat down with his back against the wall, near the fireplace, and could see the door and watch the dice game being played. He put his feet on the end of a long table, rocked back on the stool and sipped the liquor comfortably until it was gone. Then as the barmaid was walking by, he called, "Sweet maiden!" And she grinned and came slowly toward him with her hands on her hips. Redwyn's eyes were watery and he grinned all the while he spoke.

"Though my heart runneth over, my cup is empty," he said. She reached for the tankard, and he caught her between his legs and drew her in. "Your best liquor, from Venice," he said, squeezing rhythmically with his thighs. "And let the juice brim over, as my passion would also."

He put three shillings into her hand, and she left smiling and then returned with a full mug of the liquor. She smiled over her shoulder as she walked away.

He lifted the drink and rocked back in his chair again, happy. The liquor made him feel warm and he looked for Nelrum at the door then stared back into the fire. The logs hissed. He thought of the naked girl at the river. The barmaid was standing across the room and she looked over her shoulder at him and smiled again. The river girl was prettier than the barmaid. He took the sword from his belt and tapped the point on the wooden floor making tiny cuts in the planking. Then he drained the mug and set it down with a hollow knock.

After what seemed like a long moment he stood and walked over to the cask, replenished the mug, and set three more shillings on the pie board. The Innkeeper saw him and clasped his hands to his head.

There was a shout from the corner where the dice game was being played. Redwyn made his way over between the tables and stood there watching the gaming, trying to follow the dice with his eyes. The tallest of the three robed dice players said, "The game is open, sir."

Redwyn shrugged and took a sip off the mug and moved closer. All three men smiled at him. The middle-sized one shook his hand. The tall man removed some dice from a tiny velvet pouch and dropped them on the table.

Redwyn took another drink and set the mug aside. He took three stacks of shillings from his waistcoat and put them down. All three men set their bets against his. He picked up the dice, hurled them rattling to the backing, and they fell on a three. The tall man smiled and swept up the shillings and said, "It remains your roll."

Redwyn tossed the other floren onto the table. The tall man took it and pushed back five stacks of shillings. Redwyn nodded assentingly at the exchange, left three stacks wagered and put two in his waistcoat pocket. Again, all three men set their bets against his.

He shook and threw. The dice tumbled briskly, turned up three, and he pounded his fist on the table and shouted, "Another three!"

The tall man cleared the shillings and said consolingly, "A divine number that is unlucky in a sinful game. But another wager perhaps; fortune always turns."

One of the others blurted, "A drink! Call the wench for another drink!"

The Tall Robe called for the drinks, and when the barmaid brought them she didn't even look at Redwyn.

He put the remaining shillings in front of him, gulped some ale, and touched the sword handle for luck. Then he cast the dice and they rattled across the table and turned up two.

"Damn it then!" he said, and realizing he was penniless, a sudden spell of sobriety overcame him.

"A moment, sir," said the tall man. "If you haven't any money, perhaps something else?"

Redwyn shook his head No and again started to walk away.

But the tall man called loudly to his back, "I'll put ten gold florens against your sword!"

Redwyn turned back to face the Robe. The tavern grew quieter and some of the patrons were watching. "Against this sword?" he asked. The tall man nodded, small eyes black and fixed.

It was much quieter now. Redwyn grinned and said, "No, I feel a kinship with it–"

"Fifty florens!" the tall Robe countered.

The tavern reacted noisily. Redwyn removed the weapon from his belt, inspecting it.

"Still I–"

"One hundred florens!" the tall Robe said. Then he leaned toward his companions and whispered something.

The crowd was murmuring and Redwyn could feel them growing quiet and motionless around him as they waited for his decision. He heard himself say, "Of course! For one hundred florens you have a wager." Then he returned to the dice table, and the spectators closed in noisily to watch.

Redwyn swallowed dryly and laid the sword down on the dice table. The Tall Robe counted ten stacks of gold and set them near the lion-headed handle. *Even a wastrel could live well on that much money for two years*, Redwyn thought. He pushed his hair back, rubbed his moist palms on his coat sleeves and picked the dice up.

He shook and threw. Both dice tumbled against the backboard; one came up two as the other spun like a top across the table. It caromed off the side of his tankard, struck the sideboards, then wobbled back and hit the sword blade with a soft "clink," fractured, and the broken halves came openly to rest: one half simple clay, the other revealing a barley sized droplet of lead.

A rush of whispers carried the news to the rearward spectators, then the tavern fell to dead silence. In a pretense of composure the Tall Robe pointed an unsteady finger and said, "This was a trick!"

Redwyn reached the sword across the table, crushed the other die, and used the blade to separate another lead bead from the crumbs of clay. "But since they were your dice, the trick is at your expense," he stated quietly.

As the Robe reached for the gold Redwyn jerked the

sword point up and stopped him. The tall man froze and shuddered angrily, then swept his hand across the table and scattered the stacks of coins. He glared at Redwyn and nodded slowly, then turned and retracted, with his two companions, into the crowd.

The spectators began turning away, commenting on the incident. Redwyn put the sword down on the table and started to regather the coins.

After a few moments he heard a familiar voice say, "You were going to stay out of trouble." He looked up and saw Nelrum standing amidst the thinning crowd.

"Look at this gold, Nelrum!"

"You were going to stay out of trouble," Nelrum repeated. Then he frowned and shouted, "Look out!" just as Redwyn felt the blade of a forearm cut up against his throat–someone choking him from behind.

Redwyn reached for the sword on the table, but the attacker jerked him backward and he was just able to grab a metal tankard off with his right hand. He swung it back behind his head and felt it connect soundly. The strangler squeezed harder and Redwyn started swinging the mug back rapidly, each time landing it with solid clunks. The choke hold weakened a little and he tore it loose with his free hand and turned. The middle-sized Robe was standing there, unsteady, clasping his right hand to his forehead. Redwyn swung the heavy mug roundly into the left side of the man's jaw and dropped him, senseless, to the floor.

Then with the crowd reacting to something, Redwyn turned and saw the Tall Robe shoving his way toward the fireplace. The Tall Robe pulled the poker out from between two burning logs and came back jabbing it, the end red hot and sputtering. Redwyn picked the sword up from the dice table. The Tall Robe grinned confidently and stepped in, swinging the poker hard from the side with both hands. Redwyn lifted the sword crosswise to block– the two metals clanked sharply and the poker was shorn off, its hot end smoldering across the floor. The Robe looked uncomprehendingly at the stub left in his hands and Redwyn punched him in the face with the clenched sword butt and put him backward into the furniture.

Now the third and shortest of them advanced with a wooden bung mallet, circling, his arm cocked and the mallet raised above his head. Redwyn threw the sword down and laughed. For a few moments they revolved circularly, facing each other in the center of the tavern, the spectators quiet all around.

The first attacker, the Strangler, tried to raise himself and groaned– Redwyn turned his head momentarily to look– and the short man rushed in bringing the mallet down hard upon Redwyn's shoulder. Redwyn stumbled to the floor. The Short Robe rushed over him with the mallet raised, but suddenly the Innkeeper appeared overhead and caught the Short Robe's arm and they struggled and Redwyn got out from under them and scrambled to his feet. Freeing himself from the Innkeeper, the Short Robe started to circle again, but now Redwyn had had enough of it. He stepped in and jabbed with his right fist, again, hitting the Robe solidly around the eyes both times. The Robe bent over to protect his face and Redwyn swung up and hit him again and blood started spilling from the Short Robe's nose. The Robe put his hands up and cried, "No more! No more!" and Redwyn stepped back– but then the little man came up swinging the mallet wildly, landing glancing blows to Redwyn's throat and forehead. Redwyn punched him hard in the chin, caught him dazed and unsteady by his robe, then slammed his right fist down overhand onto the bridge of the man's nose and eased him, limp, onto the floor.

"This belongs to you, sir," the Innkeeper said. He had come up with a pouch containing the gold. Redwyn stuffed it into his waistcoat, and the Innkeeper picked up the sword from the floor and handed it to him.

"Thank you. The damages to your inn though, I–"

In the front of the tavern the Tall Robe and Strangler were lifting a bench.

"No, sir. Don't even think of the damages." The Innkeeper motioned frantically, and they both started backing toward the door of the vestibule that led to the bed lofts. The two Robes with the bench coordinated themselves for what appeared would be a battering-ram like charge. The Innkeeper said, "This way," and pulled Redwyn backward inside the vestibule.

Redwyn swung the door closed, leaned against it, and a split instant later came the loud "bang!" of the impact and shock stinging his hands through the door as the bench rammed it partway open. A hand came around from the other side and clawed aimlessly near his face– Redwyn threw his weight forward and wedged the hand tight and a curdling scream split through the cacophony of crowd noise. Redwyn eased off and the hand retracted feebly. He rammed the door closed again with his shoulder, flipped the iron latch down, and pulled the string in through its knothole in the wall.

The Innkeeper said, "This way. I am glad you remembered the latchstring."

Redwyn turned and saw the little man standing at the top of the stairs now, holding a candle in front of him so that his face looked ghoulish by the light.

Redwyn began climbing but thought he might vomit before he reached the top. At the last step the Innkeeper took his arm and said, "I thought you might eat something, sir, so I brought this for you." In his other hand was a meat pie.

Redwyn leaned forward against the wall, the Innkeeper waiting with the candle.

"That was a fine thing, sir."

"I will pay the damages," Redwyn gasped.

"I can fix the furniture, Master. Don't think about that. Come, I'll show you to your room."

They went down the hall, and the Innkeeper opened a

door. There was a candle burning on a table inside.

"Goodnight."

"Your meat pie, sir."

Redwyn took it and went in. Nelrum was inside, peering onto the streets through the half-opened shutters. It was quiet and they could hear the Innkeeper going back downstairs and then the groans of the beaten Robes and the Innkeeper's voice demanding payment. Redwyn set the meat pie on a small table. The voices of the Robes grew threatening, and Redwyn started toward the door again, but Nelrum whispered, "Wait!"

A clatter of horse-hooves came from outside. Nelrum clutched the drapery and retracted into the shadow.

The voices below in the tavern stopped. Then a single voice boomed out of the stillness, "Fools!" and there was the hiss of the Tall Robe's voice interspersed with coughs and barely distinguishable.

"Shut up, fool!" boomed the strange voice again.

The Innkeeper asked for damages, and the voice answered, "You'll be paid, runt. More than you bargained!"

The Innkeeper's voice came back pleading. Then there was the sound of footsteps and more clatter of hooves.

Redwyn went to the window and saw the three Robes hobbling away from the tavern, being led by a man on horseback. In the first glance he hadn't noticed the animal— but there was the familiar rhythm of hoofbeats, the muscular contours unmistakable even in the dim light— and he shouted "My horse! You ride my horse!"

The rider turned: it was the bearded monk from the clearing the night before. Redwyn lurched from the window, but Nelrum caught his arm and said, "Not now! Wait for another time!"

Under the yoke of fatigue and drunkenness he acquiesced and watched as the horse and rider passed from the light of the tavern, the three men following and afterward the hoofbeats from the darkness echoing on.

Nelrum continued to observe the street as Redwyn went back to the table and sat down sluggishly to the meat pie.

"You must be wondering where I've been tonight," the old man said. "I should have told you more from the beginning. Yes, I should have told you. Well, you are involved now." He went on soberly, "Why did you gamble the sword? You said that you would stay out of trouble. You have risked much. More than you know. But of course you could not–"

Nelrum turned back to finish, but Redwyn was slumped forward in his food.

The old man came up and shook Redwyn, then propped himself beneath one arm and moved him to the bed. "Goodnight," he whispered, then took the candle from the table, went to the chamber door quietly, and left.

Chapter 9
In Town

"Needles! Needles! I have needles!"

The shrill sound of the peddlar's voice rang in the bedchamber and broke the quiet solitude of Redwyn's sleep.

"Needles! Needles! Soap and needles!" it went on rhythmically.

"Christ's blood," said Redwyn. He shifted beneath the quilts.

"Needles—" the voice choked, cleared itself gruffly and resumed, "Needles! Needles! Soap and needles!"

Redwyn pushed the quilts down. There was a bedbug on his pillow. He flicked it off and saw Nelrum sitting in front of him, beside a window that was open to the light and to the noise from below.

"Can't you close those shutters, Nelrum?"

"Soap!" yelled the peddlar.

"Can't you?"

"Why did you gamble the sword last night?" the old man asked. He was looking out the window, his body rendered a diffuse outline by its glare.

"Needles!"

"What?"

"Soap! Soap!"

"I'd forgotten how I hate cities," Nelrum said. "The filth and stench. The ugliness that breeds here."

"The noise," said Redwyn.

"Soap! I sell soap!"

Nelrum stood, leaned out the window, and called, "You there!"

The peddlar looked up from his plot, red-faced like a ham, and heavy-set, with a peasant's smock and brown leather sacks strapped all about him. He shouted belligerently, "Needles! Soap!"

Nelrum's hands tightened on the window ledge.

"Can't you move a little further down?"

"Soap! I sell soap!"

Nelrum shouted, "I will buy some if you will move away from here!"

The peddlar shifted his straps and shouted back, "All right, sir! All right! All right!"

Nelrum raised his hand to stay the voice for a moment, walked to the foot of Redwyn's bed and picked up the sack of coins. He brought them back to the window, threw one down, and it landed ringing on the street. The peddlar waddled with the soap sacks flopping against his body, picked up the coin, flinched, and the soap sacks quivered.

"Why, this is a floren!" he shouted.

Nelrum frowned. "So?"

"Well, I can't change a floren, sir! You'll have to come down now!"

Nelrum turned from the window. His face was taut with anger and he walked quickly between the beds and slammed the door hard behind him. Redwyn rolled on his breeches and went to the window. He saw Nelrum come out from the tavern, gesticulating with his hands.

"Say, Nelrum," he called down. "Why don't you ask the fellow if he knows where the bath is?"

The peddlar bellowed, "It's just at the end of the street,

sir. On that hill that overlooks the sea. But you will need soap if you go there!"

"My friend will buy some from you!" Redwyn said, and he turned from the window grinning. He had just finished pulling on his boots when Nelrum came in again and tossed a lump of grey soap on the bed.

"The idiot!"

"Why do you malign him so," said Redwyn, grinning.

Nelrum answered sharply, "Why should he be so reluctant to trade a gold floren for a piece of soap?"

"You gave it to him?" Redwyn's smile vanished. He had picked up a meat pie, but now set it down.

"For the soap, yes. But it was difficult."

"Wine!" came another voice, "Wine! Wine! Wine!"

Nelrum went to the window ledge and snatched up the sack of coins. "We had better find your bath," he said.

Redwyn took the sword from the table and slipped it through his belt. He was perspiring and somewhat red-eyed. Nelrum came over from the window and gestured to the sword. "I would not risk that weapon again," he said.

"Wine! Wine! Wine!" came the cry.

"Well, I don't want any wine," Redwyn told him.

As they descended into the tavern, sunlight was falling through the doorway and the barmaid was straightening furniture. The Innkeeper was sweeping the floor and he stopped when he saw them. The Innkeeper said, "He was here looking for you, sir."

"Who was?" Redwyn asked.

"I told your friend. It was that black-faced devil who was here last night."

"His name is Brech," said Nelrum.

"Aye, that's him," said the Innkeeper. "He's a devil, that one."

"The man who took my horse— is he one of these Robes, Nelrum?"

"Aye," said the Innkeeper. "He came back last night, and

this morning too."

"I heard him threaten you," Redwyn said. He looked about the tavern and saw the smashed dice table, broken benches, and lying on top of the counter the two halves of the shorn poker. It all seemed unreal now as he saw it clearly, without distortion from the liquor.

Nelrum urged him toward the door with a gesture.

The Innkeeper looked at both of them for a moment then awkwardly averted his gaze and began sweeping again, staring blankly.

Redwyn said, "If he returns, tell him I will be back here to meet him!" and he immediately felt Nelrum's grip upon his arm. The Innkeeper looked up and smiled.

Redwyn went along with Nelrum to the doorway, and they stepped outside.

Nelrum said, "There is great, great danger here! You must listen to what I tell you, and in the meantime be very careful! Now let us get ourselves to that bath."

Redwyn nodded, understanding none of it, and followed him into the street. Since earlier, when the lone soap peddlar had barked beneath their window, traffic had become heavy. Clusters of people gathered around the merchant stands now, and goats were being herded through the street. The two men became separated around a crowded turn and Nelrum was pushed far ahead. Redwyn pried his way through, and as the crowd in front of him cleared he saw the girl from the river standing just across the street. She was clothed in a peach satin dress, and her dark hair was pressed into a delicate net of pearls. He was shocked that it was really her. She was buying eggs from a merchant, and Nelrum was walking toward her.

She turned and saw the old man and they embraced.

Redwyn stayed against the far wall, watching. She clutched Nelrum's robes and pressed her cheek against his shoulder. She was speaking to him, frowning with her eyes closed, her delicate mouth stiffening as a woman's mouth will when she is about to cry. Then Nelrum's hands rose higher on her back and her thin fingers clenched tightly about the folds of his robe. She cried, shaking slightly, taking short quick breaths, and after several moments seemed to relax and breathe easier. Her eyes remained closed for some time though, and when she finally did open them Redwyn could see them flash, luminous grey and moist with tears. They were bright eyes and he could see them clearly from where he stood.

She wiped the tears with her fingertips and stood facing the old man, talking at considerable length. As Redwyn watched between the passing pedestrians, he saw Nelrum lift the bag of gold and extend it in an offertory gesture. The young woman was shaking her head No. A crowd of people and a donkey cart passed. Then Nelrum was empty handed and the young woman was walking away.

He kept an eye on her back and moved as fast as he could, reached Nelrum, and caught a final glimpse of the peach dress as it was digested into the dull, full blending hues of the crowd.

"Where is the gold?"

"She has it."

"What!"

"I said she has it."

"You mean you gave it to her!"

"Yes, all of it, except for this." Nelrum extended a floren. Redwyn grimaced and took it from his hand.

"You would have done it, had you understood her needs."

"I don't believe it!"

"But I will show you."

"I want you to take me to her," Redwyn said with violence in his voice.

"I will take you to her and you can see what the money is for. But after the bath. I want to explain some things first."

Redwyn shouted, "By bloody Christ! I would like some bloody things explained!"

"Then we should go," said Nelrum quietly, "To the bath."

They began walking again, without speaking, and remained close together through the crowded street. Free of the confines of the town, the road made a wide turn and they found the bathhouse sitting atop a hillock on the edge of the sea. Steam was rising from its windows into the morning air, and they approached by walking through a yard of rain barrels and broken slate. As Redwyn pushed the heavy door open a cloud of steam billowed out and they walked blindly forward until it cleared.

Inside, young girls and matrons were washing laundry in shallow basins carved out of the stone floor. Huge black kettles boiled in the fireplaces, and Redwyn was smiling at the girls, who were whispering to each other and looking at him through the steam, when a voice called, "Here now! Can I help you two gentlemen?"

An attendant stood beside a half-opened oor with a sop-rag slung about his neck. He was very thin and had red watery eyes.

"Is this the bathhouse?" Redwyn asked.

The girls giggled.

The man pushed the door open to expose another room and said, "This way, gentlemen."

The girls made funny noises as Redwyn walked past them into the bath chamber where there was a tall open window and sunlight slanting in across several tubs of pitch-butted slate.

"Two baths?"

Nelrum shook his head. Redwyn answered, "Just one."

The man sniffed constantly from the strong soap fumes as he used a bucket to scoop boiling water from a kettle and half filled one of the tubs. He took cold from a barrel, mixed the bath to the proper temperature, then set a piece of soap down and went out.

Redwyn pulled off his waistcoat and said, "We didn't need the peddlar's soap after all." Nelrum just grinned.

He finished undressing and got in. The water was almost

too hot, but he gradually surrendered to it and put his neck against the flat, cool stone and took several purging breaths. "I must explain some things," Nelrum said seriously.

Redwyn opened his eyes and the steam evaporating from the bath into the golden sunlight reminded him of his lost treasure. He said, "Why did you give that woman my money?"

"That is the least of it."

"But start with that."

Nelrum walked to the window and looked out at the open expanse of sea. "I knew her father," he began. "He was the Baron of Solway and a good friend. I met him many years ago when he was hunting at the edge of Grinmere wood. A boar had charged him, and his party ran off and left him to face the beast alone. He managed to drive a lance into it, but it reached him nonetheless and gored his leg. "I met him by accident a few hours later. He was sitting against a tree with the leg all torn above the knee and bleeding. I took him under my care and for two weeks during his convalescence we talked and, thus, became good friends. When he was well enough I went with him back to the castle. I returned there often on visits. And he would visit me sometimes in Grinmere."

Nelrum paused, and Redwyn heard him sigh in the quiet room.

"Lynn was his first born child and only daughter. In the spring of this year she traveled with her maidservant to Venice, to witness an important wedding; but the Baron, his five sons, and the Baroness all ventured to Edinburgh to attend the coronation of the Duke. They stopped in their journey's course at a little town half-way between here and Edinburgh called Godwyne."

"I have heard of it," Redwyn said.

"Then perhaps you have heard that the Plague struck there."

"No."

"It came suddenly, without warning; struck into every

71

corner of the little village. Nearly every living thing died, even the horses and livestock; everything except the Robes."

"What!" Redwyn looked up, frowning. Just then the door from the laundry swung open and two men dressed in huntsman's garb came in. Nelrum glanced at them, walked to the window again and stared silently out at the sea.

Redwyn finished bathing, dressed, and the huntsmen watched him as he slipped the sword through his belt. He paid the attendant and sold back the extra lump of soap. Then he and Nelrum continued their conversation while walking up the steep hill road that meandered from the town.

"When Lynn returned from Venice, she had no notion that tragedy had befallen her family. She learned of it from them."

"The Robes," Redwyn asserted.

"Yes. They had taken her castle and holdings. Now all her father's wealth is in their hands."

"But they couldn't just *take* them."

"Oh, they had documents. Wills that were signed under oath and bequeathed everything to their order."

Where the road turned at the top of the hill they left it and started across a meadow, toward a stone building set back amid some trees.

"Where are we going?"

"I haven't finished the story yet. But I wanted you to see where your money went."

"Good. Perhaps I can still retrieve some."

They reached the stone-house door. Nelrum grinned as he lifted the latch, and Redwyn stepped in front of him eagerly, pushed the door open and stepped in.

Inside the large, unevenly sun-lit room there were children scattered all about– perhaps fifty of them. Some were playing, others lying in narrow cots along the walls. The noise had diminished perceptibly as Redwyn entered, and many of the waifs were looking up.

To the left, at one end of the room, was another door, a

chamber, Redwyn thought. His eyes swept over the cots, faces, rags and sparse grey furniture. Then in the rear of the place, kneeling beneath an open window, was the Lady Lynn. She had changed from her peach dress into a matron's smock and was wrapping a linen bandage around a small boy's knee. She glanced up and saw them and turned back frowning, her eyes fixed intently on her work.

When she finished, the child who had received the dressing stood up and tested it with a bend of his leg. He asked permission to leave, it was granted, and he left hurriedly through the back door. Lynn stood, and Redwyn could feel his throat tightening as she approached them.

"Do you know each other?" she asked.

Nelrum said, "Lynn St. Du Lac, Baroness of Solway, allow me to introduce Redwyn, an old and trusted ally."

His name sounded short, and he wondered at the *old and trusted ally* part of the introduction, but lifted her outstretched hand and bowed politely.

She spoke uncertainly, "I saw you at the Grinmere fork. You were performing a—"

"Swindle," Redwyn interrupted.

"This is the young man who donated the money," said Nelrum, frowning.

She was about to speak again and suppressed it, but with the silence building, demanding polite action of some kind, she simply looked up into Redwyn's eyes and smiled. She saw no expectation of gratitude in his face, no swagger or conceit. Rather, he wore the guilty look of an orphan, a look she recognized and understood. "Thank you," she said softly, and made a slight inclination of her head.

Just then the rear door crashed open and a short man staggered in and dropped a sack of flour from his shoulder onto the floor. He growled, "Were it filled with gold, that is still a heavy sack!" It was the Innkeeper from the tavern. He smiled with recognition and said, "Hello, Sirs. I didn't know you were coming this way."

73

"How many have you brought this time, Josh?" asked Lynn.

"Nine, My Lady: this one, eight still in the cart."

She went to the desk, removed the pouch of coins that Redwyn recognized, and took a floren from it. The Innkeeper twisted a leather purse in his hands.

"If it was my grain, My Lady, not one pfenning would I charge. But the farmers–"

"I know," she said, stopping him.

The Innkeeper took the coin from her and placed it into his purse, feeling the lining carefully for security. He said, "I'll store the other sacks in the grain house."

Redwyn started forward, but Nelrum moved in front of him and said, "I will help you."

The Innkeeper turned back and acknowledged Nelrum with a nod, and they both walked out through the rear door.

Now Redwyn and Lynn were alone with the orphans whose voices made a soft collective murmur in the cavernous room. Lynn's eyes flashed as she moved forward with her hands folded in front of her. She passed through a shaft of sunlight, stepped into another shadow and said, "It seems odd that you know Nelrum."

"Do you uphold this orphanage by yourself?"

"Yes, I live here now. My family have fostered this home for generations. It was the only property that the Robes neglected to claim. I didn't think that I would see you again, after the river. It was terrible the way they beat you." Her voice was growing softer; her eyes opened and closed slowly, luminously from the shadow, reminding Redwyn of an animal that watches from a hidden lair.

She said, "I *am* sorry for the way I behaved at the river. That I shouted that way. We left at dawn the next morning. I sat in the front of the wagon to watch for you along the road. I was afraid that if they saw you again they might start chasing you. I did not think that anyone would stay the night in Grinmere. Not really. But I suppose that, being a close friend of Nelrum's, you aren't afraid."

"Of what?"

"Of Grinmere," she said.

"No," he said.

"Neither was my father," she said, and looked at him with a slight turn of her head, as if by that new angle to detect whether he had understood the compliment paid him.

He *had* understood, but took no comfort in it. Not because she was a lady and he an orphan who lived from wit to penny. For she was the master now of only a room full of orphans. It was her beauty that unsettled him– that, up close, made him ashamed of the glance stolen at the river.

"Do you not feel well?" she asked, lifting a silence that had fallen over them, her voice doing it gently, as a skilled surgeon's hand might lift a dressing from a recent wound.

"I do not," he admitted. And it was true. Looking at her, Redwyn felt the same dull ache as from a sunset, or the smell of the earth in spring, or the summer forest when the light filtered through the dark green leaves and made it dim and church-like. Such beauty was to be witnessed but not apprehended, he thought– and was far easier to turn away from than to try to hold on to or understand. For he saw her in waves of realization about himself, contrasts of his own low character to the perfection there before him– that rare composition of earthly sensualities and human virtues that can live its fragile existence only in the face of a woman.

Just then a little blonde girl pushed open the front door and said:

"My Lady, William has thrown six stones at the beehive. I let him throw three but then told him to stop or I'd fetch you."

Lynn said, "Excuse me," and walked quickly past him out the front door. The little girl glanced suspiciously back, then followed.

Now alone with the orphans he sat down at the small, drawered table. There was a bowl of fruit on it and the drawer had been left partway open, the pouch of gold clearly visible inside. He reached out to take something, either a pear or the pouch of gold, he himself not certain of which, but his hand halted as a crumpled mass of clothing animated itself in one of the darker corners of the room. It sprouted hands and feet then moved toward him into the sunlight. He saw, then, it was the little boy from the street fight the night before, and said, "Hello, Master."

The boy was still wearing the too-big merchant's coat and carrying, by one corner, a blank sheet of parchment. He came closer and looked seriously into Redwyn's face. Redwyn looked back at him without smiling, and the boy reached into the drawer of the table. He removed a quill pen and pot of ink from it, then standing, resting his elbows on the table, began to write.

The quill tip scratched the thick paper, and he dipped the pen and wrote some more. Redwyn leaned forward and read:

My name is Donny Gwaith.
I am here because my house
burned down.

The pain of Redwyn's battered shoulder tightened across his back. He grimaced then noticed the boy grimacing too.

"Donny Gwaith, eh? And a scholar no less. If I may present myself, I am Redwyn, your humble and miserable slave." He smiled nervously. A half-smile twitched onto the boy's face and he never took his eyes off Redwyn.

"Have you been here long, Donny?"

The boy shook his head No.

"Do you like it, though?"

The boy shook No again, then pointed at his mouth and shook once more, signifying he couldn't speak.

Redwyn nodded that he understood, then asked very quietly, "Could you talk before the fire?"

Donny Gwaith picked up the pen again and scratched out another message. Redwyn followed the printing and read:

It was not me.

He frowned, uncertain of what it meant; the boy seemed puzzled too, his eyes shifting erratically but then settling onto Redwyn's face.

"Listen, Donny. If you know that something is true, you believe it, don't you? Well, sometimes you have to believe in something *before* you can see it's true. And no matter what people say, you have to believe in your own graces. Sometimes they're all you have. You can lose them, but you can always fight to get them back." He added, "You have to fight *yourself*, sometimes."

The boy shifted his eyes blankly to look at some odd spot in the room.

Redwyn said, "Listen. Last night we fought those men together, and we won, didn't we? You can fight this too. It's inside of you, but you can fight it– the same way."

Donny frowned and looked up.

"I'll help you fight those bad voices that are inside of you. You hear them sometimes, don't you?"

Donny looked at Redwyn's eyes and nodded.

"They are blaming you, but they are wrong. You try to talk, and whenever you hear those voices I will shout louder so you *cannot* hear them. Are you ready?"

"Are you ready?" Redwyn asked again.

Donny nodded and shut his eyes hard and Redwyn said, "Come now. Try."

The boy shook his head and Redwyn said, "Try!"

Donny took a deep breath and held it and Redwyn shook it loose and yelled, "Fight, Donny!"

The boy moved his mouth silently. Redwyn shouted, "Fight!" Other children were gathering around. Redwyn shouted, "Fight it, Donny!"

He moved his mouth agonizingly, making tiny clicks. Just then Lynn's voice cracked from the doorway, "Stop it! Stop it now!"

She rushed over with the small girl beside her and pried

Donny away. Redwyn stood up quickly, his legs knocking the bench over behind him.

"Get out!" Lynn yelled.

"No," he said, stepping backward over the bench.

"Get out!" she screamed.

Donny was weeping, tugging on the folds of her smock. She shouted, "Blackguard! Get out!"

Redwyn went out through the front door. The little girl rushed to slam it behind him. Lynn stood there for a moment, quivering. She righted the bench and then loosened her smock and sat down at the table to cry, though thought of nothing, nor any reason that she should cry. But she did. And it seemed to her a long while later when something touched her forearm. She wiped her eyes with her fingertips and saw the note that Donny Gwaith had laid there. It read:

That man would help me.

She looked at the boy and asked, "What do you mean that he was trying to help you, Donny?"

Then the rear door was opened and Nelrum came in followed by Josh the Innkeeper.

"Hello, lad," Nelrum said, and Donny moved quickly around the table to meet him.

"He seems to know you," said Lynn, her face displaying plainly the effects of spent emotions.

Nelrum looked about the room. "Where is Redwyn, Lynn?"

"Donny seems to know you, Nelrum," she said.

"This is the boy he rescued last night," Nelrum said.

"What?"

Nelrum glanced down at the child who was clutching him. "He saw some men molesting the lad, so he taught them a lesson. Where is he?"

"He wrestled three Robes!" the Innkeeper interjected, then with Lynn breaking down again seemed suddenly dumbfounded for having misplaced his enthusiasm.

"Where is he?"

"I told him to get out," she said.

The Innkeeper flushed. Nelrum looked quickly through the open window and said, "Josh, you had better bring your cart around."

"Aye, I'll fetch it." And the portly man hurried through the back door.

"Please don't be angry, Nelrum. I couldn't stand that now."

"I won't be."

She put her head down on her arms. "Who is he, truly?"

"A friend," he told her.

"Why did you bring him here? When I came in a moment ago he was shouting at Donny Gwaith."

"He was probably trying to help him."

She looked up from her forearms, wet eyes narrowing, and said in a demanding tone, "Who is he?"

Nelrum started toward the front door.

"Who is he!"

But Nelrum just kept walking. He opened the door and stepped out. The Innkeeper was waiting outside in his two-wheeled cart. Nelrum climbed in and said, "We have to find him, Josh."

The little man answered, "Aye," and snapped the donkey with a willow branch to set the cart in motion.

Chapter 10
Brech

Redwyn had walked briskly from the orphanage, the sun glaring on the dry road and gusts of wind raising dust into his face as he squinted to avoid the wagon ruts and jutting stones on the steep, eroded drop into Solway. He was angry. The road was irritating with its hazards and glare, so he abandoned it halfway down the hill and cut left across a gently down-sloped meadow that was tall with late summer growth. The field was nearly shoulder high, but the ground was hard and even underneath the weeds and the walking much easier.

Grasshoppers lit off shining from invisible perches into shallow arcs of flight, landing to become invisible again in the tall weeds. The whir of grasshopper wings was soothing, and the sun was ripe-yellow and felt good across his back with the wind cool and steadily freshening into gentle breezes from the sea. But he thought of Lynn again and cursed her in his mind.

He could see the image of her face as she scolded, and the hatred he felt grew furious and complete. Through the hatred he knew that it had been foolish to come to Solway. It had been foolish to follow the Old Man out of Grinmere, or to listen to his stories, or to trust him. "The Old Man gave away the gold," the hatred's voice reminded him. And he agreed with the voice. It told him other things that he agreed with, and he felt very satisfied as he stepped blindly into a thicket of burrs, lurched, then shouting gutturally, cursing himself, backed out slowly from the dense, high-bushed cockleburrs that detached stingingly onto the thin cloth of his breeches and, because he had backed out, covered his buttocks and the backs of his legs as well.

He picked off all the burrs that he could reach, then removed his boots and breeches and sat half-naked in the weeds to pluck the rest of them and to extract the tiny needle fragments from the cloth. Sitting down in the deep weeds he heard a cart go by on the road. Then his clothing safe to put on again, he dressed, stood up and caught sight of the bath house– small on the low horizon and issuing wisps of steam against the deep blue of the sea. He thought of going back to try one of the girls there, but reasoned that it was too far away now, and cursed himself for having left the road in haste.

He moved carefully between the burr thickets in the last stretch of field, then walked swiftly between the gardens that were behind some merchant houses, and passed between the high walls of the houses into the cool, foul smelling darkness of an alley.

The short cut had brought him into the center of town, onto the main street near the place where he had first seen Lynn again and watched her talk with Nelrum. He shoved through the crowded turn and, as the street widened and the crowd dispersed in front of him, began moving quickly and impatiently toward the Inn.

"You have a floren," he told himself. "Almost that much. That is something. You have had far less in your pockets before this, and you have never been at a loss for ideas. So think of something to improve your lot and just go on from there." But instead he thought of Nelrum. There was something about the Old Man that made him feel very deeply, but he wasn't sure what it was. Then Lynn's image returned, and with his mind bogging into emotions he decided to give up on thinking altogether.

Next door to the tavern, the cheesemaker was boiling goat's milk in large, barrel-like kettles outside his stall. Redwyn knew it was goat's milk from the bad smell it made, and a fat man had purchased a bowl of the curdle and was drinking it on the tavern porch, standing where his body's massive bulk had blocked the door. Redwyn reached the base of the steps and said, "Excuse me." But the fat man did not move; he was wearing a tight leather hood and just turned his head away vaguely and lifted the steaming bowl up to drink.

"You know, you're quite impressive," Redwyn said to him.

The man drank from the bowl sloppily, so that rivulets of milk streamed down his chin. Redwyn attempted to squeeze by. He could feel the man resisting with deliberate pressure, and he eased off and tried to pass on the other side, but the man grinned and moved over to block him.

Redwyn's muscles tightening with anger now, he tried to calm himself, thinking of peaceful courses of action, such as waiting for the man to leave, reasoning with him, or finding a back door to the tavern, but it was no good. For the fat man chuckled with his big face, squinted with his tiny pig-like eyes; and infuriated, Redwyn flew into him shoulder first, stabbing hard into the caving bulk with his elbow, shouldering the man backward until he had him off balance at the edge of the tavern porch. The huge body hung there a moment, quivering on the edge. The man rocked backward, his stubby fingers released the bowl of curd, and then he plopped off into an immense pile of filth.

A resounding cheer went up from a small crowd of pedestrians, and they began to shout at the man as if they knew him, jeering as he wallowed, like a stranded tortoise, in the mire. Redwyn watched for a moment, grinning in satisfaction, then stepped inside the tavern. The bearded monk was there, sitting at a small table in the light from the doorway. The monk was glaring at him. The barmaid was standing near the fireplace, looking frightened. There was no one else that he could see, though it was dark while his eyes adjusted from the sunlight.

The monk stood up, his face expressionless and made more so by his thick beard. He had a strange unwavering aspect in his eyes that glared motionless and flat, and his hands were huge but relaxed at his sides. This was a hard man, Redwyn realized; not like the bloater he had just shouldered into the filth heap. This was a man of enormous muscle: a human bull, relaxed at the moment, without any apprehension that a meeting with a normal man could harm him. As the giant approached, the floor boards conducted the impact of his steps.

"My name is Brech," his voice issued in a hoarse, almost cough-like whisper. "I was sent here by My Lord, Morcar, to return the lost animal to you." He extended a thick right hand, and a hump of muscle climbed up the side of his neck. Redwyn became aware that his own hand had folded unconsciously around his sword handle, but he immediately released it and accepted the greeting, feeling the stone-like texture of the monk against his own yielding flesh.

"My name is Redwyn," he said.

"I know," the giant grunted. "The barmaid told me before you came. I was ordered by my master to return the lost horse, and to ask your forgiveness for our three brethren of last night's brawl."

"Why did you take the horse?" Redwyn asked, and he searched for some expression, perhaps a jitter in the brown, doglike eyes. But there was none. The man's face told little about him.

"The fire was close. You will see that by the hair on the horse's ears and by the shrivelled bristle of his snout. I untethered him before he burned and took him to care for the wounds."

"Wounds?"

"Splinters from the explosion; also, when he bolted, the bridle thong must have scored his mouth and neck."

"I did not see him bolt."

"All horses bolt from fires. But perhaps you were lying on the ground and did not see him as he reared from the explosion and fought against the rope."

"If he bolted," said Redwyn, "the thin tether I used would have broken. The bridle thong has been broken for three weeks. I did not ride him often since acquiring the wagon."

The monk said tonelessly, "Such a stallion. With courage that it does not bolt from fires. And to pull your wagon, yet. Such an animal would be a prize for the finest knight in Christendom."

"I did not see him bolt," Redwyn answered, now annoyed. He felt the anger coming up in warm waves. "When you came in last night you threatened the Innkeeper. I heard you tell him that he may get more than he bargained for. What sort of behavior is that for monks? What sort of monk rails like a drunken heathen?"

The barmaid whimpered in fear. But the huge man just stood there, his glaring eyes motionless, his expression flat and unchanged. Then he raised his hands and turned them so the palms were facing upward, and said, "As you can see. I have come here, sir, unarmed."

Redwyn followed the flat gaze to his own sword and found, again, that he had unconsciously gripped the handle. He coughed at the discovery and shoved the weapon back down in his belt, feeling ignoble for having drawn on an unarmed man. nable to think of anything to say for a moment, he stammered, "I am sorry, Friar– I don't know why I did that."

The giant lowered his hands and rumbled, "The men who brawled with you last night will be punished. I spoke in anger to the good Innkeeper, but I am prone to this, sir. I am not used to people. My charge was to invite you to the castle. My Lord would greet you there and return the lost animal himself."

"You are a cloistered order?"

"We are solitary unless needed."

Redwyn's anger was dissipating. "Forgive the impertinence, Friar, but if you would return my horse, why haven't you brought it with you?"

"Brother Morcar asked to meet you," the monk said. "Yet if you wish it, I will bring the animal back here. Allow until nightfall because the street is crowded and it will be difficult to get him through."

Redwyn began to think that perhaps it was only the monk's voice and giant, brutish body that he mistrusted. The voice irritated him like the sound of an axe being turned on coarse stone, yet the words were reasonable and by themselves seemed true enough. *"So don't be a fool,"* he told himself. *"Horses always bolt from fires, and yours must have gotten himself tangled in the rope and suffered some minor wounds. There is nothing unusual in this. You are spoiling for a fight and, by God, the Friar is the wrong man to have it with! Maybe it is only a voice that makes a reasonable explanation sound as false as any lies."*

He glanced back toward the doorway and said, "There is no need to bring him, Friar. It is time I left this place. Thank you for rescuing my horse. And I will meet your master, to thank him as well."

The monk nodded and turned slowly and started toward the door. Redwyn followed and again could feel the quaking floorboards, the heavy, penetrating impact of the giant's steps.

Outside, the crowd was still jeering at the soiled fat man who was now out of the quagmire, but engaged in some argument with the cheesemaker. It grew quieter as Brech moved into the doorway. A path opened up for him on the street. Redwyn stepped onto the porch behind the monk and saw the fat man looking over, his mouth hanging open and fat face mottled with black mud. They turned right into the street. Redwyn noticed people giving them both strange looks and keeping well out of their way. "Well, after all," he told himself. "Monk or no monk, this is a very big man."

Chapter 11
The Robes

They passed along the stands and merchant shops, people watching from doorways, and held an uncompromised course through a thinning late-afternoon stream of pedestrians. Brech walked with his arms folded in front of him, head forward, so that Redwyn could see the skin on the back of his neck, heavy grained and bristly like the hide of some great beast.

A little way down the street they stopped at a fowler's concession. The clerk asked what they wanted. Brech told him to bring a goose. The owner of the concession seemed nervous, standing back and watching from his doorway, and he came out finally and dismissed the clerk and continued looking over the stacks of willow branch cages himself. He put a cage holding a husky, very alert looking goose on the counter; and as Brech reached for it the big goose bit him through the rungs. The monk's face showed no expression at all as he smashed his thick hand into the pen, caught the goose's writhing neck and crushed it, the bird fluttering a moment, then collapsing into a pile of grey feathers. Its head swung loose between the rungs as Brech picked up the cage again. He paid the fowler with a schilling and walked away.

Redwyn caught up alongside him and said, "Do you think

it was enough?"

There was no answer.

"It's just that– a schilling doesn't seem like ample payment for such a fine bird."

But again the monk was silent. Redwyn fell back behind him and they continued that way without speaking.

The street ended at the city gates. The two men walked through the fairgrounds, ignoring shouts from vendors, and then between the tents and wagons to meet the dusty uphill road that led to the castle. It was steady climbing on the hill in the hot late afternoon, and they did not speak and climbed until the road levelled and there were crop plantings stretching flat on both sides. The castle seemed just ahead, then, but because of its size it was farther than it looked, and they had to walk some distance between the plantings before reaching even the outer grounds. A farmer in a distant corner of his field stopped working and leaned on his scythe to watch them.

At the limits of the baronial estate two stone pillars marked the only opening through a border of dense, high-grown hedge. The two men passed between the pillars, crossed another wide field that formed the outer portion of the castle grounds, then stopped at the edge of the castle moat. It was a dry moat, very deep, and Redwyn looked down into it and saw the inward-slanting sides, ground spikes and jagged stones at the bottom that made it discouraging to cross. From where they stood the drawbridge was just across the space of the moat, flanked on either side by turreted rook towers and a high, continuous, crenelated wall that fused with the towers and surrounded the inner grounds in stone. There were two robed men in each of the rooks. Brech waved and one man from each tower disappeared and then the drawbridge started down. It groaned on its great hinges, shaking as it slowly fell, huge, square-timbered and girdled with iron, timbers creaking, and the thick black chains that suspended it clanging as they slipped through holes in the stone walls.

"Expecting visitors?" Redwyn shouted over the din.

The drawgate boomed onto its landing.

The monk grumbled something as they crossed, and Redwyn noted the bridge's guardrail had been freshly removed. Then they traversed the outer square, passed under the main arch into a walled garden where flowers were in bloom though heavily burdened by tall weeds and undergrowth. The hedges were lush but untrimmed, and ivy had grown unbridled from the walls into the terraced flower beds. Dry leaves rustled over the stone paths as they walked. Then they passed under another arch and were out of the garden, into a vestibule, and then climbing inside a narrow turning staircase into darkness.

As the light faded, Redwyn felt the close walls for security. He could hear Brech's movements in front of him. The breathing was magnified by the enclosure. Then it became completely dark and he slowed his steps a little in order to let Brech get ahead. Above, the yellow light of torches began to flicker on the curved staircase wall. Redwyn climbed the last spiral and Brech was waiting for him inside a dim, low-ceilinged corridor.

Two torches were burning sootily in grated iron sconces. There was a black door– maybe iron; off to one side an antechamber where a tapestry was hung with a gleam of natural light showing around its dark blue edges. There were murmurs from that direction, clinks, the unmistakable rattle of ale mugs, then a crash as if a tray of mugs had dropped onto the floor. Brech walked over and pulled the tapestry aside. The voices hushed, and Redwyn caught a glimpse of men sitting at tables inside a deep, sun brightened room. As the drape fell back into place the light was gone again and the antechamber was dim. Brech returned, walking directly to the black door. He struck it with his fist and made a deep gonging sound that rang on in the quiet halls. Then he left without saying anything, and Redwyn watched him disappear down a darkened passageway.

Alone, waiting for the iron door to open, laughter broke out with more clanking of tankard mugs. He reasoned that the room behind him must be the great hall of the castle and, judging by the noise, there were a lot of men inside.

There was the click of a metal latch, and as the door was being pulled open he glimpsed a shadowy looking figure moving in the interior the chamber. Then a small, boyish looking man stepped out from behind the door. He was very thin and had a slender nose and high cheekbones, and wrinkles formed around his sallow eyes as he focused them on Redwyn's sword. The man was wearing an Italian brocade vest and embroidered breeches, and one of his tiny hands was resting on a silver rapier that was slung through a leather belt loop at his side. Redwyn judged his age to be about forty, though at first glance he could have easily mistaken him for a juvenile. The wrinkles around his straining eyes and a few around his mouth told his age.

The man stepped backward, and the door swung wider so that the interior of the chamber was exposed. It was dark, save for a single shaft of sunlight that entered through a small high window and shone upon a young woman's portrait on the opposite wall. The torches were unlit in their sconces. Beneath the glare of the lone window the shadowy looking figure was sitting now, sideways, behind a massive piece of furniture.

"Are you Redwyn?" its voice asked out of the glare.

"I am," he answered, and went in.

The figure rose and motioned for the boyish man to leave. "My name is Morcar," it said, floating around what resolved itself, in the bad light, as a massive carved desk. "I am the guardian of this order of charity which the townspeople, you have doubtless heard, refer to as 'The Robes.'"

"I have come for my horse," said Redwyn, remembering to add, "And to thank you for returning it."

"But do not thank me, young man. And yes, yes, you shall have your horse. With my deepest regret over your misfortunes."

The door clanked shut as the other man left the room.

"Misfortunes?"

"Yes," the figure said, moving closer and out of the glare. "I was led to understand that you suffered the loss of your magic troupe to some sort of...explosion?"

"There was no troupe," Redwyn told him, "Only myself. But I did lose my wagon to an explosion and fire..."

Redwyn went on to describe the event, stalling in a effort to study the half-illumined being that stood before him now and still appeared more as a shadow, in its dark robe, than a man. Its face remained invisible inside the deep cover of the hood, and the robe hung loose and flowing enough to re-move all contours of form. Its shoulders were narrow, that much Redwyn could tell, but height was harder because of the peaked hood. He continued his story as the figure swayed slightly, nodding its hooded head, a subdued voice commenting, "Yes," or, "Such is fate," but nothing more. And after the soliloquy had passed through several incredible stages and Redwyn had come to making lame philosophical comments about the "upheavals of fortune" and the "furious turnings of its unpredictable wheel," still trying in vain to see the face, two grotesque hands rose against the solid black background of the robe and floated, he imagined, as disem-bodied fragments of the demon that lived inside. Long nailed and bony, with the thinnest fingers he had ever seen, the skin on them was a strange red color and deeply creased with wrinkles.

"You were saying," the hood asked quietly.

"I can't remember. Yes, I was saying something. I can't remember now."

The gruesome hands vanished into the robe, and the face-less hood said, "But I find it interesting. Especially the part about the flame engine. Brech claimed that you could con-jure a flame of no small volume, control this fire, give it direction, and quench it as you wished. It was so fantastic that I couldn't believe him. But after what you have told me; Redwyn, is it true?"

"It *was* true. But it was a swindler's trick. I have abandoned those arts forever."

"Still, it *is* a curiosity. And yet this flame engine caused the destruction of your wagon."

"I believe the lard pot must have exploded."

"Lard pot?"

"Yes, excuse me, Friar. I don't mean to flout your hospitality, but I can see by the angle of the sun's ray that the day is nearly gone. I would pack my horse and be away now if I could."

The hood rose in the direction of the woman's portrait. The rusty sun was striking just above, missing the picture and faintly illuminating the stone wall. As they were both watching the diminished ray expired.

"How right you are about the sun," the hood said, directing itself toward him again. "I hadn't noticed it myself but you are correct, Redwyn. And since I have kept you– you must allow me to pack your horse with some provisions."

He said, "You needn't." But the figure brushed lightly past him to the door. It opened, and the form of Brech appeared. Brech and the figure murmured for a moment, then Brech reached up to take one of the torches from the wall outside the door. Then the figure had the torch and as it turned around, Redwyn could see a face flickering inside the hood in the torchlight. The face came toward him, seeming to float above the darkness of the robe, features forming vaguely between shadows– fiendish at first, changing into uncertain human forms– the face of a man leering hatefully, drawing nearer and grinning, at last smiling in front of him, a pleasant face smiling and flickering in the torchlight.

"Now we can see each other more plainly."

"Yes," Redwyn agreed, feeling foolish and relieved. "This is much better."

"I saw you looking at her earlier," the man, who had been the figure, and who called himself Morcar, remarked. He turned to the portrait on the wall.

"I thought I recognized her," Redwyn said.

"Really?"

"Yes. She is the Lady St. Du Lac, I think. But younger."

"You are correct again. The poor girl."

The Head Robe lit the two torches on the wall and set the other to burn inside a narrow cylindrical holder in the middle of the floor. As he moved back behind his desk, Redwyn looked at him, seeing plainly now in the fire brightened room that he had a normal face, really, that would fit well into almost any crowd. The pointed chin and somewhat lengthy nose gave it an angular appearance, but it was not at all grotesque or unusual. His eyes were bright black and careful moving, with faint circles under them and a mild bulginess that gave him a vulnerable or humane quality. He sat down behind his desk and smiled. His age was about fifty; the sagging of his cheeks, and line of dusty grey bangs that cut straight across his forehead, and slight squeaky quality of his voice revealed his age. But it was a normal face; not like the hands had suggested it might be; the only unusual aspect being the ruddy-orange tone of its complexion. Redwyn checked his own bare arms and thought they looked a little ruddy, too, and reasoned it was probably just the strange cast of light thrown by the torches. It was a normal face, he decided. And it was comforting after the visions of his apprehensive mind.

"I've offered to share it with her. Did you know?"

Redwyn looked at him, puzzled.

"The castle. Everything else, too. In truth, it was the only *just* thing I could do. When I learned..."

"I'm not sure I understand."

"Then perhaps I shouldn't burden you."

"Please. I would like to know now."

"Would you like to sit down?"

There was a chair beside the desk and Redwyn seated himself.

"This castle," Morcar said, his face brightened by the torches, "was donated to us by the late Baron himself. In truth, it was his dying wish of gratitude that we continue our work here. So after attending to his stricken family in Godwyne, and after our other duties were concluded in that unfortunate village, we came to Solway to accept our bequeathment. But we had no knowledge that a child of the Baron had survived him. You see, he had made no provision for her in his will. Can you read?"

"Yes."

One of the grotesque hands appeared and set a scrolled parchment down on the edge of the desk. Redwyn picked it up.

"Now I am torn," Morcar said. "By my faith I am deeply grieved for the girl. But our work must go on here as well. I am the trustee of this order; but it is beyond my power to alter any bequeathments. In truth, it is regrettable that this has happened. The townspeople are against us now, and the baronial crops have not been tended properly. Because of this we shall have to *buy* our food to survive this winter." He drifted on that thought for a moment. "As you can read for yourself, the will leaves *everything* to us. It revokes all former wills and grants everything to our order."

"Leaving the Lady Lynn bereft," Redwyn said. He put the parchment back down, and Morcar picked it up again.

"As I told you, I have offered to share this castle with her; I offered her all the privileges she once had. At times, I am afraid My Lady can be quite hot-tempered and unreasonable."

"I have noticed that too," Redwyn acknowledged.

Morcar shifted uncomfortably in his chair and looked about. "It may interest you that this was the Baron's study. I venture he hung My Lady's picture here, so that her beauty would illuminate this dreary chamber."

They both looked at the portrait that seemed alive now in the torchlight.

"Friar Morcar, how do you explain the Baron's lack of charity to his own daughter?"

The Head Robe sat more upright at the desk. He grinned faintly and one of his ugly hands appeared with a ribboned, gold-looking object which he began to tap, punctuating his words with the sharp rapping sound it made on the heavy wood.

"When the Baron died it was *our order* who came to his deathbed. We *cared* for him and for his family. It was his dying wish of *gratitude* that bequeathed to us his possessions."

"But surely at the hour of a man's death he does not forsake his family."

"No?"

"I do not believe so," Redwyn said.

"Have you ever seen The Plague, my son?"

"No."

"Ahhh," said Morcar. "Then you cannot imagine it."

He put the gold object down, stood and walked beneath the window. The sunlight was gone but there was still a faint natural glow coming through, and with his face turned away from the reflecting torchlight he looked like a shadow again, and formless. "But I have seen it," his voice intoned quietly. "In a hundred cities. And if you have not seen The Black Death, then you cannot conceive of the fear it spreads. Or the inhumanity."

The simple thought of the disease made Redwyn uneasy. He had heard stories of the plague before and he did not like them. His feelings were showing plainly on his face, but Morcar did not turn around to see. He only paused for a moment, then went on.

"It always begins with people hearing of the catastrophe in another village. They invariably hoard, so that within a week a famine has begun, and with the first child's cough

they shut themselves behind their doors to starve. The streets
may be empty for a few days, then, the village quiet until the
fever starts. After that, of course, the screaming will tell all
that death comes in spite of latched doors.

"And then some odd thing happens. You never know
what it will be. Perhaps from their windows they can see a
cow jumping in the street from fever. Perhaps it is the
village idiot banging on their doors. But something always
touches them off, and then, well– madmen running into the
streets and shrieking with the knowledge of their impending
deaths. Others looting, killing for bread. Wanton brutality,
stealing, debauchery. Murder. Above all there is fear. You
see, the panic spreads until the whole city flees. All at once
mothers abandon infants; townspeople trample each other to
escape into the countryside like wild beasts. I remember
Troyes, where the seven gates were not enough to discharge
the escaping throngs in order. They panicked, clambering
against the walls until they could finally climb them on the
bodies of their fellow townsmen."

Morcar turned so that Redwyn could see his face again.

"Of course, if you have not seen it, then you could not
understand. But when a man falls victim to The Black
Death, Redwyn, he becomes an outcast, childless and friend-
less. His family deserts him. With all his gold not even a
drop of water could he buy. But it is then, when all hope is
gone, that *we* are with him."

Redwyn said, "I understand. If you will return my horse,
I'll leave now."

"But where will you go?"

"Away from here."

"Of course," said Morcar. "Then I will ask Brech about
your provisions."

He went to the iron door and knocked once. Redwyn
heard it open and looked over his shoulder and saw Brech in
the doorway. The big monk nodded and walked away. Morcar
closed the door lightly and returned.

"It is all arranged. Brech has prepared your horse and will have it waiting for you when you leave."

"Thank you." Redwyn stood, and the two men were facing each other in the quiet room.

"May I ask again where you would go?"

"I don't know, really. Perhaps Edinburgh."

"Will you leave tonight?"

"Yes, tonight, I think."

"I have supplied you with a saddle. The horse had none when Brech found him. But I trust it will make your journey easier."

"A saddle, Friar? You needn't have."

"No. It is the least gesture of apology. Brech told me of your scuffle with three of our brethren. Unforgivable. I assure you they will be punished."

"You needn't punish them."

"The argument was over this sword, was it not?"

"It involved some loaded dice," said Redwyn.

"May I see it?"

He took the sword from his belt and laid it across Morcar's outstretched ugly hands.

"Yes, interesting," the Head Robe said. He had noticed the inscription. "There is something written here. It is an old form of language." He was grinning, squinting, trying to focus in the shifting light. Then Redwyn watched his face change from a look of curiosity to disbelief, to blankness, then to disbelief again. His bulgy eyes widened as a look of horror came over him, and he dropped the sword suddenly and it rang against the stone floor.

"What is it?"

"My hands," the Head Robe gasped. "My hands are bleeding! There are deep cuts in my hands!" Blood was dripping from the wretched claws and had already formed a dark pool on the floor. Redwyn picked the sword up and saw blood running on its blade.

"But I don't understand how you cut them!"

Morcar was shaking. He moved behind the desk and began to search the floor, then bent down and came up with a man's linen undergarment in his hands. He put it on the desk and used a tiny dagger to tear the cloth, then ripped it into two pieces for bandages.

"Perhaps this is one of your magician's tricks," he said accusingly.

The hood had slipped down from his head, but he was intent on the bandaging, trying to use one of his injured hands to wind the other in the cloth. Redwyn had said nothing more. Morcar looked up and saw the path of his eyes, realizing then that the hood had fallen down, that Redwyn had seen the mass of rippling scar tissue that covered the right upper quarter of his skull and curled slightly into the shrivelled vestige of an ear. Morcar said, "No, of course not," and grinned strangely, and left the bandaging for a moment to pull the hood back up. He finished winding his hands and sat down, embarrassed, his black eyes darting about the room as if searching it for something to say.

"And yet you are a magician."

"I was," said Redwyn, hesitantly taking his seat near the desk. "But I assure you, Friar, I had no notion the blade was so quick."

"Did you sharpen it?"

"Yesterday," he lied.

"Then you should have warned me," Morcar said in the forced tone, now, of an understanding priest. He relaxed a little and took a deep breath and brought his bundled hands up to study them.

Redwyn felt sincere pity for him, this plague friar with strange, misshapen hands and a disfiguring scar on his head that was probably the bad result of some fire. Yet there was another feeling, an odd satisfaction he felt from the possession of the sword that he could not fathom. It was this feeling that had made him lie about the sharpening, and it was queer that he should feel it, it or any satisfaction at all, he knew. The emotion troubled him and seemed to belong to someone else.

"This is strange," he muttered.

"Yes," said Morcar, apparently relieved about his hands as they flexed feebly in the cloth. "But as you say, Redwyn, the turns of fortune are unpredictable and strange. However, you have your horse now, and a saddle."

"Thank you. I am afraid that gratitude is all I can return."

"It is more than enough, my son. For though gold may be the treasure of life, compassion holds its riches."

"Thank you. I should bid you goodbye."

"Then goodbye, my son. A fair journey to you."

Redwyn was halfway to the door when Morcar said quietly, "Your flame machine. You never finished telling me how it worked."

He turned back.

"It is a trifle, I know. But please, since you no longer practice the art of magic there is no shame in telling its secrets. Consider it a trade, if you will, for the saddle."

"Hardly a trade," Redwyn frowned. "A beggar's bargain, more likely."

"Nevertheless. If you do not tell me, I shall be forever curious."

"There is little to tell. I used a bellows to pump hot lard through swamp reeds. The reeds were joined with supple clay. And I used tiny oil lamps to set fire to the stream as it passed out. It was a simple trick. I practiced it in road camps to swindle peasants out of their coins."

"It does sound simple," said Morcar. "But clever. And do not be ashamed of your past. All such swindling is behind you now."

"I would like to think so. Perhaps it is now that I have confessed it. Well, goodbye, Friar."

"Goodbye, my son. Know that my blessing travels with you."

Redwyn walked to the iron door, lifted the latch to go,

but turned back. Morcar was gathering torches in the room. His hands were still in the bandages, and he took the two torches awkwardly from the wall and extinguished them head-first into the copper cylinder. He held the last one, burning low in his hand, and the room was dark again as he looked up and saw Redwyn still standing at the door.

"Did you forget something, my son?"

"I was wondering, Friar, how it is that you face certain death and yet remain, yourself, immune."

"Why, of course," whispered the faceless hood. "By the grace of our Lord God."

Redwyn nodded silently, turned and opened the door. Brech was there.

"Your horse is ready," the big monk rasped. "It has been tethered outside the gates."

Chapter 12
In View

They walked across the open courtyard. Brech threw his torch aside and Redwyn saw two men stand up at the drawbridge and start to work the winches that lowered it. He could hear the men shouting above the chain noise and, drawing near, could see the serious looks on their faces as they pumped the winch levers in a hurried but synchronized way.

The chains unwound sluggishly from their big maple chain spools, and the gate lumbered toward its landing. Redwyn looked at the men perspiring while they worked, and he considered that they must have lowered the bridge and then raised it again when his horse was taken across. He wondered why the horse had not simply been tethered inside the walls, and thought, "These Robes could save themselves some effort, if they would keep this bloody bastion halfway down."

As the timbers thudded to rest he stepped onto them. Beyond the western walls the sun was red and swollen, starting to flatten over the horizon. Looking back to the castle he located the tower he must have been in and found the small square window of the study. There was a steep ridge ascending the castle's western flank, and the ridge's shadow had climbed the tower and covered the little window. It explained the premature darkness in the study. But now he could see the sun and knew that there was still at least the twilight to travel by, and felt the prospects for his journey were much better.

"Your horse is there," Brech grunted from behind him. The big monk was pointing down the road that led from the castle's gate. "Your horse is there. You can see him."

"I see him," Redwyn said. "I was puzzled, because I thought the sun had gone down when I was in your master's chamber."

Brech said nothing. Redwyn took the meaning of his silence and started away.

To his left the sun was now burning behind the outline of some distant pines, rendering them black and spindly against its crimson light. The horse was standing bulky with saddle packs, out where the hedge broke between the pillars, and there were pink streaks of sunlight over the open field. The scene reminded Redwyn of the first time he had seen the horse in the yard of the big livery that was fifteen miles north of London. He had walked there after leaving a boat one morning because he knew the livery sold the best and cheapest horses. And when he had seen the lean, deep-evergreen tinted stallion standing apart from all the other animals in the late afternoon sunshine, he had wanted him.

He remembered how the squareheaded liveryman with a purplish face had said, "That's a fine hoorse! Aye, if you want *him* than I hope you brought a heavy purse wi' you."

Redwyn did not do very well in the bargaining, failing completely to conceal his desire for the horse, and finally was made to empty his purse to convince the liveryman he was not a "shrewd bag'ner," and paid everything he had, save a few pfennigs retained for supper that evening.

"You see," he said to himself. "You had forgotten that. You are rich now if only you remember how poor you have been at other times."

From about ten paces away the saddle Morcar had given him looked fine. The bridle seemed of good quality too, and there were saddle packs bulging with provisions on both sides. The horse had a long, horse-like shadow that stretched oddly across the field. Redwyn grinned and muttered, "Well, my stubborn beast, your old tormentor has returned to you." Then just ahead the bushes rustled a little. He froze and drew the sword halfway from his belt. Nelrum stepped out from behind the hedgerow.

"Nelrum!"

The old man walked in front of the horse and held up his hand. He was frowning and said, "It is best not to come any closer. They have done something to your mount, Redwyn."

"What is it?"

"I am not certain, but there is something tied to the understraps of the saddle. If what I suspect is true, simply touching the horse could kill you."

Redwyn grinned, searching the old man's face for the disguise of a jest.

"This is a jest."

"It is *not* a jest!" said Nelrum, suddenly angry. "I told you about them. I warned you of the danger here: about Brech, to stay away from him. Now this has happened. This fine animal must be destroyed. You have nearly been killed yourself! In the future, you must not fail to obey me!"

Redwyn was speechless for a moment, the onslaught of ill-temper having shocked him utterly. Then he thought of something that was tragic yet readily explained many of the old man's strange behaviors. In a voice filled with deliberate calm he said, "Listen to me, Nelrum. These men you hate so, these 'Robes,' are a strange lot. I will allow you that. But they could do nothing to make a horse into a blood-thirsty creature. Look– he is not vicious. These men are friars, of sorts, with a purpose to attend the sick and dying. Strange though they are, they must be brave as well. I think you are too much at odds with them."

The queer old face tightened a little, but Redwyn went on, "We should go to the tavern; a meal and a night's rest; and in the morning we can start for Edinburgh. Perhaps buy a wagon there. It is strange, but I don't care so much about the gold any longer. I won't abandon you. I told you in Grinmere I would find some way to repay my debt. Here it is. We shall talk, make some plans. But first a good meal. What do you say? Huh?"

"I am not a lunatic," Nelrum answered quickly. "You have only to stand here for a moment and I will prove my words are true. No, the 'Friars,' as you call them, have not made the horse bloodthirsty. Brech tied something to the cinch straps of the saddle: a 'poison,' of sorts, he put there to kill you. Now lend me your sword to cut it loose. For unless I show you what it is, the rest of what I say would not make sense."

"What you have said this far does not make very much," Redwyn answered. But he was somewhat relieved that Nelrum did not sound so much like a madman any longer, just angry, so he pulled out the sword and handed it to him.

"Stay away from the swishing tail. Especially the tail. It would be better if you kept behind me."

The old man knelt and extended the blade toward a small burlap parcel that was tied to the understraps of the saddle; the horse champed nervously from the presence of a stranger beneath him. Nelrum cut the sack ties carefully and the bundle dropped lightly to the ground. He said, "Stay there," rose, and led the horse by its tether to the other side of the hedge. Then he came back and bent over the parcel frowning, and using the blade tip delicately he lifted the folds of burlap to expose the tiny carcasses of three black rats.

"This *is* a jest!" Redwyn said. "Brech put these rats here to offend me. He begrudged the return of my horse, but his master ordered him. So he put these rats here to insult me."

"To kill you."

"What!" Redwyn grinned. "Is this what you expected to

find? These rats are not poisonous. Who would eat them, besides?" He moved carelessly forward, reaching toward the carcasses, but Nelrum swung the sword point over to stop him.

"I beg you to save your life– do not move another inch closer!"

Redwyn stood up slowly. Nelrum's eyes were steady and his hand was steady holding the sword.

"Would you kill me, old man?"

"Not in ten thousand years. But perhaps now you will listen. You are my great hope, and I have known you all your life."

Redwyn exhaled with a faint moan of exasperation. "Old man, you take this prank too far."

Nelrum said, "Very well. You were an orphan, apprenticed to a copyist in Edinburgh until you were fifteen. Then you ran away to London. You worked in a copy shop there for little more than three years, then traveled about: Paris, Troyes, other places. Eventually you settled in Venice, where you lived, four years, in a room on the third floor of a house beside the Grand Canal, fighting incessantly, drinking and incurring huge debts, working only when you needed money for more drink, food, or further debauchery, and frequently swimming the canals at night to escape the enthusiasm of Italian husbands." Redwyn gasped, and Nelrum said, "Oh yes, I know about it. You were escorted onto a ship and expelled from Venice with the city fathers paying your passage back to London, where you managed to acquire a wagon and began your swindler's career using glass blowers' arts and magic tricks to cheat people!

"We are in danger here," he went on, his voice beginning to quaver. "I must convince you of that. Perhaps if I told you about your parents. Perhaps if you knew they were killed by the same invisible 'poison' of such rats as these!" He paused and blinked, struck by the rashness of his own words. He went on, "It was against my heart to reveal such things so soon. Your temper and self-pity have forced it. Well, but since I have spoken the truth on so many details of your life, at least perhaps now you may believe me."

In the following silence Nelrum walked around the dead rats to the other side of the hedge. He returned carrying a cloth sack and an oil lantern. The lantern's shutter was closed but smoke was rising from its top, so it was evidently burning. He knelt and untied the sack and removed from it a torch and a big silver flask that had a cork stopper in its end. He set it all out in front of him, opened the top of the lantern and lit the torch on the lantern's flame. Then he picked up the flask and looked at it a little urgently, the burning torch now occupying his other hand.

"Would you uncork this for me?" he asked, and lifted the flask over his head toward Redwyn.

"What is it?"

"Liquor from Josh's Inn."

"May I have some?"

"Yes."

Redwyn took the flask and pulled the cork out with his teeth. He had a very long draught, then another, then handed it back to Nelrum.

"Have some too," he said.

"Not yet."

"Why?"

"I need it for the rats."

Redwyn felt heavy under the burden of emotion that had accumulated throughout the day. From the morning's first meeting with the Lady Lynn, to the frightening unreality of Nelrum knowing those things about him, the emotions had been piling. Now he felt the liquor too, a little dizzy as he watched the old man extend the flask over the rats, pouring liquor onto them, pouring slowly, the liquor spattering as it fell onto their soggy fur. Nelrum spilled some in a path up to his feet and touched it with the torch. The flame ran forward and ignited the sodden carcasses. The three rats curled as they burned, bloated and hissed. As the fire consumed them, the flesh shrank over their skulls, and he could see their needlelike teeth glowing, incandescent splinters inside the veil of bluish flames.

Nelrum closed the lantern and extinguished the torch by rubbing it into the dirt road. Then he rose and handed the flask over to Redwyn.

They both stood there a moment, silent. The little fire went out and the ensuing smoke carried the stink of burned fur. Redwyn filled his mouth with the remaining liquor and swallowed it in one strenuous gulp. He fitted the cork into the flask and drove it in with a slap of his palm.

"I want to know everything. About my parents, the rats, everything."

"You do not," the old man answered, and he walked behind the hedge with the sack. He returned empty handed, picked up the lantern and said, "You only think you want to know because I have revealed the most alluring fragment of a great and horrible truth."

"Yet, you *will* reveal the rest?"

"Oh yes, I must. But only by a great treason to us both."

"You talk rot sometimes," said Redwyn. The liquor had taken a firmer hold now, and it was beginning to get dark.

Chapter 13
The Cell

"For reasons you will understand soon, you must say nothing of the things you will see here."

"What things?"

"The 'horrible truth' I mentioned."

"You're talking rot again," said Redwyn.

"If there were any other way, I would not subject you–"

"Rot," said Redwyn.

"Very well," said Nelrum.

"Rot."

"Listen to me. There is a ruined castle inside the grounds. You can see the walls from here, if you look."

"Rubbish!" said Redwyn.

"I thought you wanted the truth."

"I'm sorry. I have seen the walls. What about them?"

"We are going inside. There is a dungeon beneath the ancient foundation. You can see the mounded earth from here and the foundation walls sticking up a few feet above the ground. There are slits to let in air. But look for the big mound with the sod covering it."

"Yes?"

"The Baron used the dungeon to store grain. I am afraid

that Morcar and his Robes have found their own purposes for it."

"We'll never get in without being seen. We have been in view all this time."

"That was necessary. But now they will see us leave."

Nelrum opened the lantern's shutter wide, then went over and untethered the horse and brought it back to the center of the broad, straight path that led to the castle's gate.

"Get the sack, Redwyn, and come over here."

He retrieved it from under the hedge and returned. The old man handed him the sword. "Here, you had better take this too," he said. "Well, they have seen us. Now we shall go back down the hill, cut over and come up again behind the hedge. Remember to stay away from the horse."

"Rot," said Redwyn. He grinned, and by the light of the lantern could see that Nelrum was not grinning back.

They left the shutter of the lantern open until well enough below the hill that only the upper-most parts of the towers could be seen outlined against the twilight in the western sky. Then they moved slowly along the side of the slope, came up again into an open field of crops. The horse kept stopping to eat whatever it was they were trying to hurry through. And Nelrum kept jerking the tether gently, trying to urge him with whistles, clicks, and commanding whispers. Finally Redwyn took the rope and demonstrated how hard one needed to jerk to get the stallion's head up from a fresh vegetable. Nelrum understood and they made better time and reached the hedge rather quickly, a little out of breath from having plodded through the soft field.

"There is another break, less conspicuous, a little further down from where we stand. Stow the sack far enough away that the horse can't reach it, and we'll leave him tied here to the branches."

Redwyn nodded and went some distance down the hedgerow and pushed the sack underneath it and returned.

"On the other side there is an apple orchard. Once through

the break, we'll make for it– then just beyond, an entrance to an ancient tunnel. It was an escape tunnel from the old castle, and it surfaces again quite close to the dungeon. It ought to get us in without being seen."

"I hope it does. What then?"

"As I told you, the Baron once used the dungeon to store grain, that his subjects might not starve in times of famine. I want you to look inside, to see for yourself what Morcar has done with it."

"It will be too dark."

"Use the lantern. Once we reach the air slits open the shutter wide enough to produce only a small ray; nothing more; we dare not risk any more than that."

"And what shall I see?"

"Simply promise that no matter what you see, no matter what your feelings are, that you will tell no one."

"I promise," said Redwyn. "But why don't you tell me more about it?"

"Words would only strain at a vision you are not likely to forget."

"You enjoy being mysterious, don't you, Nelrum."

"No. It is treasonous, but necessary."

"Rot!"

"Remember your promise. Don't talk now, follow me and keep low."

They crept along the hedge until reaching the overgrown break. Nelrum went through first, moving briskly, his grey robes flowing as he passed between the dark trees of the orchard. Redwyn followed and caught up to him just as they reached an overturned flat cart at the edge of the open field.

"Do you see any guards along the walls?"

"It is too dark," Redwyn answered. "But I am sure there is a four man watch in the gate rooks. But they won't see us."

"Stay low, then."

Nelrum started running half-crouched across the field, Redwyn behind him, both checking the castle's facing parapets for sentinels. After about fifty paces they stopped again at a waist-high, grassy mound. Redwyn whispered accusingly, "Why have we stopped!" But he saw the old man's hands working over the grass, then heard the sod tearing and saw the side of the mound coming up, a sod-covered wooden door. Nelrum started down into the tunnel. "I've got it," Redwyn said, and took the door and followed onto the slimy stairs, letting the hatch close on top of him. It was utterly dark and he said, "Let out some light!" And his voice came back seeming louder than before, echoing in a chorus of repetitions. He felt Nelrum grip his arm, but already knew not to speak again.

They made their way along, feeling the damp wall, hearing only the splashing of their boots and a sound like droplets falling in a cave.

After what seemed quite some distance Nelrum opened the lantern just a slit and cast a faint ray toward the end of the tunnel. They went a little further. He whispered, "The stairs are here," and closed the shutter. Redwyn slid his boot forward, found the first step, and together they climbed the stairs and felt overhead for the passageway door. They started pushing against it in the darkness. There was the sound of ripping sod again, dirt sprinkling down on their faces, then the rush and smell of fresh air and the stars above. Climbing out they could see the castle, close and bluish in the twilight.

They eased the door down and smoothed the sod where it was torn. Nelrum whispered, "Hurry now," stood up in a crouch and started running toward the ruin's foundation. Each time he ran this way he had to hold his long robe up, so as not to trip.

They reached the dungeon and fell down with their backs to the wall near one of the air slits. There was a very foul smell and a trilling sound like a hundred tiny wheels that faintly squeaked. Redwyn said, "What an awful stench!"

"Take this." Nelrum handed him the lantern. "Put it up to the air slit and open the shutter a crack; a crack, mind you, and look inside."

Redwyn hung the lantern rope in his mouth and crawled on his hands and knees toward the air slit. The smell was worse there and he heard the trilling sound more distinctly as he rose upon his knees to look inside. It was too dark to see anything, so he put the lantern up to the slit and moved the shutter open, just a thought, and threw a faint yellow ray upon the opposite wall. The cell was very large; and deep, he saw, as he tilted the lantern toward the floor. The squeaking had grown louder, but from no source that was apparent, and he moved the ray around the cell to gauge its dimensions. It was about thirty feet across, and wide, and just as deep; then he thought he'd seen something moving on the floor. He opened the lantern a little wider, muttered, "Yes, something is moving," and widened the shutter further. The floor was glistening, an undulating surface that looked like tar. He opened the lantern nearly halfway to illuminate the watery blackness and gasped quietly, "Not tar– the floor is covered by a swarm of rats!"

When he tossed a rock down through the slit, the noise rose to an uncomfortable screech, the rats swirling from the impact in a whorl of motion. The floor was laid bare in a spot and he saw the sleeve of a man's garment projecting into it. Then Nelrum whispered, "Quiet! Close the shutter. I told you, open it only a crack."

"Rats!" said Redwyn. "Thousands of them."

"Close the shutter. Keep your voice down."

Redwyn shut the lantern completely. Nelrum whispered, "We have to hurry now, they may have spotted the light from the castle. I am sorry for what you are about to see. If there were any other way, I would spare you–"

"If we should hurry, then let's get on."

"Go down to the end."

They moved along the full length of the dungeon, passing

air slits. Redwyn stopped to look inside one, but saw only a bin of coarse grain, hurried along, and Nelrum was waiting for him at the last cell. "Be careful with the light," he said. And Redwyn nodded and positioned himself in front of the slit.

The smell was even more putrid than before and nearly made him retch. He backed away and found the shutter latch with his finger, ready to slide it open when he got up close again. He turned his head and took a deep breath and held it, then moving quickly, leaned forward, and resting his body against the dungeon wall brought the lantern into position and nudged the shutter sideways. He directed the light toward the floor and suddenly the smell didn't matter anymore as the breath he was holding rushed unbridledly out of him and he began to gasp in fear.

The ray had fallen upon the face of a dead woman. She was sitting against the wall on some sort of bench, and her eyes were closed, but Redwyn knew that she was dead because of the frozen contortion of her face, and her complexion, and finally because he noticed one of her ears partly missing and saw the rat that had been eating it. The rat looked up into the lantern's ray and then resumed his chore, and Redwyn widened the shutter and saw that there were other rats in various places on the woman's body. She was sitting on a bench-like slab of stone that projected out of the dungeon wall. He moved the shaft of light from side to side and saw that there were other corpses sitting with her. He opened the lantern wider and it seemed all the victims had shared a common agony that had sculpted their faces into differing masks of death, that some had born their pain better than others– some had died grimacing, while others had screamed– but that none had died peacefully. By the pallor of their faces they had gone at different times, the most recently dead still bluish white, while others had turned yellow or pale green, dark purple or black; it was difficult to tell shades accurately by the lantern light.

The cell floor was defiled with excremental filth and there were dead on the floor as well, some of them missing clothes. Redwyn could see huge oozing boils under the arms and in the groins of some of the naked ones; he remembered something about boils and what they could mean, and he quickly made a survey of the naked bodies and saw that they all had boils, and there were crusted streams of blood trailing from some of their noses. His heart was jumping as he started to move the lantern rapidly from face to face. Bloody noses, bloody ears, swollen necks, blood from the eyes; he had heard stories of it all before: Blood from the mouth, purple faces, red faces, yellow, black faces, many black faces, blood from fingernails, black hands, feet, tongues— Yes! My God, he thought. Yes it has to be! "Oh Christ!" he said out loud. "Oh sweet Christ in heaven. Oh of all the hells on earth! Oh, my Lord, sweet Lord, Christ!"

"Who are you!" came a voice from the cell.

He looked away from the slit, to Nelrum, but the old man was crouching silently, his back to the dungeon wall.

"Who is that!" the voice came again. Redwyn went back to the slit and started searching with the lantern's ray.

"Here!" said the voice.

He swept the lantern into a corner and there was a living man sitting among the dead. His face was ghostly pale and he struggled to his feet and said, "Sweet God in heaven, help us!" Just then two other figures started moving on the bench. They had been asleep and they lifted themselves groggily to stand. "What is it?" the shortest one said. "There's someone here!" said the tall man.

Redwyn recognized them now as the three Robes he had brawled with at the tavern. "No!" he said. "Oh God, please no! Oh no! No! No!"

The men started moving toward his light.

"Help us," the tall one said. "Who are you? Oh, brother, savior, help us!"

"It's *you*!" another of them gasped. "Oh, help us, won't

you? Oh please, for merciful God!"

"Rope–" Redwyn managed to choke out.

"Yes, a rope!" said the tall one. "Get a rope!"

"Come," said Nelrum.

"A rope!" came the horrible cry. "Rope, God save us, a rope!"

"Come, we must leave *now*."

"We can't leave!" Redwyn disgorged.

"*Now!*" And Nelrum pulled his shoulder backward, causing him to fall onto the sloped earth. The lantern rolled down the bank and its shutter came fully open. Nelrum snatched it up and closed it. Then Redwyn saw the line of torches moving toward them from the castle. He felt Nelrum lifting his arm. Then he was up, and they were both running hard for the tunnel door.

Chapter 14
A Tidemark

When they reached the overturned flat cart in the orchard, both of them were wet from having splashed through the tunnel. Nelrum made sure the lantern's shutter was still closed. They crouched there, looking back at the wavering line of torches that filed up slowly to the dull outline of the dungeon's mound. Neither of them spoke; they only watched the movement of the torches, trying to control their heavy breathing to hear the voices from across the open field.

The word "Rope" came on an ebb of wind, the first of the night breezes to disturb the acquiescent air of dusk. Then Morcar's voice was clear.

"Search the grounds. You were correct, Brech. Someone must have been here."

Brech's voice responded, a low, indistinguishable grumble. Then Morcar's voice came back.

"Clean it up then. Pour oil into the cell and burn it. I am certain we have a good source now; certain. There is no need to risk spreading to the other cells."

Half the torches came slowly together and began moving along a path toward the castle. The others congregated about a figure which, by virtue of its large outline, could only have been Brech. The figure was motioning with it's arm, and the torch bearers broke off into smaller parties and started in different directions over the field.

Redwyn felt a tap-tap on his shoulder. He and Nelrum cut back into the cover of the orchard. Keeping low and moving from tree to tree, they struck the hedge and followed it, staying low until they found the overgrown break and, pushing through its stiff tangle of branches, at last were out of the castle grounds.

The horse was tethered a little way down. Nelrum said, "You pick up the sack, Redwyn. I'll get the horse– let's move quickly now."

But Redwyn did not move. He was staring at the lights from the village below. He said, "I would never have believed any man was capable– but if it is true then we must leave here. Not only from Solway, but far away. Far away, Nelrum, at once!"

Nelrum stopped and turned around.

"But where shall we go?"

"On a ship perhaps."

"The Lady Lynn?"

"I thought of that– we could take her. She might come."

"And the orphans she cares for?"

"For God's sake!"

"She would never leave them."

"Then we might steal a ship for them. Steal it, or use the gold to buy their passage. I haven't thought of everything yet."

"No place is safe now, Redwyn; it would be of no use to run. But perhaps we could find some way to fight this. There is a way, I think."

"No! There is nothing!" Redwyn countered. "Not you, nor I, nor the King could fight this! Don't even think of it!" Then calmer, "There are no weapons to fight a thing you cannot see, Nelrum. It is something that comes on the wind, like a phantom!"

He turned in the direction of the horse; but the old man moved over to face him.

"You saw the rats in the pit?"

"Yes, thousands of them. This Morcar is a lunatic of some kind. Perhaps he worships rats."

"He uses them to spread plague. But are rats not easily enough destroyed?"

"We have to get out!"

"He uses rats to kill people," Nelrum said. "Like those in the plague cell. The rats he put beneath your horse were supposed to kill you. They would have. As they have killed your horse already."

"My horse stands here healthy enough! In truth, I'm going to ride him far away from this place!"

"Are you? Then hurry. Because soon the animal will drop, to become an unmovable infestation of the plague."

"No."

"It is true."

"You are an insane old man!" Redwyn said disgustedly. "By some sorcery you believe that a bundle of rats can conjure plague. Rats that are everywhere, especially in stables. Horses don't die from them. I should have known you for a lunatic when you gave my gold away!"

"And yet, Redwyn, you stand here yelling to an insane old man. Why? Is it because I know things about your childhood– things that seem impossible to know? Why don't you mount your horse and leave? Are you too cowardly to ask the question, or have you guessed, finally, that Morcar killed your parents?"

Redwyn muttered, "What do you mean?" Then he was silent and the two men stood facing each other in the darkness.

The Old One understood what was happening. But the young man, his heart turned over in his chest, his mind exhausted by the incomprehensible events he was enmeshed in, felt only the emotions that ran in cross currents of fear and anger and self-hatred for the cowardice he harbored and detested more than anything. For him there was a sudden strange edge upon the night. His skin crawled over with goose flesh, and he looked uncertainly about.

But there was no place to go, and so relying only upon the darkness for shelter he shut his eyes, and for a moment a numbness prevailed and he could no longer hear his heavy breathing or feel the ground. There was only a shuddering like the wind blowing over a fire, then silence– save for his short gasps of breath– and a vague sense for the thing he was losing, perhaps that was already lost to him: a rare, intangible childhood thing, like the memory of some secret playmate he had had, and loved, and told his deepest confidences to a long time ago when he had been a little boy. And although he had never had such a playmate, he felt the same peculiar vacancy of loss. And as he had not fully understood the origins of the spell, he did not know why, when the numbness trickled tinglingly away, he found himself gripping the sword handle. His mind just grew gradually clear again, and he looked up and saw Nelrum standing in the darkness.

"Can you still trust me, Redwyn?" he said. His voice sounded strange. "I had hoped to spare you this. I am sorry. I promise to tell you everything now, but first we have to take your horse from the city and destroy him. Can you trust me once more?"

He shook his old white head. "It is a terrible wrong to tear at a man's innocence with horror– to assault him with the knowledge of evil and put outrage where innocence belonged. Why must we always hurt the dearest things?"

"I have been a coward, Nelrum. I can see that I've been. I'll get the sack now. We have spent too much time here already, with the search parties out looking for us."

As he spoke he knew for certain something had changed in him. It had happened as quietly as when the tide changes in the open sea. But now he felt it, deep and irrevocable inside.

"Can you trust me?"

Redwyn started toward the place where the sack was hidden. He just kept walking and said, "I trust you well enough."

Chapter 15
Before the Storm

They descended the hill road. Below them a scattering of campfires burned throughout the fairgrounds. The air was warm and damp feeling with the smell of rain, and sometimes big gusts of wind would make the fires all wave and sweep drifts of sparks into the darkness beyond. Once amid the concessions they were careful to keep a safe distance from anyone who happened to be out walking on the road. But the merchants stayed beside their campfires mostly, voices ebbing in low campfire tones; or their shadows moved against the candlelight on the walls of the big tents that would flap and rumble when the wind blew.

Outside the fairgrounds the road turned and ran close along the beach. Redwyn could see it was high tide, the surf crashing with the heavy wind and turning white beneath the moonlight not forty yards from where they stopped.

Nelrum started back toward the fairground and, as prearranged, Redwyn stayed behind with the horse. He followed the old man's grey robes in the moonlight, saw him walk into the glow of the liveryman's fire. The liveryman stood and shook his hand, and they walked off together toward the corral.

Redwyn muttered, "It is a mistake to buy a horse in the dark, Nelrum. Especially at one of these fairs. They only sell what they can't get rid of anywhere else." He looked back to his stallion, burdened with heavy saddle packs, its head lowered in a posture of defeat, and thought, "Strange how he keeps back. Usually there is nuzzling, snorting and horse-type affection. But maybe the plague is in him already."

Then he put the sack and lantern down and looked out over the sea.

The moon was skipping in and out of clouds, droplets of spray sometimes reaching him in the wind. Along a line of squalls on the horizon heat lightening flashed, and then, as the moon broke through the clouds again, the unmistakable shape of two lovers formed against the shimmering of the brightened beach. The pair was facing the sea in a posture of lovemaking that is convenient on sand, coupled and bumping rhythmically. And Redwyn turned away but he could still hear them on the dampened gusts.

For a while he watched only the ocean and the whitening surf. Then when he looked back the couple was finished, kneeling and facing each other in a locked embrace. The moon was swept behind a cloud bank again and he could no longer see them.

Later, Nelrum came up the road from the liveryman's camp leading a horse. "I bought one," he said.

"Is it a mare?"

"I didn't ask. Does it matter?"

"I told you I was against buying a horse at night. Does it have four legs?"

"You did not buy it, I did. I owed it to you."

"You owe me nothing."

"Why did you ask whether it is a mare?"

"I thought that for his last night on earth we might provide him some companionship. But I suppose that, being an unclean beast, he is not fit for amorous encounters."

"We had better keep them separated," Nelrum said. "I'll

take this one and go in front of you. The wind is too strong to light the torches here. Why don't we wait until we're inside the forest; it won't be nearly as windy there."

Redwyn nodded, and looked back and searched the beach. But the lovers were gone now, and he wondered whether he had ever really seen them.

Chapter 16
An Older Place

Distances are always made greater by the darkness, and while their journey into Grinmere had taken little more than a quarter of the night, it seemed, to Redwyn, ten times what they had travelled the day before. It was not nearly as windy on the road in the forest, but the wind rushed through the treetops and howled and roared when the gusts came. Branches broke loose, sometimes a heavy one landing, "crack" upon the forest floor.

On the road ahead, Nelrum waved his torch and then disappeared into the right side of the forest. Redwyn found the place where the broad, well worn path connected, followed the firelight through the trees and saw the old man tethering the nag at the far edge of a clearing. There were stone artifacts all about; pillars and a sundial close by, other structures too far away to be distinct in the torchlight. Nelrum finished tying the horse and walked into the clearing's center and sat down at the base of an enormous, towerlike construction– an alter, Redwyn perceived– perhaps twelve feet high, with a staircase rising sidelong to its summit. At its base was a large circle comprised of closely fitted boulders, and upon one of these Nelrum sat, his head down between his arms, white hair flagging in the wind.

Redwyn tethered the stallion and approached, surveying the structure for the task at hand. "They must have been giants to build such massive things," he observed. "The alter stone would weigh a hundred tons."

"Not giants," Nelrum muttered tiredly.

"I suspect they would have needed such an alter to sacrifice large animals. You were right in saying this is a perfect place."

The old man said in a dispirited quaver, "You have only read what another, less civilized cult has written about them— one that uses its own alters to ritualize the cannibalism of a gentle man, revels in death and exalts suicides to sainthood—" He stopped without finishing, and his torch snapped and fluttered like a banner in the gusting wind.

At such blasphemy Redwyn's first reaction was the familiar tension that flowed into his neck and arms, that had always and involuntarily hardened his fists for battle. But he said gently, "I meant no disrespect to them— only to remind you why we came here. Shall I bring the horse over now?"

Nelrum sighed and looked up. The torchlight gleamed faintly on his forehead and on the balls of his cheeks. "Yes. We'll gather some wood first. The circle, here, will shelter our fire from the wind. And, Redwyn, I have been thinking— there is a chance we may be able to save the beast, after all."

"Just tell me what to do, Nelrum."

"A large fire to start with. We need more light to work by."

There was plenty of wood beneath the ancient oaks of Grinmere, and as the two men gathered, the wind brought down more. Redwyn thought to himself that the old man must indeed be mad. For although his living alone in a forest and his obsession with the artifacts of an ancient race could be considered eccentricities, his scornful blasphemy seemed nothing less than insane. "An old man, especially, should be close to God," he thought. And while he himself had sworn occasional oaths upon the various parts of Christ's body, it was unthinkable to him that the Lord God should be called a "gentle man" or holy communion an act of "cannibalism." And yet he felt no true anger or aversion toward Nelrum. They were on a very strange journey together, and wherever it led, even if hell itself were the destination, he was bound to go. In spite of the weariness and confusion he knew that somehow he had asked to go.

When the circle was filled, the torches were set deep inside the lattice of weather seasoned branches. The wind spread the flames until the blaze roared toward the summit of the alter and all the clearing's artifacts were illuminated in the brilliant light.

About the circular periphery of the expanse there were casket-like stone boxes on elevated platforms. The sides of these sarcophagi had been engraved with swirled patterns, sunbursts and constellations. There were four maze-like arrangements of stone, compact and very exactly built, and next to each one a sundial, each with a slightly different orientation. In the clearing's center, seemingly placed there for prominence, boulder had been carved into a gigantic two-visaged head. The faces looked in opposite directions, and though moss mottled and pitted with age, one was unmistakably a child's, round and plump and smiling, while the other seemed the sunken death mask of the world's most ancient man. It was not a man's per se, for gender disappears from a human face when it is very old and, of course, a child's face has no gender. They were deliberately and universally the aspects of Death and Youth. And as the wind caused the fire to waver, Youth seemed to change slightly in expression, while the death mask remained as lifeless as the stone from which it had been carved.

Redwyn pointed to the sculpture and said, "There is one exception to your rule: an inscription older than the rock that bears it."

Nelrum grinned. "You learn quickly," he said, and then

went on to explain how the horse might be saved. He said that if an animal had absorbed the plague already, then by no means on earth could it be driven from him. But if the rats had been removed in time, by soaking the stallion's hide with a mixture of oil and extract of tannin bark the corrupting agents could be kept from infesting him. Redwyn did not understand fully, but knew that tannin saved pelts from rotting, so agreed that it made sense.

Nelrum went off somewhere and returned with a clay pot of the acrid smelling mixture. Redwyn did not ask where it had come from, but, as instructed, removed his clothing and rubbed a light application onto his skin. Then he brought the stallion into the firelight, so as not to miss any part of him, and used an unlit torch to swab the potion on.

After the work was finished, Nelrum said that only time and fortune would decide the animal's fate, but that the ritual had made him safe to ride and he could not spread the disease to any living thing. Redwyn decided to tether the horses together beneath the alter. Then Nelrum lit a brace of torches. The two men crossed the clearing, found a path on the other side, and followed it down to the river's edge.

The moon was mostly behind clouds now, showing itself only rarely to dapple shimmers of grey upon the black water. The current was high and swift, and from the debris floating by Redwyn knew it had been raining further upstream. Nelrum planted the torches in the bank and urged him to hurry, warning the dye would stain if left upon his skin too long. Redwyn waded into deep water, submerged, and when he surfaced again he was a hundred feet from the torches and had to swim hard against the slowest part of the current to get back. A big cedar tree had been washed down in the flood and nearly struck him, it's spiny roots and branches scraping as it plunged by.

They grabbed his clothes from the bank and returned quickly to the fireside. The water had left him invigorated, more alert– and he felt better about the horse, at least having done something to help a creature that for some time had been his only companion. The night was sharply cooler. And now the gusts of wind tore at the treetops and sent flurries of debris into the firelight and over the ancient stones. Redwyn dried himself by standing in front of the fire until it almost burned and then turning his overheated body to the chilling wind. The stars shone brilliantly through windows in the racing clouds and the night felt savage with the coming storm. As he was dressing, the first thunder rumbled in the distance, warped and muted by the surging wind.

"I noticed Morcar's hands. Is that how he keeps himself immune— with tannin? His hands were deep red, his face too."

"Only one of the ways," Nelrum answered. "Another is his ritual of burning, purifying with fire. And he knows how to handle the rats— with long rods that keep the corruption away from him." He frowned into the declining blaze. "He was a rat catcher once. Perhaps he noticed that in a plague house they are the first things to die."

Redwyn prompted, almost whispering, "My parents."

And Nelrum nodded, as if acknowledging a vision he saw there in the vaporous flames.

Chapter 17
The Gift

"From the first moment I saw Morcar he was like a blackness," Nelrum said. "A shadow that fell deep into my heart and turned me cold inside. Twenty four years ago in Troyes he was still a rat catcher. I used to travel in those days. I ventured to that city and met him a year before the plague struck.

"In my tavern late one evening, when most of the other guests had left the dining hall and gone to their beds, I heard an argument in the next room. The Innkeeper had accused Morcar of smuggling rats into the tavern to collect his fee dishonestly. He denied the charges, but the Innkeeper ordered him to open his sack and enlisted the aid of a knight who was sitting drunk at a nearby table. Morcar struggled with the knight, and the scuffle aroused several nobles who came down from the sleeping chambers with their swords drawn. The Innkeeper explained the charges; Morcar was seized and his sack was opened. Not only were there dead rats in it but valuables stolen from the rooms. He went to prison for two years. But in that miserable hole of cruelty and filth, two years must have been a lifetime."

"Did he escape?"

"He was released to serve an abbot."

"Why would an abbot want him?"

"That," answered Nelrum, "Is the power of the plague: to make all men equal beneath a sentence of death. You see, a city in the final throes of plague has no civic servants, magistrates, courts–only the dead and dying. Men were needed to burn corpses, to extinguish a multitude of fires–"

"And to attend dying nobles," Redwyn interjected.

"Yes. When Morcar was taken from prison he was given a bath and some new clothes, then turned over to the stricken abbey. It was a pardon, of sorts, for a simple fraud. But Morcar is no simple fraud. Within an hour the abbey was burning– the abbot and remaining monks died in a blaze which no one even tried to extinguish. Later, it was discovered the gold, livestock, even the monks' robes had been looted. Two days afterward the prison was overthrown. Most of the escapees were heretics slated to die by torture. Brech was among them. They joined forces with Morcar, and this was the beginning of 'The Robes.'"

"Hasn't anyone tried to stop him?" Redwyn asked in astonishment.

"Well, his scheme is clever. He will travel to an afflicted city, offer the local authority the services of his robed 'Hospitaliers,' then begin to burn and loot at will. There is no one to stop him and his legion of filth. Torture, mayhem, rape. Cruelty beyond a sane man's imagination. And never a living witness to complain. You see, no one will come to the aid of a plague house."

"But how can *he* survive."

"Tannin protects him. He must have discovered that furriers and tanners rarely contract the plague. But Morcar takes few of the risks himself. His henchmen– the 'heretic prisoners' and recruits– do most of his bidding. Many of them have died by plague or fire."

"I observed that his face had been severely burned."

"Yes. Yes. That occurred in his first meeting with you."

"What!"

"In Edinburgh, when you were an infant," Nelrum said gravely. "Morcar and his Robes were painting red crosses on doors and nailing them shut to ensure those inside would contract plague or die from fire. The door of your house had been nailed shut as well. But your mother lowered you onto the street in a basket. From the window she begged Morcar to show mercy. But he laughed and poured the bloody stain over your body. His henchmen had started to burn the houses on the street. As I approached they warned him of a blazing wall about to collapse behind him. He drew his sword, perhaps to finish you, when that wall broke loose and leaned onto your mother's house. He was knocked unconscious and burned. His henchmen rescued him from the fire and led him away from the street and Edinburgh."

Redwyn stared into the flames. The high gusts tore at the treetops and the embers seethed and brightened with the surging wind.

"My father?"

"Dead," Nelrum said. "You became my property. I named you, or rather Morcar did. For when they were leading him away, he screamed 'The Red One! The Red One!' His cohorts probably thought he was delirious. But I took you from that holocaust and named you from his own words, hoping that some day–" And without finishing the old man just shook his head.

"I did not help you very much I am afraid. My life was consumed by the evil I had witnessed. His evil. I placed you into the care of the Copyist and gave him gold. But you must have been unhappy there."

"I ran away," Redwyn said absently. "My God, Nelrum, is there nothing to do?"

The old man waited a moment then uttered, "There is vengeance," half whispering it, so that it seemed almost an incantation of the surging winds.

"Is that another Druid word?"

"As I have told you, the race of the Druids is extinct. Men have passed the time of verdure when they could have chosen to live as moral beings. The decision was made long ago– and since stamped indelibly into the earth by a thousand armies' heels."

"I don't believe that."

"Then perhaps you misunderstand. Morcar will wait no longer for the plague to strike. He now intends to spread the seeds of death himself. The rats in the dungeon, once infected, will spread the plague anywhere he releases them. Cities, whole kingdoms will be at his mercy. And mercy he has none."

"Oh, I am going to kill him," Redwyn said in a deathly monotone. "There is no doubt of it. But I had not taken you for a hypocrite. Why haven't you killed him, if you knew what he was?"

"It is not my destiny to kill Morcar."

"Rubbish."

"No, not rubbish. It is not within me to kill him. You do not understand, Redwyn. Each man's character is a wish, a prayer, if you will, to the stars. And destiny is the star's reply. It is not my destiny to kill him. And do not think it will be easy for you to do so. For he has his own destiny, one of pure evil. To defeat him you must know yourself, know your very heart and soul. For the portal of fate is open to each man for a mere instant. It is a flicker in time that a shooting star will perish in the night sky. But then that man is the architect of his fate. Then you might succeed."

"That is a bushel of dung. What difference does it make if I know myself, as long as I kill him."

"Lest you become like him, the evil you would conquer must be fought with truth."

"Bah," Redwyn said. But he was listening.

"And you must learn of truth. It has not one, but three intertwining threads. First and simplest is a man's integrity of speech. With it he guides himself like a ship at sea. Truth holds his course like a rudder in the currents of life.

"In the second truth, a man finds a balance between his ideals and actions. It is the correspondence between his reality and his dreams, the virtues he would have and those he truly possesses. It is the measure of his will."

"So it is for truth that I kill!" said Redwyn.

"No. Look into your heart. You must be guided by your heart and perceive your fate with faith and, above all, courage. Remember something: *There are no victories in this world—only the truths we live by.*"

The wind came down and churned the flames in the fire pit. Redwyn stared into them and his face burned feverishly.

"I don't understand it well enough, Nelrum."

"Come with me, my young friend. I have something that by all rights belongs to you." The old man led the way to a nearby casket, pitted and moss covered with age. He began pushing sideways on the top of it, Redwyn laid on to help, and the moss tore away and the stone top shifted sideways.

Nelrum reached into the casket and removed what looked like a bolt of cloth. He extended it slowly in an offertory gesture. As Redwyn took it he found the outer layer was not cloth at all but armor mail. He peeled the metal garment off and set the rest of the bolt, which did indeed feel like cloth, upon the casket.

"Put it on," Nelrum said solemnly.

Redwyn held the garment up, and he was awestruck. It was a chain mail vest, worth a guildsman's fortune, he knew. It gleamed with a dull blue iridescence in the firelight. He carefully, almost ceremoniously, put it around his neck and fastened the clasp over his right shoulder.

"There is more," Nelrum urged him.

Redwyn picked up the bolt, unwrapped the next layer and held it into the light. It was a crimson tunic of a finer weave than he had ever seen before, and the neck and arm sleeves were hemmed in gold. He slipped his head through and his blond hair fell about his shoulders.

He picked up the bolt for the third time and began unrolling it carefully, feeling something long and hard inside. As it unraveled, he found the black outer cloth was a cloak. He probed the last folds with his fingertips and felt the hard object inside, metallic and tubular, and pulled it out– a scabbard, silver, with a symbol of some kind on its hilt. With his heart beating fast he slipped it temporarily into his belt, tied the cloak around his neck and let it flutter backward in the wind. Then, with Nelrum watching, he undid his belt and buckled the scabbard on, lowered the sword down into it, and it locked into place with a solid click. Lightning flashed above. The symbol on the scabbard shown brilliantly in the blue arc.

"Redwyn– I should tell you–"

"No, please, Nelrum," he said urgently. "Don't say anything at all."

And thunder exploded in the heavens, and Redwyn looked up and raised his arms to the inflamed and furious sky.

"Then follow me," the old man shouted against the wind. "I live close to here. We can wait out the storm tonight and talk of things to come."

BOOK II

Passage

Chapter 18
The Letter

The wind howled outside the orphanage, and in Lynn's chamber drafts through the shutters caused the heavy blue drapery to move. Her bedchamber was in the back of the orphanage, and she lay awake in bed, a lone candle flickering in the drafts and shadows moving around her chamber walls. She thought of Redwyn as the thunder rolled down from the highlands of Grinmere. She remembered the evening at the river when he had seen her bathing nude. She pinched out the candle and imagined he was with her in the dark. The wind blew hard and the thunder rumbled softly away, farther and softer, until she drifted off to sleep.

The next morning Lynn awoke and sat up on the large oak bed that Josh had built from ship's timbers that had washed onto the rocky shore near his tavern. He had planed the big pieces of oak and pegged them together, and the townswomen had quilted a goose-down mattress for her. Lynn loved Josh. She looked at the bed and it made her happy to think of the townspeople.

She took a dressing gown from the back of the chair. Sunshine through the cracks of the shutters made bright stripes on the wooden floor. The stripes went across her body as she put the gown on. She opened the shutters. The landscape and morning were beautiful and she wanted to set her mood now and make those feelings last all day.

From her window she could not see the castle, only the hill that dropped off steeply then came back into view as a grassy slope down into town. The town was far below and the white and rusty houses were pretty in the morning sun. The houses looked very small and the donkey carts and people smaller still. Off in the fairgrounds, very far away, the horses and people were almost too small to see, but there were mottled colors and reflections in the sun. Her view swept over the dark green of the forest, over the sea with the sun shimmering brightly, then back to town and around the grassy slope. Where the road came up the hill toward the orphanage she saw a man walking. He was dressed heavily for August, and as he disappeared behind the steep part of the hill Lynn closed and latched the shutters.

She dressed, brushed her hair, and scrubbed her teeth with the fibrous end of a willow stick. Then feeling curious about the man on the road, she walked over to the shutters and opened them. He was coming over the top of the hill now. His coat was dark green and thick and his face was very sunburned. He left the road to come across the meadow. Lynn did not recognize him from the town, but by the cuffs of his breeches, upturned sleeves, and heavy buckle she realized he was a shipman. She closed the shutters quickly and left the room.

Gwendy the big cook was standing at the fireplace stirring a pot. She looked up and said, "I have cheese and boiled apples, My Lady."

"No thank you, Gwen."

"I'll boil eggs then."

"No, Gwen, not just now."

Lynn opened the door, and the Shipman was coming from between two Poplar trees. He saw her and stopped. He took a paper from his belt and removed his cap. His hair was streaked and dirty-looking, face haggard, and he smoothed his hair with his palm and stepped forward awkwardly.

"Would you be the Lady Lynn St. Du Lac, Baroness of Solway?"

Lynn smiled nervously at the strange soft sound of his voice. "Yes. You look tired. Have you just come from your ship?"

"Yes, M' Lady."

"Take some water," she said, gesturing toward the well.

"No thank you, M' Lady. I have only come to give you this, then I'll be gettin' back to town."

Lynn frowned as he came forward and handed her something. She didn't see what it was at first because his face had drawn so dark and taut that it distracted her. Then she saw he had handed her a letter. Her father's seal was set deep in the red wax, and her own name was on the other side. She turned it over again, but there was nothing except the seal and her name, and she had gone all sick inside.

The Shipman spoke, "I'm sorry I was so long in coming. I was told that no one else should know of it except you. I brought it as soon as I could. I have been ill with the coughing sickness, My Lady."

Lynn was frightened now.

"How did you get this?"

"Your father gave it to me, in Godwyne."

She didn't want to open the letter, so she asked again, "How?"

The Shipman's face grew even darker. He said, "It was my ship your father was taking to Venice, right after the coronation of the Duke. So I went to see him in Godwyne, and he threw this letter down to me from his window. He paid me for the ship and said I was to bring this letter here instead of taking him to Venice. That was all I was supposed to do. But then the plague broke out there. I escaped the plague, but I caught the coughing sickness for three months. Then I came. I'm sorry for you, M'Lady."

Lynn heard her own voice shaking. "Would you like some water now?"

The Shipman hesitated. "Yes, I'll take some."

They walked over to the well, and after he finished drinking he set the gourd down in the bucket and looked away.

"Thank you, My Lady. Goodbye."

"Goodbye," said Lynn.

The Shipman put his cap back on and walked across the meadow and down the hill. Lynn watched him go, then leaned against the cool stones of the well and opened the letter slowly. It read:

> My Loving daughter,
> I pray this letter reaches you in
> time. I am held prisoner inside this
> tavern with your mother and the family.
> There is a group of men who call themselves
> Hospitaliers who have killed the Innkeeper
> and are threatening to kill mother and one
> of your brothers each day unless I do
> certain things. They are after our home
> and lands and I am afraid that unless I
> cooperate with them, they will fulfill
> their threats.
> Whatever happens in the future will
> depend upon the turns of fortune. But
> you must never give up our home. The
> Duke will help you, and God looks after
> the kind. Pray for all our souls.
> Your Father,
> Bret St. Du Lac, Baron of Solway

After she read it, her body convulsed into deep breaths and she cried without thinking of anything for a long time. Then a balm of numbness ensued, and except for the germ of a single purpose she was calm and horribly empty. The long morning shadows of the poplar trees had become round pools of shade for the children to play under before Lynn splashed her face with water from the well, dried it with her dress, and went back into the orphanage.

Gwendy stood up from the spinning wheel with a distaff in her hand,

"Will you take breakfast now, My Lady?"

"I don't think so, Gwen, I'm going out."

A little boy came in crying through the back door, dripping mud, and he held his arms out at his sides and bawled. Gwendy went back to attend him.

Lynn went into her chamber. She put her hair into a net and took a shawl from her trunk of clothing and placed the letter inside her dress.

When she came back into the big room, Gwendy had taken the boy's clothes off and sat him in a wooden tub. She was about to douse him with a bucket of cold water but stopped when Lynn came out.

"Could you find us some needles, My Lady. So many things have to be mended now."

Lynn nodded and opened the door. Donny Gwaith was just outside. She turned back to Gwendy, and again the muddy boy was spared.

"Gwen,"

"Yes, My Lady?"

"If Nelrum or his friend come back, please tell them I am at Josh's. Tell them I must see them– that I am looking for them."

Gwendy raised the bucket over the boy's head and said, "Yes, M'Lady."

Lynn felt like crying again as she pulled the door closed behind her, but Donny Gwaith was playing there. He had fashioned a sword from two lashed sticks and was thrusting it toward a tree. He turned quickly when he heard the heavy door close, rushed to face her and bowed with the sword in front of him.

Lynn bowed too, and said, "Sir Knight, will you be my

escort to the doorway of King Arthur's Inn?"

Donny nodded, smiling. He held out his hand. Lynn took it and they started down the hill toward town. They walked along in silence, and Lynn looked down at Donny's too-big floppy hat bobbing beside her.

"Donny, I know that Redwyn was trying to help you yesterday. I misunderstood, and now I am trying to find him."

Donny nodded.

"If I *do* find him, I am going to apologize."

Donny nodded again.

Lynn shook her head lightly. "He is very brave isn't he?"

Donny looked up at her, put his hand under his coat and shook it like a fluttering heart. Lynn laughed, then said sternly, "A good knight never taunts a maiden in distress." Donny hurried quickly in front of her and held out the sword and stamped on the ground as he walked, swinging his head from side-to-side as if searching for danger diligently. Lynn laughed again.

"That is better, Sir Knight."

They entered the town and began searching as they made their way through the crowd. Donny stayed close to her, and when they reached the Inn she put her hand on his back and they stepped into the tavern and saw Josh. He was carrying a large basket of apples to the counter.

"My Lady, you should have told me you were coming. I would have brought my cart up to get you."

"But I have enjoyed the protection of Sir Donny Gwaith, Knight Templar and Guardian of Maidens," she answered.

Josh handed an apple to Donny then stood erect with his shoulders pulled back and said, "Sir Knight, I thank you for protecting this Lady."

Donny just looked at the apple absently and left through the tavern door.

Lynn asked, "Have you seen Nelrum or Redwyn?"

"No, My Lady, not since yesterday when I brought the

older gentleman here."

"Do you know where they went, Josh?"

"Well, when we arrived at the Inn the maid told us that the young man, Redwyn, had gone up to the castle. I suspect that Nelrum went there after him."

"And you haven't seen them?"

"They didn't come back last night."

She frowned and turned to look out the doorway. "It is not like Nelrum to leave without telling me. They must be at the castle. But why?"

Josh closed one eye. "The barmaid said..." He hesitated, and Lynn searched his face... "said that Redwyn was going to meet with the Head Robe so that he could get a horse and *leave* M' Lady."

"What time was that, Josh?"

The Innkeeper looked to the doorway where the sun slanted through onto the tables and floor. "Oh, after noon I'd say."

"Late afternoon?" asked Lynn. "Was it late, toward evening?"

"Yes," said Josh. "I'd say so. Fairly late I'd say."

She frowned, "He couldn't have traveled last night; it would have been too late for that. If he did not stay here, then he must have slept at the castle and perhaps he is still there. Oh, this is terrible. Please, if one of them should arrive, tell them I have gone to the castle and send them there right away. Better yet– do you have a quill?"

Josh took a tally sheet from the counter and set it on one of the long tables with a quill and pot of ink. Lynn sat down to write, speaking as the feather waved before her beautiful features. "If Nelrum or Redwyn should arrive here while I am gone, give this to them. You mustn't let anyone else see it, Josh." She rose and kissed his cheek. "And you mustn't worry, either."

"But to the castle," he moaned, "My Lady, you shouldn't be going there alone."

"I shall be safe enough. I am certain those two will be

there."

Josh felt a faint prickle go up his back. "But why, My Lady? What if they aren't there? What are you going to the castle *for*?"

"I am going to get my home back."

He felt the prickle again, stronger. "I don't know what you mean, but suppose they aren't there. You mustn't go unattended." He was pleading with his eyes.

But Lynn shook her head with finality.

"Dear Josh, If Redwyn or Nelrum *are* there, I shall be protected. If they are not, I shall return here; after all, I have met with Morcar before, I have been there unattended, and there simply is nothing to fear."

Josh was sweating, "I'll go with you, My Lady."

"Then who will give them the note if they should come here?"

"Very well." He reached into his apron and took out a metal prong, "At least take this."

Lynn smiled and shook her head No, and walked out of the tavern.

Josh felt sick with himself. She had made it easy for him. "I don't like this," he muttered. "But cowards don't have to like things."

Chapter 19
Pranksters

As Lynn hurried through the crowded street, townspeople recognized her and bowed and smiled politely. Some of the older women stood in their doorways, dressed in black and whispering to each other as she passed. She walked along the shops and around the livestock being herded through the street, and held her breath near the stables. Then, passing through the city gates, the fairgrounds opened up. The road was dusty and busy on both sides where the merchants sold their wares. The air was sweeter, and she turned to face the sea. Ships filled the quays, flying bright crests from Venice, Portugal, and Spain. The same crests fluttered on poles above the ware displays. As she made her way along the merchants tallied, grinned, and assumed postures of dignity over their goods. Because they wore stripes and satins and rich embroidery while eating and working in the road dust and hot sun, Lynn thought they were grossly overdressed.

Outside the fine goods there were livestock pens and fowlers. Then the road branched off and started up the hill.

To her right there was the deep, dark green of Grinmere. And to her left the grassy slope that ran all along the edge of Solway, rising steeply to the skyline of the hill. Following the skyline to her left, way off amid some trees she saw the orphanage. It was small and dark looking, the thatching of the roof was yellow in the sun, and on the wall that faced the hill there was a squarish fleck of green that Lynn knew must be the shutters of her room. She thought back to the morning, how the Shipman had appeared upon the road. He was only a figure on the landscape, then, but he had brought the letter and now everything had changed. She reached up and pressed it underneath her dress and heard it crinkle. Ahead, the castle loomed large and grey, and as the road grew steeper she put her head down to climb.

At the plateau there were two farmers in their field. She knew them. They saw her and brought their hoes and came over to the roadside.

The two men were brothers, their fields were part of the castle holdings, and the crops looked very poor. Lynn greeted them. They both looked bad and awfully hungry but they were trying to be cheerful. When she mentioned their father's recent death, in sympathy, they looked worried and then moved awkwardly back to being cheerful and polite. It made them happy when she asked about their sisters, and they reminded her of how they used to play together when they were all just little girls. Lynn recounted a time when she was playing with the sisters and the brothers had crept up behind some trees and run out and, in spite of their girlish threats and screams, dumped sacks of wheat chaff all over them. The brothers laughed hard and leaned on their hoes. Lynn reached into her purse and took two florens out.

They did not seem as happy, then, but accepted the coins, smiling and thanking her, and then they all said goodbye. When Lynn had gone on a little further she looked back and saw the brothers walking downhill toward the town. Their hoes were left abandoned in the road.

She continued on and entered the castle grounds through the pillars, then raised her head and walked briskly toward the moat. The sentinel stared down from his perch in the shooting turret as she approached. She stopped directly beneath him and called, "I am here to see Morcar. I am Lynn St. Du Lac, daughter of the Baron of Solway."

The sentinel turned and disappeared. After a considerable time the drawgate began to fall. The giant chains clanged as they slipped through the stone wall and the ground pulsed joltingly when the huge gate landed.

The two winchmen stared at her as she walked through the gateway, and a Robe with a crossbow stepped up. He scanned her body, raising his stare slowly from the ground, and said, "Brech is coming," and licked his lips in a slow, vulgar way.

Lynn said scornfully, "How wonderful for you."

The guard had a stubbly beard and he thrust his face in front of hers and clasped her shoulder. He grinned with his rotten teeth and held his crossbow up in front of her eyes. "I am supposed to stay close to you!"

The man clasped her face with both hands, almost the same instant that Brech came up behind him. Brech caught the man's hair and yanked him backward, and the man fell elbows-first onto the ground.

The giant turned to the winchmen and snapped his fingers. The drawbridge started up. He snapped his fingers again and pointed. Two guards came forward and picked up the fallen Robe.

"Hold him here," Brech rasped.

Lynn followed him to the castle. They ascended an outer wall staircase, passed under an arch and went down the cool dark corridors to the great-hall antechamber. They stopped there, and Brech held his arm out to barricade her entrance to the study.

"Wait," he grunted.

He went in and shut the door behind him. Lynn stood in the antechamber and touched the big blue tapestry and listened. Inside, the mens' voices rumbled in a low murmur. Then Brech came out and pointed to the open door. As she went in, Morcar was standing in front of the desk.

"Hello, My Lady. To what am I indebted for the pleasure of your company?"

"I *had* thought my friends were here."

"Oh?" said Morcar, "Who might they be?" He seemed amused with himself.

"An old man named Nelrum," she said.

"He hasn't been here."

"His companion, then, a young man. Redwyn."

Morcar nodded slowly and turned his back to her. "You say this young man was companion to Nelrum?"

"Is he here?"

The Head Robe turned around and faced her. "He was. But he seemed impatient to reclaim his horse and leave."

She shut her eyes for a moment. Morcar said, "Have I disturbed My Lady?" Then as if reflecting thoughtfully, "Yes, this Redwyn was quite a good looking lad. Big and strong, quite virile I'd say. Hmm, M' Lady? Is that the breed of stallion to fill your stall?"

Lynn flushed with anger, but the thought of the letter in her dress kept her tongue. She turned around. Brech was standing at the door.

Morcar's voice came back, "I don't believe that you will see our young stallion again. When the stable stinks, the horse longs for greener pastures."

At that she turned to face him, her eyes flashing steely grey with hate.

But Morcar came toward her and grinned, "You shouldn't be angry, Lynn. A rogue like him could never give you the rights of your station. On the other hand, I offer all the lands and titles that befit you; you could have them, you know."

His angular face and round bulging eyes smiled. He reached out to touch her– she was rigid– and he sniffed and turned away.

"Very well then. *Be* a common waif, if it pleases you."

It was too much. Her voice rang in the silent room, "Maggot! I will see you twist from a gallows' arm. Maggot! A filthy maggot you are!"

Morcar turned his head in a slow, almost theatrical gesture, keeping his body taut. As he leered at her a grin flickered onto his lips. "You are a foolish girl! Your discontent is born of a newfound poverty and your father's willingness to leave you without a crumb."

Lynn's breath grew short, she lost her composure and burst out weeping, "The Duke will know!– You weren't careful enough!– I have the proof to hang you now!"

The Head Robe's eyes glistened, then he erupted into shrill peals of laughter. Even Brech laughed in a quake of muffled rumblings at the door. The joke was over.

"I sent the letter!" he cried. "Yes, Lynn. You poor pathetic fool! I sent the Shipman to your door!"

Chapter 20
Josh

The willow branch whistled through the air and cracked as it struck the donkey's hide. "Hah! Come on, you hop sack! It's the Lady Lynn at the top o' the hill– hah!" Josh's face was feverish and he mumbled to himself, "I never should have let her go. Fine man that lets a lady walk into a rats' nest." He whipped the donkey again. "Hah! Come on with your creakin' bones!"

Brech climbed into the archer's rook and scanned the castle grounds, his black eyes shifting beneath his thick eyebrows. "Have you seen anyone outside the gate?" he asked the sentinel.

"No. Only the donkey cart that now climbs the hill."

Brech turned to leave, but the cart stopped and a short figure stepped out and tethered the donkey to a pillar.

"What is it?" asked the sentinel.

Brech was staring at the short man that stood beside the cart. "Lower the drawbridge," he said.

"Why?" asked the sentinel.

Brech snatched the crossbow from the guard's hands and glared at him. "Lower the drawbridge."

"Yes, Lord."

A moment later, Josh crouched beside the hedge as the noisy gate started down.

The sentinel returned from giving the order and as he stepped off the top of the stairs, Brech kicked his legs out from under him, the young man's face smashing into the stone floor of the turret. He groaned, and Brech whispered, "Quiet."

Josh was moving along the hedge. He craned his neck toward the gate rook and squinted nearsightedly. "Oh My Lady..." he mumbled. "What have I done to you?"

Brech raised the crossbow up and growled, "I said you'd get more than you bargained for," and his finger found the trigger.

The Innkeeper started across the open field. There were no sentinels along the parapets, but he would not have known what to do had he seen one. He was there on an impulse, looking for just what, he knew not, hoping to see the Lady Lynn emerge from the drawgate and perhaps redeem himself for the cowardice he had shown. About fifty yards from the bridge he heard the faint quick whir of the arrow– and then "crack!" his legs were out from under him and he fell backward to the ground. Staring up at the sky, all but senseless, with a sudden warmth spreading under his shirt, he could hear Brech shouting something, groped over his stinging shoulder and realized an arrow had gone through him and exited through his underarm. He raised himself but fell forward into the grass– stood again and started for the cart, groping, sometimes losing it in the blur and intermittent darkening of his sight. He felt as though he were suffocating. But at last at the cart, he took his hand from the bleeding shoulder, loosened the donkey's tether and climbed in.

Brech was bellowing behind him as the cart lurched forward. There was another whirring sound, and a second arrow stuck into the cart's floor. The donkey was running down the highland road. Josh tucked the reins into his belt and looked behind him to see four Robes giving chase on foot, their dark figures getting smaller and blurrier as they lost ground. The cart bounced, and he fell down hard upon its floor. The jostling came through the rough hewn planks and hurt him.

*****

Donny Gwaith had been playing outside the stone house as the shadows lengthened across the field. Now he raised his wooden sword and was about to strike a tree, but stopped and looked up the highland road. A donkey was running briskly toward him pulling a cart behind. When it came to the turn it pulled the cart off the road onto the meadow, and lowered its head at a puddle.

Donny approached slowly and looked inside.

Josh lay bleeding on the floor; he peered up and said, "Hello lad." Donny shook his head silently. "You mustn't tell anyone that I'm here. You've got to hide me and... You've got to hide me."

Donny hurried to the donkey's reins and tugged on them. The donkey would not move and Donny tugged and leaned, but the donkey was stubborn. He took his wooden sword and swatted its hind, and it lurched from the puddle and away.

When they reached the grain house the boy leaned over the side of the cart and touched Josh's cheek. The little man opened his eyes and nodded. Donny took his arm and pulled him from the cart and Josh walked hunched-over into the grain house and settled there amid the sacks.

Donny went away then came back with some blankets and a rag. Josh opened his eyes when he felt the weight of the blankets on him. He said, "You mustn't tell anyone. Hide the cart and tell nobody I was here." Donny knelt down near the wounded shoulder and began to tie the rag on. "That's a good lad. I'll be all right. Just need a little while. The two men that were here yesterday– do you know the ones I mean?"

Donny nodded seriously.

"Tell 'em that Lynn's in danger and bring 'em here. Bring 'em here, lad."

Donny stepped from the grain house and closed the door. The sun was setting into the sea and the shadows were fading. He wiped his face and climbed into the cart, and the tired donkey started down the hill.

Chapter 21
The Assassins

The boy waited in the shadows of a doorway and watched Josh's tavern from across the street. It was very dark, except for the squarish patterns of light that fell dimly from the tavern's door and windows, and he watched the shadows of the men who moved inside. The night grew sharply colder. Then the moon rose over the rooftops turning the black street to midnight blue and grey.

Two men came out of the tavern. They walked toward the boy, against the opposite wall, then stopped near some tethered horses. One of the men was Brech. He pulled the other man closer and they both stayed close against the wall.

"He should have bled to death by now," the low voice rumbled. "Wait some more– not very long– then meet me in my chambers."

The other man whispered, "Yes. Yes, I'll meet you."

Then, as they stood there, Brech pulled the other man toward him until their breath came together in the cool night air. A shout broke from the tavern, and the other man looked over quickly and stood away. Brech watched him go back inside, then he turned to the horses and fumbled to untie one in the dark. He stepped back and gripped a crop of the horse's mane and tried to pull himself into the saddle, but slipped joltingly onto the street. He cursed and reached up to the mane again and awkwardly mounted. Donny held his breath as the horse turned clatteringly around. He kept still in the shadows as the giant rode past his doorway and disappeared into the night.

More men came and left. The night seemed very cold, and now each of the damp cobblestones held a reflected moon. A mist was creeping in, and the boy retracted deeper into the shadows and pulled his knees against his chest. He had been scared and wide awake, but now fatigue took hold, and while the noises from the Inn droned on, he let his chin rest upon his knees and fell into a sound and deafened sleep.

*****

A voice broke the silence, "Donny? Donny?"

The boy stood and rubbed his eyes, groggy. The moon was shining brightly into the doorway. Redwyn was crouched down, smiling, with Nelrum standing back holding two horses.

"Come inside and eat," Redwyn said.

The sleep left Donny. He shivered.

"Come stay with us."

Donny shook his head No and started backing down the street, motioning with his hands.

"What is it?"

Nelrum was looking into the tavern window. He said, "We had better follow him."

The two men climbed onto their horses. Donny ran in front of them into an alleyway. He came out driving Josh's donkey cart and turned onto the street whipping the donkey hard. They went on, Redwyn and Nelrum riding at both sides, Donny with the cart in the center. When they reached the edge of town, the buildings cleared and all three saw the luminous glow of fire on the hill.

Redwyn and Nelrum broke into a gallup and went ahead, kicking their horses hard at the incline. Redwyn's horse was faster, and topping the hill's crest the meadow flattened in front of him and he rode across its brightened openness, between two burning poplar trees, then drew reins violently to a stop. In front of him the orphanage was being ravaged by flames. The roof was mostly gone, the thatching had burned away to leave a criss-crossed frame of sticks that dripped with fire. The flames fluttered from the windows that belched black smoke. Redwyn dismounted, ran to the buckled sheet of embers that was once a door, and kicked his way in.

Inside, the plank floor was a bed of seething coals. The heat was coming quickly through his boots. He could feel his feet blistering as he searched carefully into the corners, with the smoke in acrid billows clawing at his eyes. The roof began to collapse, but he searched as the burning sections dropped, found Lynn's door and kicked the burning planks down and stepped in.

Her chamber was only halfway gone, the bedding pouring out luminous clouds of biting smoke. Flames were roaring up the walls and Redwyn felt his head turning light. He looked with eyes wide open to the smoke and shouted out Lynn's name, waited another moment, then turned and started back for the door.

Outside when the tears had washed his vision clear, he saw Donny standing near the grain house. Nelrum was kneeling inside of it; and walking closer Redwyn saw the legs, rms, and lifeless face of Josh. Nelrum was peeling Josh's shirt back from a wound that was clotted like dark jelly. He looked up over his shoulder and said, "He has lost a lot of blood."

"Is he alive, then?"

Nelrum shook his head and said, "A *lot* of blood."

Standing outside the grain house with his boots cooling in the damp grass, Redwyn could feel the first true waves of pain from his blistered feet.

"There is no one in the orphanage," he said.

"I did not expect there would be. Here, you had better read this." Nelrum picked up an unfolded letter from the

Innkeeper's chest. Redwyn took it and turned it toward the fire. It read:

> I have proof my father was murdered.
> You will find me at the castle.
> Lynn

Nelrum went on working over Josh. He poured some liquor from a flask into a cloth and started dabbing off the wound. Then he said, "While we were outside the tavern I saw some of Morcar's men. They were dressed in huntsman's garb, but they were *his* men nonetheless. I see, now, what they were waiting for."

"Josh must have gone to help her," Redwyn said.

"We have to take him to a bed somewhere–" But hearing the champ of hooves, Nelrum turned and saw that Redwyn was no longer there. Donny pointed in the direction of the town. Nelrum nodded he understood and went back to work on Josh.

Redwyn tore across the soft earth of the meadow, hunks of sod flying from the horse's hooves, and then he galloped recklessly down the hill, feeling weightless with the wind rushing in his ears, caring not about the deep ruts in the road that could trip the horse and send them down the hill, send him into somersaults beneath the horse's crushing weight. He flew around the sharp turn into town, the horse slipping on the damp cobblestones, and galloped without bridle down the narrow, cobbled street, though he could scarcely see before him in the dark.

At the tavern lights he drew reins and skidded clatteringly to a stop. A drunk stood in the half-light of the inn's windows, pinned with his back against a wall. He looked up dough-faced and said, "I heard you coming." Redwyn dismounted and handed him the horse's reins.

The three henchmen sat at the back of the tavern, two with crossbows on the table, the third with a broadsword leaning against the wall. Redwyn stayed outside the tavern door and watched them. All three were drinking. One took a long draught of ale and put his mug down. The other two picked their mugs up.

He thought, "That's two off guard," backed up to the opposite wall, and pushed off running.

He bounded up the tavern steps and leaped through the door. The men saw him and started reaching for their weapons, but far too late. Redwyn charged forward, caught the table's edge and threw it over on top of them. They all fell from their stools, wedged between the long table and floor. Redwyn drew his sword out and waited.

The first one crawled out with a crossbow already in hand. Redwyn slashed at the bowstring. The sprung bow jumped from the man's hand like a frightened animal and the heavy string lashed open his right forearm so that a purple bulge of muscle protruded wet and quivering through the cut skin.

The Robe wailed and rolled protectively onto his wounded arm. The two others pushed the table off and scrambled across the floor.

The second archer found his crossbow and rose up sighting quickly from his knees. Without hesitation Redwyn lunged at him and pushed his sword, with a sickening crunch, into the man's chest, withdrew it, and the crossbow discharged into the ceiling. The man eased himself forward to die upon his knees, but a nudge from the advancing Broadswordsman toppled him sideways.

The Broadswordman's eye twitched as he hoisted the heavy weapon up over his head and the six foot blade whirred in a complete revolution through the air. Then, all in one motion, he swung the huge sword downward– knees bent, arms fully extended, wide back and shoulders rounded against the great weight he swung– then he sprang forward and leveled the blade flatly into Redwyn's chest. Redwyn held his own weapon against it with both hands. The tavern rang as the two metals clashed. The broadsword came loose, and the force of the blow lifted Redwyn from his footing and threw him into the door jamb. He fell winded to the floor. The barmaid screamed. Redwyn stood up again, gasping, and tossed a table from his path. The broadswordsman reached his weapon, lifted it and charged forward bellowing, this time wielding the blade overhead like an axe. Redwyn lunged low to the attack; shoulder first, he hurled himself into the swordsman's body and plunged his sword in low and up to its hilt with both hands. The two men fell thunderously to the floor planks, Redwyn still gripping his sword handle– the assassin disgorging torrents of blood from his mouth, his dying eyes agape in disbelief. He made one last effort to clutch at Redwyn's throat, and then succumbed.

The man whose arm was cut now sat in the corner, crying, a puddle of vomit in front of him on the floor. Redwyn stood, picked up the broken crossbow, and waited a moment to settle. Then he went over and said, "Take this back to Morcar. Tell him two more rats have died."

The man stood and used his sleeve to wipe the vomit from his chin. Then he clutched his forearm and hurried out through the door. Nelrum and Donny stood aside to let him pass.

The barmaid was crying and to Redwyn's astonishment she stood over the body of an old man. He was to learn later that when the broadsword was deflected, its handle had struck the poor fellow's neck and broken it. In the frenzy of battle Redwyn hadn't even noticed.

Several of the townspeople went out to help carry Josh in from the cart. They brought him through the narrow doorway on their shoulders, as pallbearers would bear a corpse, and gravely and carefully lowered him onto a table. Other inn patrons came forward, some murmuring Josh's name.

Nelrum told the barmaid to bring a mug of liquor and a clean cloth. She did so. He put the cloth over Josh's wound and poured some liquor on to soak it. He heated the metal mug over a candle until the liquor fumed, and waved it under Josh's nose.

Some color came back into the little man's soggy face, and he coughed.

Nelrum called, "Bring some cider!" and a patron handed a mug of it over the heads of the crowd.

The crowd huddled close now as the fuming liquor was waved under Josh's nose again. Some color rose in his cheek, and the folds of his eyelids quivered.

Nelrum shouted, "Stand away! Give him room now!"

But the crowd moved in and pushed their astonished faces over one another to see the life in Josh. He opened his eyes. Nelrum quickly supported his neck and helped him drink the cider.

The Innkeeper coughed, "They have Lynn at the castle. I shouldn't have let her go alone. She didn't come back, I–"

"Don't speak," said Nelrum. "We will move you up to bed."

"It was Brech," Josh groaned. "He shot me. They have Lynn. They have her at the castle."

Redwyn took his groping arm and eased him back on the table. The room was very still.

Then an old man stepped forward. He had strong eyes set in a strong brown face, and his shoulder length grey hair shimmered in the candlelight. His thick white mustache trembled as he gestured to the aged figure whose neck had been broken and was now a crumpled corpse against the wall.

"He was my oldest friend," he said to Redwyn.

"I am sorry."

"You need not be." The old man's voice was deep and clear. "My friend was from an old and noble line of knighthood. We fought many battles together. We thought we were the last of our kind to fight for honor and not for gold. That is– until tonight."

He raised a trembling hand. "You see, it shakes. Not good for anything now." He pointed with the hand. "Do you know what is on that hill?"

"No," Redwyn answered.

"Camelot," the old man said. "It's ruined walls are all that is left.   An old knight could always find a home in the Baron's castle and be near to those bastions of chivalry. My friend was once the finest swordsman in Christendom. While you were fighting, he took my arm and said, 'how good this knight!' And we both knew that we were not the last who would fight for honor."

Redwyn's eyes set deeper in his brow. He knew what was coming next, and he said quietly, "But I am not a knight."

The crowd reacted and, "Aye!" "A knight you are!" were repeated again and again. A big Miller advanced from the crowd, broad faced and embarrassed, and he only glanced up briefly from the floor. He said, "The Lady Lynn was our last hope, sir. She was all that's left of the Baron's line. I have no place to store my grain now. In the winter it is very likely many of us will starve–"

A skinny farmer yelled with an intoxicated voice, "The heel of death clatters outside the door. Listen! The wind howls through his hollow mask!"

The crowd reflexively listened: outside the horse champed the cobblestones and snorted from his run.

"You hold your tongue!" the Miller shouted. He looked back to Redwyn and said politely, "You see, sir, the Baron was a good Lord."

"Aye." "Aye," they said.

"His generosity kept many of his subjects alive. The Lady Lynn is in trouble now. It is our loyal duty to save her."

"Yes," said the Old Knight, "And restore the castle to its rightful heir."

"Aye!" "Aye!" came the cries.

Redwyn shouted, "Wait! If you men try to storm the castle, Morcar will cut you down!"

"You can wear my armor," said the knight.

Redwyn looked at him, and into the close crowd's hopeful

faces. "I want Lynn back too. But the Robes are dangerous. Let me do it another way. Alone."

"Let us help," said the Miller.

"You can help," said Redwyn, looking about him, "All of you– by keeping your tongues about this."

The men nodded to each other, and the big Miller asked, "Is there nothing else?"

Redwyn said emphatically, "No. Simply do not say a word."

With a nod the Miller acquiesced. The mood of the crowd softened into disappointment. Nelrum walked over to supervise the men who were carrying Josh up the stairs, rockingly, on a table top.

Redwyn went out and thanked the drunkard who was still holding his horse in the street. Groups of townsmen carried the Robes' bodies out and bid 'fair morrow' and 'good night,' and disappeared into the darkness.

Finally all the townspeople had gone, save for the Old Knight. He came out to the street and said, "It is lonely to be brave, isn't it, Lad?"

Redwyn asked, "Where will you sleep?"

The old man started away. "At the fairgrounds, likely. Always a fire burning there."

Chapter 22
Peril

On the morning after the fight Redwyn had slept late. There was a knock on the bedchamber door. He opened his eyes and saw Nelrum walking over to answer it. The Barmaid entered with a tray. She walked slowly up to the bed and very softly and politely said, "I have some breakfast for you, sir."

As Redwyn sat up the blankets fell down from his bare chest. The Barmaid's eyes widened and she leaned over and set the tray down in his hands. "Oh, it is for you too, sir," she said in an afterthought to Nelrum.

The old man's mouth twitched at the corners. "Shall I eat it from his chest?"

She ignored him and said pleasantly to Redwyn, "Can I bring you something more?"

"No, thank you. This is enough." He picked up a rose from the tray. It had pink petals and a tiny yellow button in the center. He twirled and inspected it awkwardly.

"It is an August rose, sir, from the second bloom. There aren't many left, it being so late in August, but I found one for you."

"Thank you," he said.

There was a moment of silence. The Barmaid nodded and backed toward the door, all the time watching Redwyn, even as she pulled the door closed, smiling through the door crack until it shut.

Redwyn took the mug of cider from the breakfast tray and drank some. He smacked his lips and tipped the mug again. He saw Nelrum was watching, and lowered the mug self-consciously.

"Have some, Nelrum."

"No, no."

"Why not?"

"I will eat later. Besides, you are going to need your strength today."

Redwyn propped himself higher in the bed. He reached onto the tray and took one of the apple slices that were spread out like a fan with a drop of honey in the center.

"Imagine the barmaid bringing all this."

"Yes."

"It surprises me."

"Does it?"

There was a clamor from below, as if furniture were being slid across the tavern floor.

"It's noisy," said Redwyn. "Do you know how Josh is?"

"Yes. Better."

Redwyn slowed his chewing and put a half-chicken down on the tray. "I cannot eat this," he said with his mouth full. "We must free Lynn. The orphans too; they are a complication now."

"Really?"

"Yes, really," Redwyn answered, flashing his eyes with consternation.

Then from below in the tavern a pounding started– becoming rhythmic and quickly growing so loud that the shutters vibrated in the window frames. Redwyn grabbed his sword from the bedside and said, "What in hell!"

He stood and pulled on his breeches and went to the

shutters. Through the cracks he saw a crowd of men jamming the tavern doorway. They held up scythes, hoes, axes and plain sticks, moving them rhythmically, as they stamped their feet on the ground. Then a fat man waved his arm and barked, "Lead us! Lead us!" Other voices joined his in unison, "Lead us! Lead us! Lead us! Lead us!" and the chorus grew to a thunderous resound.

Redwyn turned around and Nelrum was opening the door. Josh came in, held up by the barmaid. Other men stood back from the doorway and looked inside; they, too, had scythes and axes.

Nelrum helped walk the unsteady Innkeeper to the bed. Redwyn left the window and went over to him.

"How are you, Josh?"

"They want to storm the castle, sir."

"They cannot," Redwyn said.

"They're planning on it. They're hoping you will lead them."

"Morcar will kill them, shoot them down! They have no weapons, and there are other things, too. They mustn't try!"

"Some of them have weapons," said Josh. "There is a whole pack of them downstairs. They're waiting for you. Every one of 'em has a weapon of some kind." He was pale and sweaty. Nelrum eased him back on the bed and said, "You are too weak for this."

The cheering and thumping had grown louder and more rhythmic below. Redwyn went quickly to the door and opened it. The men who were standing there backed away. He walked past them and passed others on the stairs. As he came down into the tavern the crowd at the base of the stairway parted and the thumping ceased. The hush went out the door, and in a moment the room was nearly still.

Redwyn frowned and shook his head. "This isn't good. You men don't know the risks that you would take."

"We'll fight," said the Miller as he pushed his way forward. Redwyn looked at his hands and saw the weapons he held.

"With what? An axe and club?"

"Aye," said the big man, brandishing them. "And a vengeance!"

"Aye! Aye!" cheered the crowd.

"You will be shot down!"

"Will you lead us?"

"No! Not to your deaths I won't!"

The Miller stepped back into the crowd. Red faced, he glanced from side to side and mumbled, "Better to be shot than strangled."

"Aye," said other voices. "Aye its true."

Redwyn asked, "What is true?"

The peasants glanced nervously about them, but an answer was postponed by a disturbance out in the street, a metallic clanging as if a pot vendor's cart had overturned. The crowd cleaved to the doorway, and the Old Knight stood there holding a tarnished suit of armor on a wooden pole. After exhaling, he threw back his head and declared, "I am Sir Perceville Thorne, Knight Templar of the house of Lancaster. Command and we shall follow!"

"Ayyai!" rose the cheering.

Redwyn rolled his eyes and clenched his fist. He shouted, "Sir Perceville, all you men– hear me! Lads, if you can wait–"

But Sir Percy cut him off, "There is no time to wait!"

The crowd went wild.

The Miller's courage had been stoked, and he bellowed with his big red face, "If we don't take the castle, we'll starve by mid fall!"

"They have no food," Sir Percy shouted, advancing between the waving arms. "The Robes have taken nearly all of it."

"The wheat has ripened," said the Miller. "There is no place to store it now."

A farmer blurted, "The Robes 'been takin' the food and

watching the wheat and livestock. When the time is come they'll take it and put us by to starve!"

"The land is owned by Morcar now," Sir Percy explained, his brown and sweaty face now close to Redwyn's. "Even if these people *could* move away, there is no place for them to go. The plague has been within just two score miles. A famine has begun. The food they planted in the spring is all the wealth they have. All the hope as well."

The crowd grew quieter to listen.

"Food is getting scarce already," said a nearby farmer. "Aye," said another. The men nodded among themselves.

The Miller looked up self-consciously. "So you see sir, we will be going to that castle. If we cannot save the Lady Lynn, and somehow earn her mercy—"

Sir Percy interrupted, "Morcar snatched the Lady! She never would have gone by her own free will. Perhaps if we begin a siege the Duke will come." He added more softly, "But we are going. Your sword could only help us."

Redwyn heaved a sigh of exasperation. The men were watching him anxiously. He looked out the brightened doorway, then into Percy's eyes.

"It must be understood that this is perilous. And if I am to lead you, my orders will be obeyed with fidelity."

The crowd cried, "Aye! Ay-yai!" Someone yelled, "Onward, to the castle!" And Sir Percy put his hand on Redwyn's arm and said, "I thank you." But now his voice was drowned out by the cheers.

Chapter 23
The Procession

Redwyn squinted as he stepped out through the doorway into the glaring sun. Close about the tavern were the farmers, the herdsmen, the fathers and sons, the men who toiled earliest and long. Their faces were reddened, their hands were cracked and grimy, and arms though worked by endless strain had not grown strong but were skinny sticking from their ragged shirts.

He started slowly down the street, giving the crowd time to fall in behind him. Perhaps it was the strange self-consciousness of leadership that made him keen to his surroundings, the sense of being watched that made him look into the darkness of the livery with its dampened straw and acrid urine smell, to see the faces of the tired boys who all day tended horses to sleep amid the dung-straw and the rats. And across from the stables, the leather shops where the hide pits gave off tannin fumes that charmed the flies and made them drop so that now, in August, the pits were filled with flies and the Tanner had to reach in with his hands and pull the leather sheets out of the black ooze. Just ahead, the Butcher with his meat hung up on slabs, and more flies from the piles of entrails heaped by his door. And next the Fowler with his stacks of willow pens, loose feathers all about, and tethered, desperate geese. The bloody bandage pole where the surgeon kept his razor finely honed to amputate the broken and infected limbs from the peasants he made drunk and lay upon the board that now attracted flies as it leaned against the wall dangling chains and iron rings. Around a turn, and Redwyn passed beyond the shops and along house rows where the widows kept themselves in black, clutching their rosary beads with thoughtless faces, chalky from the darkness where they dwelled. He noticed all these things and more.

Free of the town walls, the crowd spilled out behind him, spreading like an army forming lines. They turned along the sea and started up the hill toward the orphanage. The dust rose behind them from the road and fallow fields. Then at the summit, the orphanage's charred stone walls and stalks of trees were still smoking, black against the bright blue sky. Here Redwyn stopped for a moment and while the procession caught up he stared at the ruin in silence. Sir Percy stepped up beside him, breathing heavily, and put his hand upon the young man's shoulder.

"Poor orphans," Redwyn said. "Truly they are Life's forsaken lot."

The old man's brow was creased over his hot blue eyes. He glanced back to the crowd plodding up the hillside, their anguished faces burning in the sun. And he said, "The truth, Redwyn, is that Life makes orphans of us all."

And as the crowd came off the slope and again formed a column behind them, the two men led the way together toward the castle, along the rutted highland road.

Chapter 24
Proclamation

Redwyn and Percy entered the baronial grounds through the pillars, and Redwyn motioned for the crowd to stop outside.

"There is no sentinel," he said.

Percy shielded his eyes and squinted at the castle's rook. "I cannot see one." The heat rose from the parapets and wrinkled the air in waves.

Redwyn turned and gestured the peasants in through the pillars. But he shouted, "Stay back along the hedge here!"

"Good tactic," said Percy. "Keep them out of crossbow range." He turned and yelled, "Stay back!" and moved over to tend the ragged band.

In all, about two-hundred peasants filed in, with Percy pacing the line to keep them back. The leaders from the tavern had formed a loose platoon and along with Percy were shouting at the crowd to, "Move along the hedge now!" and "Stay back!"

When they were all in, seeming quite nervous to be on the castle grounds, they fidgeted and did not speak. The other men had re-formed their platoon.

Redwyn advanced toward the castle with Percy beside

him.

"There should be a sentinel."

"There probably was," the Old Knight answered. "They saw us on the road, and now have set the bait out for a trap."

"They have seen us," said Redwyn. "But I don't think that Morcar wants to fight– not like this, in the open."

He drew his sword and turned. "You men take the flanks," he said, bringing the blade down to divide the platoon in half.

Percy drew a short-sword with many nicks in it. "I'm with you," he said. "Good idea to keep the others back."

Redwyn waved his hand to signal the advance.

They all moved up, Redwyn and Sir Percy leading, and the tavern's men spreading from their vanguard in a 'V'. The peasants advanced from the hedgerow in a very straight line about thirty yards behind.

The heat waves made the castle seem to quiver in the air. The glare was painfully bright and the muscles in Redwyn's forehead were pulling tautly as he scoured the roofs and parapets for Robes.

Some dust swirled against the drawgate and tightened into a vortex against the wall.

"It's too bloody still," said Percy.

Distantly, a thin warble of a voice teased the young man's ears.

"Did you hear that?" Redwyn said.

"No, what?" said Percy. "No."

"Listen."

The noise grew louder until a woman's voice could be plainly heard. The next moment the Lady Lynn rose up from behind the parapet wall, with Morcar following, and they both walked into the gate rook and stepped forward.

Percy's eyes flashed. He grunted and raised his sword. His face was angry and he pursed his lips to speak, but Redwyn clutched his arm.

"No, Percy. Don't say anything."

"What the devil?"

"Just wait."

Morcar came to the edge of the turret and looked over the field. He glanced at Redwyn then put his hand against Lynn's back and held the other arm open as if addressing an assemblage there to honor him. "Approach!" he called liltingly, turning slowly with his open arm. "Please, all of you. Come closer!"

Redwyn held one hand up, and the peasants halted their advance.

Morcar looked at him. "Why did you do that?" he called, the politeness in his voice now strained.

"Why should they come closer?" Redwyn shouted back. "They can hear you."

"I want them to know their Liege Lord," the Head Robe declared loudly, again turning regally on the parapet.

"What nonsense!" spat Percy.

"People!" Morcar began, "You are invited to partake in a great feast– one that will celebrate the marriage of The Lady Lynn, Baroness of Solway, to me."

The crowd stirred, the peasants turning in dismay, some cat-calling their words of disbelief.

Morcar went on, "In two days hence, at noon, you may come upon these grounds to eat and drink and pay a tribute of respect to your new Baron."

"No!" shouted Percy. "You force the Lady to wed your rotten hide!"

Lynn was silent, staring, her grey eyes fixed and, invisibly to the spectators, building tears.

The Miller advanced in angry strides from the flanks. "What about the harvest?" he shouted, and lurched up to the edge of the dry moat, directly beneath Morcar's gaze. "What about the storage of our grain!– the famine that will come because we have no food!"

The line of peasants began advancing.

"Where are the orphans?" someone called.

Morcar just stood rigidly and glared.

"Stop it!" Lynn cried. "All of you, listen! I marry him of my own free will!"

The crowd gasped. Sir Percy lowered his sword.

"No," moaned the Miller. Others whispered, "No, no."

Lynn beat her fists together. "Try to see! You will have your grain bin back. And you farmers won't starve this winter–Your tax money can be used to purchase food!"

She paused in the quiet that comes of disbelief.

"I have my future husband's pledge that these things will be done."

"Where are the orphans?" Redwyn called.

She tensed at the sound of his voice and turned toward him, but her powers of speech were lost in the conflicts of her mind.

Suddenly Morcar gripped her arm. "The orphanage caught fire!"
he shouted. "My Lady came to me for shelter, and the orphans here reside."

"Take the knife from her back!" yelled Percy.

Morcar leered over the head of Lynn. Then he stepped aside from her and held out both his hands at the edge of the parapet, and said, "I have no knife, Old Fool!"

Redwyn glanced quickly to the stones in the dry-moat below. "Who shot the Innkeeper?" he yelled. Morcar's shoulders flinched and his eyes shifted hatefully toward Redwyn who raised his sword in the sunlight. The blade caught the proper angle and a blinding flash shot straight to the Head Robe's eyes.

Morcar clutched his face and gasped. He turned and dropped his shoulder and tilted beyond the ledge. His eyes blinked and blindly stared, and he groped out with his arms and leaned into the fall. But Lynn's hands shot forth and snatched his robe and jerked him back. And he fell upon his knees, safe.

"God in heaven!" said Percy. "She saved the Devil's life!"

Redwyn grinned.

"Now I've seen it all!" Sir Percy said.

The crowd had been watching. The scythes, sticks, hoes, and axes were lowered.

Morcar rubbed his eyes and cursed. Lynn looked at her hand in revulsion, only now comprehending her act.

"Let's away," said Percy. "The world has gone to hell."

Redwyn met her searching eyes. He nodded once into them. She swallowed, nodded vaguely in return, then turned away.

Morcar had recovered. Panting, he glared with vicious hate and pointed down at Redwyn and cried, "Be gone by the wedding! Or my first act as Baron will remove your handsome head."

"Do you really think it handsome," Redwyn called.

The crowd laughed. Morcar spat into the moat.

Lynn turned and descended behind the parapet wall. Redwyn raised the sword again and Morcar flinched with fear. The crowd laughed again. Redwyn let the blade fall on his shoulder and grinned broadly. The crowd broke into cheers, and Morcar twisted himself around angrily and disappeared.

Percy clutched his jagged sword. He looked at its tarnished blade and frowned and shook his head. "I am sorry, sir."

Redwyn clasped the Old Warrior's arm. "Call me Redwyn, if you will."

Percy smiled with his deep blue eyes and then glanced back toward the pillars where the peasants filed slowly from the grounds. "That was their last hope," he said, and he sheathed his sword. "It's a scoundrel's world all right. We might as well go with them."

"I am coming back," Redwyn told him.

"What?"

"Lynn is desperate. If I can talk with her tonight, perhaps she'll find the strength to see this through."

"Good God," said Percy. It shocked him.

"I am going to talk with her. I am going to stop the wedding."

"I believe you mean it," Percy said.

"I do. Come on."

"Good God!"

"Come on," said Redwyn.

Inside the castle walls, Brech waited at the base of the stairs. He took Lynn's arm and held her as she stepped onto the landing. She twisted in his grasp and spluttered, "Let me go!"

Morcar descended the stairs behind them. "Yes, Brech, let her go. The Lady saved my life today. I, at least, can show some gesture of good will."

"It wasn't deliberate," she snarled.

"No, I am sure," said Morcar. "It seems your brimming with *irrepressible* goodness." He gestured, and a guard stepped forward.

"Escort the Lady back to her chamber."

Lynn started walking, and the guard followed awkwardly behind her.

"What about the men?" Brech said.

Morcar looked along the parapets at the hundred or so Robes that were crouching there with crossbows. "When the townspeople have gone you may call the archers down," he said. The sentinels will be tripled."

"Yes, Lord."

Morcar's gaze became thoughtful. He took a step forward and slowly looped his arm through Brech's. "Redwyn isn't dead," he said in a soft voice.

Brech's nostrils flared, and he exhaled heavily.

"No, My Lord."

"He frightens me, Brech. It's a feeling– as if the earth could crack and I'd be swallowed into it."

Morcar caressed Brech's hand. As his eyes focused on a distant thought, his realization escaped in a thin whisper.

"Today he nearly killed me with a beam of light. With his leadership these peasants–" He did not finish his thought, but said, "Well, I shall kill them all tonight. We have enough rats to do it."

"Yes, Lord."

"Then see to it."

Morcar started back inside the castle. Brech climbed the gate rook and looked out across the meadow at the last of the townspeople trudging wearily toward their homes.

Chapter 25
The Power of
the Sword

The tavern was empty when Redwyn and Percy returned. The barmaid was standing behind the counter. She pointed to the stairs and said, "Josh asked that you go up, sir."

Percy sat down near the doorway beside his stand of armor.

Redwyn walked in darkness up the stairs to the low, beam-ceilinged loft. He paused at his own chamber and rapped on the door.

"Nelrum?"

There was no answer and he looked inside. The shutters had been left open, and the room was empty.

He went across to Josh's chamber and rapped again. A faint voice said, "Come in."

Josh raised himself in his bed. Redwyn looked about the chamber for Nelrum.

"Hello, sir."

"Hello, Josh."

"I heard it didn't go very well at the castle."

"How did you know?"

"That sort of news has wings. But I wouldn't think as much of it as some do."

"What is that, Josh?"

"The Lady Lynn, sir, saving that devil's life like she did. I wouldn't think very much of it."

"I don't," said Redwyn.

"Knowing her like I do, it comes as natural– to save someone's life I mean."

"Have you seen Nelrum, Josh?"

"Yes, sir. He left you that note."

"Where?"

The Innkeeper nodded toward the fireplace. "Just there– beside those flagons on the mantle."

Redwyn walked across the room and lifted the letter from the mantlepiece. He tilted it toward the shutters where the sunlight came through the cracks. It read:

> Remember
> There are no victories

He turned toward Josh's bed, still staring at the words. "When did Nelrum leave?"

"Just after the crowd cleared out. A short while after you did."

"Did he say where?"

"I asked him because I knew you'd want to know. He said, Master Redwyn, that you would understand if I gave you that note. Is it all right?"

Redwyn smiled at the bandaged Innkeeper. "Yes. Ease back and rest."

Percy was still waiting by the tarnished suit of armor as Redwyn came down the stairs.

"Was there anything wrong?"

"No. My friend had to leave, that's all."

"Oh," said Percy, looking down. "You mean old Nelrum."

"Do you know him?"

"I met him when I was staying at the castle," said Percy. I was an instructor to the Baron's sons, in the arts of knighthood. At least that is what the Baron said."

"And you met Nelrum?"

"Yes. I met him many years ago when he brought the Baron out of Grinmere wood. A boar had gored the Baron's leg above the knee– here." Percy pointed to his knee. "He visited the castle several more times, but not often."

"He is a fine man," said Redwyn.

Percy muttered, "Fine he is."

"What do you mean?"

"Nothing."

"No, Percy; say what you mean."

Percy shook his head, and his eyes grew narrow. "It was a long time ago. I am not so sure of it."

"Go on," said Redwyn.

The old warrior huffed with resignation and blew out the long white strands of his mustache. "Well, a half-century ago, I was my father's squire. He fought the heretics in Spain, beside the King."

"Go on."

"I remember the battle. Horrible it was. The worst carnage I have ever seen. A thousand knights were dead. There were horses, men, dead on top of each other. Even cooks and camp maids had been butchered. But we prevailed in the end.

"That night the air was foul and filled with agony and death. Father had a mortal wound. I sat with him by the fire. He was lying with his head on my lap. A man came from the darkness, and I reached for my dagger, but father said, 'No!' He was staring up at the stranger and seemed to know him. The man knelt down and touched my father's side where the wound was. My father said, 'It has been so long,' and the man asked, 'Can I help?' and Father said, 'No.' The man nodded, and without saying another word he walked back into the night." Percy paused. "That man was Nelrum."

Redwyn said, "I see."

"You don't believe me. Well, he wasn't called Nelrum,

then. I asked my father who the visitor was. And he told me, with the devil on his chest mind you, that *his grandfather* had known the man as Merlin."

Redwyn was silent.

"Aye," said Percy, his blue eyes glaring, "If you say 'Nelrum' but say it backwards..."

"Have you told anyone?"

"No. It is too hard to believe. They'd think me mad. But *you* don't seem surprised, Master Redwyn. Or shall I say, 'your Majesty?'"

"What!"

Percy looked from beneath his furrowed brow and searched Redwyn's eyes. "Only one man before you has worn that sword; Arthur was his name."

Redwyn said, "You were right, Percy, it is too hard to believe. I wouldn't tell anyone else what you think. By any measure, I'm no king. I'm not even certain what to do."

Percy said, "Fate is not so plainly seen. We may look for it, but we don't always know. Sometimes the search is all we have. It is a truer scale to measure a man by– the thing's he's searched for, than by the things he has. Often, all a person has are the things he's *never* found. Do you know what that sword does?"

"Tell me."

"It answers dreams!" the Knight exclaimed. "It knows the heart that is best, and grants that heart its visions. Like Arthur's visions. Dreams of glory and honor." The old warrior frowned and shifted his gaze from his armor to the sun-brightened doorway. "Yes, the sword must have a human hand to hold it, to give it life. Aye. And what if *you* should need some help? There may be a fray that you can't handle alone. Then what? Arthur had his knights, his round table."

He waited for Redwyn to answer, then looked out the door, and the sunlight shone on his wrinkled face. "I am very old," he said. "Perhaps very useless. But I know that unless humanity itself were at risk, Merlin would not have given mankind the Sword again. Whatever your task is, Sire, you must not fail."

After a long pause, Redwyn's voice said quietly in the stillness of the room:

"Then you be my knight."

Percy flushed but without hesitation and saying nothing he put one foot behind himself and teetered onto one knee; he bowed his head, and his grey hair glistened in the shower of sunlight.

As the sword cleared the scabbard it rang in a sustained note. Percy knelt in the column of light, and the blade flashed brilliantly as Redwyn turned it flat above the Old Knight's head.

"By the virtue of your noble heart..." The blade touched Percy's left shoulder. "You are Sir Perceville, a champion of honor..." The blade came down on his right shoulder and flashed. "...Champion of truth and righteousness." Redwyn lifted the sword and stepped back, "Knight of Excalibur.

"Rise, Sir Percy."

The old man lingered kneeling, then raised his eyes and stood. The ceremony was over.

"What is it?" said Redwyn, discerning an expression of disbelief in the Knight's face that had overcome all his other emotions.

Percy held out his right hand and tightened it into a fist. "Look," he said. "It isn't trembling anymore."

Chapter 26
At the Castle

There was no moon, and the endless luster of the stars seemed to fold above the castle like pale satin. Redwyn and Percy drove a cart along the highland road. The load of unlit torches rattled over the bumps. They stopped at the hedge break. Redwyn looked at the lights in the tower and jumped out of the cart. "I am going in," he said.

Percy climbed out and began unloading the torches. Redwyn took an armful and walked with him.

"It's as black as Satan's soul!"

"Are we clear?" Redwyn set his torches down quietly.

"I've got it. Good luck."

Redwyn sprinted, keeping low to the grassy mounded opening of the passageway and fell against it. His fingers felt through the dirt and dewy sod and found the iron pull-ring. He raised the door and stepped down into the utter blackness of the tunnel. He began feeling his way along the walls, the plash of his boots and heavy breath magnified by the hollow closeness, stopped and listened, but heard only the sound of droplets hitting pools, continued along, feeling the jagged wall, dragging his feet along the muddy ground, then stumbled and fell upon the stairway at the tunnel's end. He felt the door above him, slimy and wet, and climbed up two steps and pushed with his shoulder. The doorway loosened and he lifted hard against the burden of earth, and the fresh air blew against his face. The ruins of Camelot were above him on the hill, stars shining through the gaping walls.

Redwyn pulled himself from the tunnel and eased the door silently down. From his elevation near the ruins he could see inside the castle grounds. Scattered torches burned in the main court, and groups of soldiers stood around fires with racks of weapons nearby. Along the parapets there were archer Robes, barely visible against the firelight.

Two bonfires burned in front of the drawgate. Some men were hoisting a big kettle up toward the rook on a scaffold arm. Other Robes were waiting near another fire on the rook. When the kettle reached the top of the scaffold it was swung over on the huge arm and the men on the rook guided it over the fire there.

Redwyn started running toward the towers, straining in the dark to see. A shallow wall appeared suddenly, and he caught the top ledge and swung his legs sideways and cleared it. His cape flew up behind him and snapped in the wind as he plunged downward about ten feet then struck into soft earth, his knees buckling, his whole body hitting the dirt and rolling up inside his cape.

He raised his head slowly and when he pulled the cape from his eyes he was looking over a terrace ledge; he was lucky to have hit it. For thirty feet further below in a sunken corridor, two Robes were walking. They stopped at the corridor's end. One of them set a lantern down against a big cathedral shaped door. Their shadows stretched down the corridor. Redwyn watched them.

"We'd better stop," said the small one. The whispers were distinct.

"No! We earned a share of it."

"We'll burn if we're caught– maybe worse!"

"Let's do it and be gone."

"No, please."

"No! We're doing it."

"All right. Yes, all right."

One of them took out a key and unlocked the heavy door. It creaked as they pushed it open. They glanced behind them down the corridor and hurried into the room. Redwyn moved down the terrace and listened. From inside the room came a jingling sound, the telltale ring of coins falling against the stone floor. Then the men emerged with sacks. One of them pulled the door shut, while the other was fumbling with a long gold chain, trying to lower it through an opening in his sack.

Redwyn heard the faint "champ, champ" of marching feet. It grew more distinct, then long shadows appeared from the other end of the corridor. Against torchlight that became brighter until it illuminated their faces, the two men backed up to the door. The man who had been fumbling with the chain threw it sideways, over his head, and it landed near Redwyn's feet. Redwyn picked it up and looked toward the torches.

Morcar was leading a column of Robes that filled the corridor and blocked the thieves' escape.

One of the men tried to climb the wall, scratched and jumped against it. The other had fitted a key into the door; he pushed it open as Brech came forth and grabbed him. The thief struggled and Brech clubbed him with his fist and he slumped against the doorway.

"Look, Brech," Morcar said, "Here are two men about to make the journey to a better world."

"No!" said the frightened man.

"No?" said Morcar. "What then?" He gestured, and Brech wrested the sack from the other man's hands. Morcar opened it and said, "Gold."

The frightened man looked up terrified, but Morcar smiled.

"Why didn't you ask me, Intaglio, if gold is all you wanted. I would have given you enough to last a lifetime."

The man smiled nervously and straightened himself on his knees.

"My dear Intaglio," said Morcar. "Dear sweet, Intaglio, come to my embrace." Morcar outstretched his arms, and the frightened man laughed nervously and stood. Redwyn saw a rapier dangling at his side and recognized him now as the boyish man from the study.

"Come to my embrace, sweet Intaglio, if gold is all you want."

The boyish man smiled, and the other man stood up and shouted, "Swine!"

Morcar laughed, and the boyish Robe glanced over his shoulder and laughed at his former companion. Morcar's embracing left arm made a quick jerk– there was a faint scraping sound. The boyish man's face contorted with pain and disbelief, and he slumped onto his side with a golden dagger stuck between his ribs.

Morcar said casually to the other man, "He wanted gold. What is it you want?"

Redwyn moved back from the ledge and walked silently on the soft earth to a place where the curved tower wall came closest to the terrace. He stopped and looked above him. Midway up the tower a faint light came through a window. Thick vines ascended the tower and coursed around the window's opening. The tower was separated from the terrace by the span of the corridor, about an eight foot jump. The vines would have to hold the instantaneous shock of his body and he would have only a split instant to grab them. If they tore away, or if he missed, he would drop into the corridor. At one end there was Morcar with his column; at the other end more guards. But a fall would probably kill him anyway.

He cocked his legs and felt the tension gather in them. His heart pounding, he leaned over the terrace and leapt. His hands snatched two fistfuls of the sinewy vines and as he fell back the vines ripped partially away from the wall. He held his breath and tried to stay the motion with his feet. The light from the guards' torches flickered on the tower wall and on his hands and the vine leaves. He glanced below and the column of guards stood motionless, unpiqued.

He loosened one hand, reached over his head and gripped a thick crop of vines and pulled himself upward toward the window about thirty feet above. He scaled hand over hand, legs pulled up, black cape flowing behind him like a shadow, all but his hands concealed.

At last at the ledge he swung his legs through and rested there. The muscles burned in his arms.

A curdled howl rose from the corridor below. The column of Robes backed away with their torches and the other thief fell forward at their feet.

Redwyn slipped inside the window behind a drapery. The huge room he had entered seemed vacant. Long tables were spaced evenly with half-eaten meals and mugs left on them. In the hearth, violet tongues of flame licked across a pile of embers. In the faint light Redwyn could see a tapestry. He realized he was in the Great Hall adjacent Morcar's chambers.

Silently, he cut between the tables to the tapestry, pulled his cloak about his head and peered out. A guard was standing in the antechamber, leaning next to the study door.

Redwyn pulled back, reached to the nearest table and took two tankards off. He drew into the shadow of a stairwell and then threw one of the mugs. It struck a table with a loud "knock!" clanged onto the floor and clattered across it. On the other side of the tapestry a cutlass was drawn scrapingly from its sheath.

"Hallo!" said the guard. "Who's there?"

Redwyn waited, and after several moments had passed he pulled the bottom of the tapestry up, just a wrinkle, and saw the guard lean back against the doorway, the cutlass still in hand.

Redwyn drew back under the stairway, hurled the second

mug, and quickly pulled his cape around him. The mug rang as it struck the far wall, bounced onto the floor and clattered across it.

The guard lifted the torch from the sconce above his head and hurried in. Redwyn slipped out the other side of the tapestry and into the antechamber. It was dark. He strode quickly past Morcar's chambers and down the adjoining corridor.

"Hallo!" came the guard's voice calling from the hall. "Who's lingering drunk in here?"

Redwyn smiled as he strode quietly on.

At an intersection of two corridors he heard the sudden shrill peal of an infant's cry. The squalling died out and other voices grew distinct: A woman's voice, not Lynn's, then another child's. As Redwyn followed the corridor to the left, the voices sounded louder. Then, ahead, he saw the glow of torchlight on the curved wall. There were two voices speaking in deep whispers. A knock. Then a door opening. The woman's voice again– it was Gwendy's:

"Well, what is it?"

The guard's voice was deep. "My friend and I was thinkin'– you may as well be some good to us."

Redwyn heard the door slam and the two guards laughing in the corridor. "Come on children," said Gwendy's voice sounding small through the closed door. "Bed now."

"What did they want?" asked a child.

"Time for bed," said Gwendy.

Redwyn turned and followed the corridor back to the intersection, cut right, curving round past several chamber doors, until he saw a light. He inched forward and spotted what he thought must be Lynn's room. There were two guards outside the door and torches smoking in sconces.

He eased away and turned back down the corridor, but coming toward him there were footsteps. Torchlight grew brighter as the footsteps neared. He stopped at the first chamber and tried the door; it swung open and he stepped inside and eased it shut.

The guards' footsteps echoed and their torch rays swept under the door crack as they passed.

The room was pitch-dark and Redwyn turned around and started walking with his arms out in front of him. His foot found a single step and he walked onto it and moved forward until he touched some wooden planking with his hands. His fingers fumbled across the planks and found a latch, lifted it, and he swung the shutters open.

Below, there were more torches burning in the courtyard, more men carrying things to the parapets. To his immediate left the light from what he hoped was Lynn's window fell soft-yellow on the sill stones. He stood up on the window ledge, clutched a handful of vines and swung, falling-dangling against the outside of the tower. Twisting himself around so that he faced the wall, he began scaling sideways hand to hand, finding the strong vines first with his fingers, gripping them in bunches, his black cape rendering him a shadow on the wall.

Inside the chamber, Lynn knelt at her bedside. Her fingers were knitted and her head was bowed and resting on her hands. In front of her was the open window. She picked up her rosary beads from the bed and clutched them and her lips moved silently, as unseen, Redwyn's hand caught the base of the sill.

Chapter 27
The First

As he swung himself through the window, Lynn dropped her rosary. His face was flushed and sweaty. Some of his hair was sticking to his forehead. He drew his forearm across his brow to wipe the perspiration off. "Speak softly now," he said. "The guards wait just outside."

"How did you–" she stammered, "I don't understand–"

He moved closer and whispered, "Speak softly."

"Why have you come here? If the guards see you, Morcar will–" Her eyes swept over him in disbelief. "Those clothes are familiar somehow."

"Orphans?" said Redwyn. "Will Morcar hurt the orphans?"

"Yes!" She gained composure as the anger built in her eyes. "Why did you bring the Villagers here? Morcar had a hundred archers waiting to cut them down!"

"I know," said Redwyn.

"He would have killed you all– the children, Gwendy. He would have killed them. Even now he's planning to– he said something about 'infesting' the city tonight. He's a madman! He talks about rats and plague and– wait a moment!" She went to the bed, lifted the corner of the mattress and removed something.

"Look," she said, returning with a golden, ribboned medallion in her hand. "This seal bears the crest of Cumberland. It belonged to the Duke's brother, Thragonparke, who died from plague. I took it from Morcar's– I mean my father's– study."

Redwyn took the seal, inspected it, then walked to the window and looked out over the ruins. His face was feverish. At his side the sword and silver scabbard gleamed conspicuously in the candlelight.

"I have seen those clothes," Lynn said. "In an old woodcarving that my father had. I recognize them now. That sword! From the woodcarving. I would almost swear..." her voice trailed off and Redwyn turned from the window.

She said, "Why have you come here?"

Redwyn smiled and said, "I don't know."

She looked at him questioningly. As he continued smiling they both burst into nervous laughter.

"Idiot!" she said, and laughed in high feminine gasps. To the guards it must have sounded like weeping.

"Hush," said Redwyn grinning. "The guards wait outside the door!"

Then they looked at each other and as often happens the silence said more than the awkwardness of words. She knew why he had come. And they both knew that, whatever happened, afterward she would remain a hostage. The safety of the orphans would demand it.

Softly, Lynn said, "The crest of Cumberland. If you show it to the Duke, he will come. I know him to be a hot-head and drunkard. If he *suspects* his brother's murder, he will come to fight."

"Then I will show it to him," Redwyn said.

"Leave now, before the guards discover you."

"I cannot yet."

She walked to the window and glanced below. "Of course, there are soldiers in the corridor."

"It is not because of the soldiers I would stay."

She stood with her back to him, looking out the window, and said nothing. Redwyn said, "When I first saw you at the river that evening, I thought for a moment you were a ghost. You made me promise not to watch as you ran from the water, but I did. And later, when we met at the orphanage and I saw how beautiful– when I saw *what* you were– I felt ashamed for breaking that promise. I knew I wasn't good enough to look at you that way."

She turned around from the window and her face had grown expressionless and strange. "It makes me hurt to look upon you," Redwyn went on, avoiding her eyes, "Not because you're a noble. In Venice there were noblewomen too." He frowned trying to find the words. "It is because–" he drew a deep, nervous breath and said, "When I was a boy I apprenticed in a copyhouse, you see. It was dark and all day and into the night I copied the books and contracts put before me. So I used to make up a better place. It was my own kingdom, and it was very bright. The sun shone yellow– I even used to have dreams of it. There were always blue skies and blue lakes and rivers that would take you in any direction that you wanted to go." He smiled faintly. "There was a castle with great towers. It was hot and close in the copyhouse, so I used to stand on top of the highest tower where the air was fresh and cool. I used to change the land with the seasons and sometimes it would snow in the winter and I would let it be cold so that I could look forward to when the spring came and I could smell the earth and my country would be perfect once again.

"And I imagined a girl, Lynn. She was only ten years old at first, but she grew as I grew. She was my love and she was a great friend and confidant, and at first we were completely virtuous and vowed only to love God and to keep ourselves pure and in a state of grace and share eternity in heaven. Later, when I had turned thirteen, we knew that God would understand the things we did because our love was caritas, and pure.

"I ran away from the copyhouse when I was fifteen. I took some money from the copyist and left. It was hard after I had run away, but I kept that perfect place inside me. At least I tried to. The world changes us and I learned villainy, and how to take advantage of the ignorance of other men. As I grew more corrupt, it became more difficult to imagine that kingdom I had longed for as a child. Finally, I suppose I no longer belonged there. But, nevertheless, the memory of the girl remained.

"The night before last, Nelrum took me to the dungeon of the castle, that I could see for myself this Morcar's work. The horror of his deeds made me a coward, Lynn, and I feared my death. But it was strange how I feared it; I cared not for my soul, but for having found nothing of the life that I once dreamed. An old knight told me that it is truer to measure a man by the things he searches for than by the things he has, for sometimes all a man ever has are the things he's never found. When I saw you save Morcar's life, when I saw you standing on the tower in the sun, I knew that you were something that, once, I had searched for.

Lynn had begun to weep.

"So I have come, if for nothing else, to have searched, to ask you, Lynn, to be my love. I, myself, am nothing. I know that. But the kingdom I once dreamed now lives in you." He paused and looked into the dark, wavering shadows of the candlelight and found her eyes. "Are you my strange, dark love? Enchanted nymph? Will you give me back my country in the sun?"

For a moment they both stood there, saying nothing, and he did not take his eyes from hers. Then she moved toward him through the shadows and he closed his eyes and, inside, was very still and oblivious to where he was. For a moment there was only the stillness, then all her breath upon his cheek, her soft lips searching over, and the warm, unfathomable depth of her kiss, foretold to him somehow, yet now as inexorable and vast as the depths of the ocean to a drowning man.

✳ ✳ ✳ ✳ ✳

Afterward, Redwyn held her close while her breathing changed from sighs to tranquility. But his mind was clear again and his first thought was of the seal of Cumberland that now lay atop his clothing and gleamed dully in the candle's glow.

After waiting as long as he dared, he said, "I have to go."

"Yes, go."

"There is much I have to do."

"Leave before the guards come on their rounds."

"I could stay until the candles burn half-way."

"Leave now," she said.

He lifted from her slowly, their skin warm and moist. Lynn pulled her knees up and made a hump beneath the quilts. She turned her head on the pillow and stared blankly while Redwyn dressed. And then her whisper was distinct.

"I saw your country."

He turned to her. Her eyes were watery and dark looking over the blue satin that glistened from the candle's flame.

"We are never going to leave it," he said.

"For eternity," she whispered.

"Eternity," he agreed.

She turned over and lay face down in the bed. She heard his footsteps, a metallic scraping sound and then his footsteps moving off. There was a long silence and she turned over and knew that he was gone. By accident her hand drifted down to her side and when she touched the cold metal object and realized what it was she rolled from the bed and ran naked to the window.

"Redwyn?" she whispered. "Redwyn?" But there was no answer. She tried a few more times, then listened to the faint sigh of the wind as it swept across the ruins. The stone floor was cool against her bare feet, and at last she turned away and walked back into the candlelight. His sword lay next to the depression that their bodies had left in the thick feather mattress of the bed.

Lynn crawled into the bedclothes and drew them up. The sword gleamed next to her, and she covered it with the quilt and lay there with her eyes open. The candle was casting shadows about the room.

Chapter 28
Gambit

Redwyn worked around the curved tower wall, finding the thickest vines, pulling sideways and lowering himself away from the window. He had not heard her whispers, nor had he seen the light go out in the window. For he kept his gaze below to the flat roof of the castle's entrance hall, searching its ledges for the dark outlines of Robes.

Now working again, using his feet to stay the motion of his sway, to pull himself sideways and hold there until he caught the next group of vines. Reaching, pulling, swaying, lowering; reaching, pulling, holding, lowering, he worked his way downward, then dropped onto the roof.

He saw no guards and, crouching low, ran to the brink of the outer ledge. A mist had crept up the hillside, across the meadow, and now was flowing thinly over the wall and down into the torchlight like an amber veil. There were more fires, more racks of weapons, and far off there were men at the dungeon, standing in front of it with torches.

Redwyn knew, now, that he would not be able to reach the tunnel door unseen.

A stairway ran down against the outside wall and landed in a sunken corridor. The corridor ran back toward the towers, and he thought, "All the activity is in the courtyard. It should be easy to reach the ruins from the castle's rear and work around." Without hesitating, he crept to the top of the stairway, made one last check for guards, and had gone down three steps when voices came from below.

Morcar came out from under an arch and started across the courtyard with six guards at his flanks. Brech was with him. They walked out toward the parapets and stopped at the gate.

Brech shouted and the drawbridge started down. Redwyn could hear the chains clanging and saw Brech waving his torch in the air. Another torch was waved up near the dungeon, and then the dungeon door was opened and some men came out against the doorway light.

The men carried long rods with bundles tied to the ends of them, and with the realization of what was happening Redwyn felt his stomach go tight with fear.

He kept his eyes on the guards standing watch around the gate, and descended the stairs until he was abeam the parapet ledge, just a few steps above it. It was an eight foot span between the stairs and ledge; the drop into the corridor was forty feet. He jumped off, hit the parapet hard with his chest, caught it and hung there. Then he struggled to pull himself up, stood, and started running toward the gate, the empty scabbard flopping against his thigh.

He made the turn, running along the front wall.

Morcar was waving and shouting for the horsemen to go faster. All the Robes were watching him. Atop the gate rook there was a big guard standing in front of the kettle that had been hoisted there. Redwyn flew, knee first into the guard's back, chopped sideways with the blade of his forearm, and sent him stumbling off the ledge.

Now, hearing shouts of alarm, he caught the huge arm of the scaffold and swung the kettle out over the drawbridge, the heavy timbers creaking as he slowly turned them. An arrow whirred by. The men on horseback holding the long poles with bundles tied onto them halted just short of the gate and looked up. Morcar was yelling at them to go on and waving his arms. Redwyn whispered, "Now look, Percy," grabbed the leather strap that pulled the kettle's release pin, jerked it, and the catch of the scaffold broke free and the kettle swung loose on one hinge, spilling its boiling oil onto the drawbridge below.

Men were screaming, and the horses were louder than the men, screaming bestially in the scalding flood. Redwyn kicked a burning log off the parapet and fell backward against the crimson explosion that came billowing upward and then churned in a tower of dirty flames.

He stood against the heat, saw the torches being lit at the hedgerow, and muttered, "Well done, Percy!" stepped up onto the ledge, aimed himself carefully, and jumped.

He struck the bridge feet first, rolled onto his side, and had cleared the flames entirely. As he gathered himself to stand, there was a sound like tiny hammers rapping against the wooden planks around him. He saw the arrows biting in and in the next instant he was hit– felt his side muscles tear, his backside above his right hip split where the shaft had gone through. A sharp stinging quickly followed, and a flow of warmth down his leg.

The queer thought struck him that he must have looked like a puppet whose strings had been relaxed, as the strength wilted in his limbs and he awkwardly squatted onto the bridge. There was the sound of more arrows tapping into the planks, and with a sudden pang of fear, feeling almost as if the invisible hands had yanked him up again, he stood, dazed, and started to run spastically toward the hedge.

A dozen lights were glowing in the mist in front of him, and while he moved across the meadow a dozen more appeared.

He crashed numbly through the break in the hedge and saw Percy walking along it, lighting torches hurriedly as he went.

"Percy," he panted. "Here!"

The old man looked over, his face brightened by the torch he held. "Good God!" He said and ran over.

"Give me the crossbow, Percy. Go to the tavern. Get the men– bring them here."

"You're bleeding!"

"Go," said Redwyn. "Bring the men here quickly."

"You're bleeding fast," said Percy.

"Give me the torch now. Go!"

Percy ran for the donkey cart. Redwyn limped to the hedge, and said, "Bring back horses," and he began to light the torches that Percy had stuck into the stiff tangle of the hedge.

Inside the castle courtyard two Robes rolled a water barrel up to the burning bridge. Another Robe took an axe and chopped the barrel's head and the water rushed out, spreading the fire quickly.

Morcar shouted, "Fools! Bring dirt! Smother out the flames!"

The Robes scrambled about confusedly. Then Brech came forward pulling a flat cart with his hands. "Into the garden!" he bellowed. And a squad of Robes rushed through the archway after him. The men began chopping at the soft dirt with axes, others scooping it onto the cart by hand.

The first load was brought back and dumped onto the flames– men began spreading it, and Brech pulled the cart back for more.

"Hurry!" shouted Morcar, "After him!"

The second load was dumped, then a third, and as the dirt was spread the flames diminished steadily.

"Mount the horses," Brech roared. "Bows and lances. Be ready to charge on my command."

Only small flames remained flaring up sporadically through the moist dirt. More was heaped on and spread. The fire went out completely. The Robes on horseback poised themselves.

"My Lord," shouted a sentinel from the rook.

Morcar looked up at him viciously.

"An army, My Lord– out there!" The guard was pointing.

Morcar hurried up the steps, and the guard pointed again and said, "Look, My Lord!"

There were a hundred torches burning at the hedgerow. Morcar looked at them, tried to look beyond them through the darkness and the mist.

And as Brech rode onto the drawbridge with the small cavalry behind, a shrill scream descended on him, "Hold them! Back! Back!"

He lifted his huge hand to stop the charge and looked up from the bridge.

"Raise the gate," shrieked Morcar, "It's been a trick! Look, damn you! The castle is under siege!"

Chapter 29
The Mist

At Josh's Inn the men had been drinking heavily and the tavern smelled foul of vomit and sweat. Sir Perceville stepped into the doorway. His shortsword was drawn and he whacked the blade flat against the door frame hard, then slapped it harder, "Whack! Whack! Whack!"

Some men close to him flinched. All those who recognized Percy were looking at him in disbelief.

The Old Warrior thrust his sword into its scabbard, and as it was still too noisy to speak, he shouted hoarsely, "Listen to me!" And the tavern settled to near silence.

"Lads, if you've come to drown your troubles tonight, you had better know them first! My Lord Redwyn entered the castle; the Lady Lynn and the orphans are hostage there."

The men broke into murmurs. The Miller pounded the table to quiet them.

Percy went on, "Redwyn warns us that Morcar is coming to attack the town. Unless we marshall an army and proceed to the castle at once, Solway will be razed this night."

There was a moment of silent absorption before the crowd began to stir, and Percy cultivated the pause, his eyes steady and clear, sweeping about the tavern, singling out the familiar faces and assuring them he spoke the truth. Then his tone of voice grew sharper. "My Lord Redwyn was shot tonight as he blocked Morcar's army at the castle's gate. They were coming here to murder you!"

Shouts broke through the noise, a few men rose to their feet. The big Miller was among them and he growled bestially, "If there's a backbone among you, get your lazy haunches from those stools!"

"Aye! Aye!" the shouts came. Someone cried, "We'll give the Robes their due!"

Percy shook his fist, "Are you all for it lads!"

"Aye!" rose the cheer in a loose chorus. "Aye! Aye!" it roared again in firm accord.

Then Percy knew they were ready. He wailed at them, his neck strained and his old face flushed and red. "Then move! Like the devil's on your heels. Move! Move! Gather torches— lots of torches, lads. And hold them high above your heads!"

Morcar and Brech stood upon the parapet and looked across the grounds. Diffused by mist, the torches at the hedge appeared as floating balls of amber light. Morcar focused intently, then leaned toward Brech and said, "Are they moving?"

"Master?"

"The flames. Can you tell whether they are moving?"

Brech craned his thick neck toward the hedge and squinted. As he scanned, one of the lights went out.

"No, Master."

"No?"

"They do not seem to move, My Lord."

Another torch failed. Morcar leered at the quivering row of luminous blobs. "I am not so sure," he said.

Redwyn had slumped against a tree. He held his side and felt the blood trickling warm against his fingers. His head swam as if someone had clubbed him. The stars were shrouded by the mist, and the mist seemed to take on human

shapes as it drifted overhead in the torchlight. The shapes
had limbs, sometimes faces. He began to think of the forma-
tions as a vaporous procession of souls. Some were hunched
and claw-like shapes that reached out graspingly, others enormous heads with hollow eyes and gaping mouths that seemed
to moan in silent agony. Some were in pieces, only part way
formed, or shapeless; he thought of cripples when he saw
these, the simple-minded, and orphans. Then came one that
was flowing, white, and inscrutable, and he thought of angels
and of Lynn.

He shut his eyes and muttered, "Where are you, Nelrum?"

Just then a torch went out directly before him and the
sudden darkening on his eyelids caused him to look. Down
the hedgerow, nearly half the torches had gone out. He
pushed against the tree to stand, clamped his hand against his
side and staggered to the hedge.

Brech pointed from the parapet, "Look! Another torch
goes out."

"Yes," hissed Morcar. "A trick! What army does not
move about, or keep its vigils."

Then, from the center of the line, two torches appeared
close together and moved out in front of the others.

"Look here!" said Morcar.

"Perhaps another trick," said Brech, "One man perhaps."

The Head Robe squinted, "Not one man. For look– the
one is steady in his gait, the other wobbles."

"Two men then. Perhaps just two?"

"Or two sentinels keeping watch for the Duke's legion."

The two lights disappeared. And in a moment two more
floated out.

"Look at these!" said Morcar. "Two, but both are steady.
Two different guards."

Brech glared. His eyes were fixed, his voice came low and
growling. "Let me open the gate for a small force of cavalry–"

"And learn if we've been tricked," said Morcar, grinding

his words through clenched teeth. "Yes, assemble them. Send them toward the pillars with torches. I want to know who's there."

Redwyn went around behind the hedge again and out of sight of the castle. He put the torches back, high into the stiff, tangled branches, stumbled to the same tree he had leaned against before, and slumped there. His side was still bleeding heavily and he clutched it and groaned.

Through the break he could see the lights of the castle. A big square of luminosity grew downward from the darkened line of the parapet wall, and from the faint clanging of chain he knew it was the drawgate coming down. Then several lights appeared at ground level and began moving up and down with a steady gait. "But the mist is thick now," he thought, "And the riders will have to come slowly."

He picked up the crossbow from beside the tree and slung it across his back. The brightened gap of the drawbridge closed. The bouncing lights were moving steadily closer. He got to his feet, staggered to the break in the hedge, crouched there, and in a wrench of pain pulled the crossbow from his back. The lights, much brighter now, were blurry, floating with rhythmic motions that swelled the heavy dizziness inside him. He blinked and shook his head, pressed the crossbow's stock against his chin and sighted along the dim gleam of the shaft.

It would be soon he thought. His finger found the trigger. Redwyn aimed high above the closest torch; he would wait until he heard the first hoof beat. It came in the next moment, and almost involuntarily his bow snapped and the arrow whirred into the mist. There was a low moan. The closest torch dropped to the ground and the lights stopped moving. The riders dismounted and the torches came together in a ring around the fallen one. There was a faint rumble of voices, then all the torches were dropped onto the ground.

The earth was soft. He listened for the clink of armor, the

rattle of chain mail. The moments passed and he listened for the sound of heavy breath. He couldn't let them reach the hedge he thought. They mustn't see the hedge or get back to the castle if they did see it.

He began crawling on his stomach toward the grounded torches, his wounds sending waves of searing pain, the blood flowing warm down onto his stomach and the grass cold and wet. The torches from the hedgerow flickered behind him and lit the patchy fog, and as the mist moved, shadows formed, took on shapes and vanished. He jerked as he caught a glint out of the corner of his eye, raised the bow, but there was nothing. Then the sound of footsteps running hard came from the mist and he fired where the bright spot had been– a thud and some rattling and a shrill, hideous cry that ended in a gasp. Then more voices broke the silence.

Redwyn reloaded frantically, cranking the bow back until it cocked. The voices were coming from several directions. He got up on his knees and heard the sound of horses, the rattle of armor– footsteps very near– behind him. A great shower of light turned the mist bright gold, and he whirled around to shoot and saw Percy coming through the hedge break, a column of torch bearers spreading out behind.

BOOK III

A Small War

Chapter 30
Percy's Ride

Redwyn dropped the crossbow and grunted with pain as he struggled from the ground. Percy held a torch out toward his side and said, "Good God, sir."

Redwyn cupped his hand over the wound. "You've brought the horses." Blood had soaked his left leg, and Percy just now noticed the sword was gone from its scabbard.

"Aye, I've brought the horses. Now what?"

Redwyn stumbled as he stood there. "We ride," he said.

"To where?" asked Percy gently.

Redwyn removed the medallion from his belt and held it out. Percy took it from him and turned it over. His old face frowned, "The crest belongs to the House of Cumberland," he said.

Redwyn spoke tiredly, "The Duke's brother was killed by the Robes. It's proof."

"It is what we need," Percy said. "The Duke will have to come to avenge his own brother's death."

The two men looked at each other and then Percy understood. He said, "Let me go."

Just then the barmaid stepped out of the darkness with Donny Gwaith beside her.

"Your wound is bad," said Percy. "I know the way even by moonlight."

There was a pause and, strangely, Redwyn felt compelled to look down at Donny Gwaith. The boy nodded, as if the consultation were anticipated. Redwyn reached to the back of Percy's neck and drew him close.

"Go then, Percy. Speed, man! Speed! There is more at stake than I can ever tell."

The barmaid came forward and propped herself under Redwyn's shoulder.

"Cleanse his wound with liquor," Percy said, "as old Nelrum did for Josh. Then bind it tight. Tight, do you hear?" He turned and went to the horses, pushed them apart with his hands and chose a stallion from the group. He untethered the horse, caught its mane, and without using the stirrup swung up onto the saddle as would a young man.

As he left the castle grounds, the barmaid was on her knees.

Donny Gwaith was running away.

"Probably running for some liquor," Percy thought.

He had chosen the largest stallion from the group. It had looked dark and muscular in the torchlight, and now as they moved onto the town road, the horse began to canter. Percy leaned a little forward, and the canter broke quickly to a trot. He held back the reins through the fairgrounds, past the quays, then eased the reins out a little to climb the rocky hill and move onto the high cliff road that followed the sea.

The moon was rising, a giant copper crescent to throw a dim shimmer of orange onto the blackness of the ocean. The path was narrow, and the horse's hooves clacked rapidly against the stone as it trotted, climbing the rising cliff. At last the road leveled, and the waves were breaking white against the rocks a thousand feet below. All ahead and to his left where the cliff dropped off was the sea. Percy rode, keeping close against the cliff-face, sometimes his elbow brushing the jagged rocks. He rode that way to feel the cliff, even though he knew that horses could see well at night.

The moon rose higher and its light changed to a wide river of gold upon the water. As Percy rode on, the moon grew smaller and brighter until it was silver, shimmering high and brightly onto the pitch-black sea.

He could see the outline of the cliff now and quickened the horse's pace. A warm wind came off the sea and rushed against his side. The wind was strong, and Percy felt it on his left side, pressing like a wall against the drop-off. It felt good.

The trail widened, so he shifted forward and squeezed the stallion's shoulders with his knees. The quick trot smoothed into a gallop. There was a steady wind in his face, the gusts rising stronger from the sea, lashing wildly against his side.

The road continued widening, and the cliff-face on his right was growing shallower, receding from the road and then it broke up into monoliths and boulders, then was gone entirely where the road turned inland. Percy felt the wind at his back, accelerating away from the sea now along the turn, the wind growing lighter, until at last there was no wind for a moment and then he felt it in his face again and knew that the horse was running faster than the wind.

The stallion had galloped steadily while the stars had wheeled a quarter in the heavens, and Percy marvelled at the pace. He could not believe the horse had run so hard; that any horse could run so fast and hard. But he could feel the horse's power, marvelous and unburdened by the weight of its rider. Only a stallion, he thought. Only a stallion had the strength and anger that could become such speed.

Percy could feel the horse's neck extending, the powerful muscles straining as the horse lunged forward, grabbing the road and pushing it behind in huge leaps. The animal had not been prodded or pressed in any way. He was burning, Percy knew, in his back and legs, burning in his neck and all his great muscles and yet had not been pushed to do so. "You are a young horse," Percy thought. "You are wild and you are young and you would rather that your heart would burst, your lungs, too, bleed and burst, than admit that you've grown weak." The horse's head was rhythmic up and down and, looking over it, Percy could see the breath bursts come explosively, misting into puffs as he flew past them.

"Perhaps you hate the rider on your back," he thought. "Your wild heart would throw me off; you could do it. But duty says, 'He rides.' Aye, some man has hammered at your heart, Horse, forged duty into your horse's soul." The stallion's breath came hunf! huff! hunf! huff! Very quickly, hunf! huff! hunf! huff! And Percy thought again, "If you had been my horse, what battles we'd have fought. And now we'll fight just one, but this is it. This is the best of them, Horse." He leaned further forward, felt the hot closeness of the animal's body, and knew that the horse was fighting his battle already; a battle inside of him that turned his heart to fire and made him fly upon the road.

"The battles *inside*," muttered Percy. "Those are the cruelest fights of all. And age is the worst of them, Young Horse!"

When he reached the Duke's castle it was late. There was only one guard at the gatehouse, and a boy. The horse broke his gallop reluctantly and stopped short of the gate. In the light of one torch, both the boy and guard looked bewildered as Percy dismounted and approached them.

"Take the horse, boy," the Old Knight said. "Tend him properly."

"Yes, My Lord." The lad was small and thin, and he rushed excitedly to the panting stallion.

The guard had not said anything.

"I wish to see His Grace, The Duke of Cumberland."

The guard put his head back slightly and frowned. "The Duke is sleeping now– go away from here."

The boy was holding the horse's reins and looking on. Percy spoke sharply.

"The Duke's lands and subjects are at risk. I will see

him!"

Percy pulled the shortsword partway from its scabbard and the guard looked at it, then turned without saying anything and began walking toward the castle. The drawgate was down, and they walked under one arch, up to the main door and into a Great Hall lighted with torches. Another guard, sleeping on a long oak banquet table, was startled to wakefulness.

"What's this!" he said.

"He's going to see the Duke," said the gate sentinel.

"No he isn't," said the sleepy guard. Percy stepped in front of the table, and the gate guard just kept walking toward a stairway.

"It'll be your head," said the sleepy guard to Percy. He moved off the table sluggishly then looked outside the door.

"You all alone?" he asked.

Percy said, "Keep your mouth closed. Or I'll see you flogged for sleeping."

The Duke came down with two servants. A distinguished looking man in a blue velvet robe was walking behind him. At the bottom of the stairs the robed man walked over and stood at the fire with his back to everyone.

The Duke came forward and sat down in front of Percy on a bench. He looked very tired, and his crops of bright red hair stuck up on his head like pointed flames.

"Well, what is it!" he asked petulantly. He seemed very tired.

Percy knelt with his hands folded down in front of him and kept his head bowed as he spoke.

"Your Grace, I have come to tell you that the castle of Du Lac has been usurped, and that the Lady Lynn is now held hostage there by the Hospitaliers."

The Duke looked up slowly. The other man turned a little but kept his eyes fixed on the fire.

"I already knew this," said the Duke, red eyed and angered. "Young Lynn was here some months ago. You've wakened me for *this*? I was aware of this!"

The two guards eyed each other. The sleepy one nodded knowingly.

Percy reached inside his belt and took out the medallion. He rose, stepped up smartly to the Duke and bowed to him.

"Your Grace was not aware of *this*, nor of the Lady Lynn's true peril. Morcar, the head of the Hospitaliers, plans to attack the city of Solway and destroy it. He will kill Lynn, your loyal Baron's only heir. And unless Your Grace sends a force to stop him, he will accomplish this by morning."

The Duke took the medallion from Percy's outstretched hand. The man at the fire turned.

"It was my brother's! Where did you get it?"

Percy lifted his eyes and spoke softly. "Morcar killed your brother, Your Grace. My Lord Redwyn took the medallion from him this night."

"My brother died of plague."

"But Morcar's hand was in it, Grace."

The Duke swallowed, looking awfully tired and confused. He raised his hand toward the servants and said, "Bring me something!"

"A brandy for His Grace," said the man at the fire.

A servant backed away, then turned and ran like a foot racer into a corridor. He returned shortly with two tankards of brandy and a small cask all on a big wooden tray.

The Duke drank his tankard down quickly then looked again at the medallion. "Who are you, man?"

The distinguished looking man from the fire came over and picked up the second tankard of brandy and extended it. But Percy refused.

"I am Sir Perceville Thorne, Knight of The House Of Lancaster, Knight of Excalibur."

For a moment the Duke looked stunned. The servants were mumbling, then there was a quick burst of stifled laughter. The Duke shut his eyes, turned away and said, "Throw this old fool out of here!"

The two guards came at Percy confidently. The first one had drawn his sword, but Percy knocked it from his hand with a single, crosswise motion of his fist. The sword slid across the floor and Percy jabbed his fist straight into the guard's chest and knocked him sitting onto the floor. It was quiet, then, except for the downed guard's broken gasps, and Percy knelt before the Duke again and said:

"Your Grace, I shall not leave until my duty to *my King* is done!"

There was a long pause of astonished silence as the Duke sat, his jaw clenched and his eyes fixed on Percy. Then he turned to his servants and said, "Sound an alarm! Order the Captain of the Guard to come here."

The servants rushed off, and the distinguished man offered Percy the brandy again. Percy felt good now and took it. He smiled. His blue eyes and wrinkled face were happy.

The distinguished man said, "I believe our fathers were friends," and smiled ironically and went on. "My father often spoke of a Palomon Thorne. They fought many battles together and were great friends. Palomon had a son, Perceville, who was eight years my elder."

Percy searched the man's eyes.

"I am Palomon's son."

The man spoke again, "I believe your father died in battle. In..." Percy finished for him:

"Spain, Sir. It was a battle in Spain."

The Duke looked up from the bench where he was sitting with the brandy and said admonishingly but politely, "Say 'Your Majesty,' Sir Perceville, when you speak to the King!"

Percy dropped quickly to one knee, and uttered, "Your Majesty!"

The King turned to the Duke and frowned. "Cannot two old sons have a drink together, and talk of their fathers' deeds?"

"Aye, Your Majesty," said the Duke apologetically. "Aye, that they can."

The Captain of the guard soon had the legion cavalry marshalled in the grounds. The Duke had gone to dress, and now returned armored in mail and wearing plated gauntlets.

The King and Percy stood up from the bench where they had been talking. Percy felt weak, and thought it must have been the mere presence of the King that had drained him.

The Duke approached, "Will you need a fresh mount, Perceville?
Are you coming?"

"Yes, Your Grace. Thank you," Percy answered.

They walked out into the courtyard: Percy, The Duke of Cumberland, and the King. The boy Percy had given his horse to was crying. The horse was lying dead on the ground. The boy was standing beside it and he looked up.

"Was this your mount?" asked the King.

"Yes," said Percy.

"A fine stallion," said the Duke. "He must have exhausted himself during the ride."

"It is a terrible shame," said the King.

"Yes," said Percy quietly. He ever knew the horse was Redwyn's.

Chapter 31
Battle

The mist had thickened as the night air cooled and now it glowed amber grey wherever the torches still burned. The townsmen had kept only half the torches burning throughout the night, but the mist had risen above the hedge and grown so thick that the castle lights were obscured. "They can't see our torches," Redwyn thought. "But we can still see theirs."

He took shallow breaths and kept still beneath the light blanket so as not to disturb the wound. The dizziness swept through him again as a figure moved across the light of the torches. The figure was large and black against the glare. Redwyn knew it was the Miller.

"The scouts report that nothing has happened at the castle, Master."

The big man was trying to speak softly. It seemed difficult for him.

Redwyn asked, "How close are they now?"

"They had to move right up close, Sir. It's so foggy now, they had to move up almost to the moat."

"Tell them not to move closer. Even if the fog worsens. Tell them to keep a distance back and only listen."

"Aye, Sir," said the Miller. "I'll tell them."

He moved off, and Redwyn watched his big, hunched form getting blacker against the torches and then vanish into them. The dizziness swept through him again.

"Donny?" he said. The boy scooted out on his rump from behind the tree. He sat with his knees pulled up, his arms wrapped around them.

"I'd almost forgotten you were there. I must have fallen asleep. Aren't you tired, Donny?"

He shook his head No, and then pointed to Redwyn.

"I am? Yes, you're right."

Donny twisted to look at something that was coming from behind the tree and out of Redwyn's view. Redwyn reached instinctively for the sword but felt only the dressing on his side. He heard a voice whisper, "How is he?" Then Josh walked up and stood over him. The torchlight lit half of Josh's face.

"How are you, Master?"

"Well enough," said Redwyn.

The barmaid was there too, but standing back.

"Would you be hungry, Sir?" Josh pointed to the tray of food that she was holding.

"Not now. Thank you, though, Josh."

The Innkeeper motioned for the girl to go; then he stood tensely, his unslung hand clenched into a fist at his side.

Redwyn looked straight up into the mist and said, "You go too, Josh."

"I am sorry, Master."

"Don't be."

"If I hadn't coaxed you..."

Redwyn finished for him, "The town would be dead now. Go back to the Inn and rest, Josh. Your wound will take time to heal."

"It doesn't hurt at all, Sir," the Innkeeper said.

But in that instant Redwyn had fallen to sleep, and Donny pulled the blanket over his shoulders.

In a dream Redwyn was lying in his chamber in the old

copyhouse. The blanket was too thin and the winter chill came through and pressed upon him. He opened his eyes and could see it— the chill— a mist that crept in through the cracks in the shutters and flowed steeply onto the floor. It moved directly toward him now, slowly across the floor, until it reached the bed and flowed up in a vaporous sheet of grey. It was hard to breathe as it coated his legs, chest, and made it harder still to breathe as it glazed his eyes with grey.

Donny pushed his shoulder down, but he barely felt it.

In the dream again, Lynn stood in the doorway of his chamber. He turned toward her. With the light at her back, her face was dark. She said something but he hadn't heard.

"What?"

"We'll go," she said.

"No! Please, please wait!"

Voices came into the room, the Copyist and his wife arguing in the shop below.

"It isn't enough!" he heard the wife.

"It's twenty times the average rate."

"You ask the old fool for more."

"Christ's blood, woman. He's an apprentice, not a ransomed prince."

"The little cur eats like one."

"He's a boy," said the printer.

"Ask for more!"

"But he is an orphaned boy, Alison."

Now Redwyn stood slowly from the bed and Lynn was gone from the doorway. He walked dizzily down the stairs and closed the copyhouse door behind him. His feet felt heavy as he started down the street, the suffocating mist at his back moving slowly, yet slowly and terrifyingly catching him. He jerked at his feet to free them from the invisible mire— and lurched into the awful half-wakefulness in which the horror of a dream seems real.

Then suddenly he was on his bedboard again and the suffocating mist was just over his legs but receding back down toward the floor. He could breathe, and Lynn said something from the door-

*way, "Can we leave now?" Redwyn stood up and he was small.
Lynn's face was darkened by the light that was behind her. He
grew taller as he approached, trying to see her face, reached out
with his arms to embrace her, but in that instant she had changed
to Morcar.*

"Master Redwyn! Master! Hold!"

He was sitting up, and Josh and Donny had his arms.
The dream had left his heart pounding. "How long 'til
dawn!" he asked, and for a moment was not yet certain of
being awake.

Then Josh said softly, "The nightingale's been singing for
a long while now. I'd say not long 'til dawn, Master."

"Don't let me sleep again."

"We promise." Josh nudged Donny, and the boy nodded
in agreement. "Shall I bring the tray back, sir? You should
eat something."

"Aye, bring it, Josh."

The Innkeeper went off with Donny, and they came back
with the boy carrying the tray. Redwyn had not felt the
dizziness while they were gone.

"Some brandy, sir?"

"Yes."

He drank it down quickly and felt a slight reprieve from
the chill that seemed to bite at his very bones. Donny lifted
the cask again, but Redwyn shook his head.

"Do you remember, Master Redwyn, when you drank a
whole quart
of this and wrestled the Robes? We used this to clean your
wound."

"I should be fine, then."

The Innkeeper reached out tremulously and handed Redwyn
a meatpie. He ate half of it slowly, careful not to nauseate
himself, and afterward drank a whole mug of cider. In the
meantime, Josh's face had turned white and sweaty in the
half-light of the torches.

"That was a perfect fit. Why don't you go back and rest

now, Josh?"

"How are you, sir?"

"Fine now."

The little man smiled briefly and stood, with Donny helping to lift his one good arm. "I won't be gone very long."

"Josh," said Redwyn.

"Yes, sir?"

"You're a good man."

"Yes, sir." But his voice was disappointed.

A lark had joined the nightingale. Redwyn had been listening to it for some time and he knew the dawn was close.

The Miller came back. He said, "Most of the torches are out, Master. Should we light new ones?"

"No," Redwyn answered, pausing to think it out.

Two other men moved up to stand behind the Miller.

"How many horses have you brought?" Redwyn asked.

"We'll count 'em, sir." The Miller motioned and one of the men left.

Redwyn said, "Now listen. Prepare all the horses and get riders for them. Relieve the scouts with rested men and post two more at each corner of the castle walls. The rest of the men– anyone who isn't posted– should begin to scavenge for sticks."

"Sticks, sir?"

"Gather them and bundle them with cloth so they can be carried on horseback. Use the burned torches as well."

"Aye," said the Miller. "We're going to start a fire to keep them inside the walls."

"We may need to," Redwyn said.

"Do you think the Duke will come?"

"Either way, we will need the fire."

"Just in case, sir?"

"Yes. Just in case."

The other man spoke up, "Do you think he will come?"

The third one came back from counting the horses. "Thirteen, sir," he said.

"Take two of the better ones out and choose riders for the others. Choose the best men."

"Will they be carrying sticks– these men on horseback?" asked the Miller.

"If they have to," Redwyn said.

"What sticks?" asked the man who had counted the horses.

"Get going," said Redwyn. "Post the other scouts." The Miller nodded and walked toward the hedgerow where the rest of the men were.

"What sticks?" called the third man.

"We're going to build a fire," barked the Miller walking away, the others following after.

The dawn came gradually, first as a creamy luster around the glow of the torches. Then the fog turned milky grey, then slowly, milky white. Redwyn put his head back against the tree and could see the branches now, disappearing into the mist.

The Miller returned. "It's coming dawn, sir."

Redwyn nodded. "Have you posted the new scouts?"

"They're out there, sir."

The birds had stopped singing, and Redwyn listened in the silence. He looked up to the tree branches again. "Probably the fog," he thought, "the birds have flown off above it." He struggled to stand, and the Miller esitated then moved over quickly and put his big hands under Redwyn's arms, the Miller's strength making it nearly effortless for him to stand.

"How many of them are there, sir?"

Redwyn turned toward the castle as if to see through the mist.

"At least a hundred."

The big man frowned.

"What is your name?"

"Robyn, sir."

"Robyn, I think we should post a relay between each

scout and the hedge here. Tell the lookouts to shout out
what they see to the relays. You stand about twenty paces
out and report whatever the relays say, to me."

"Aye." The Miller narrowed his blue eyes then moved off
toward the hedge. Redwyn turned and saw Donny curled up
at the edge of his blanket. He was still wearing the merchant's
coat and Redwyn knelt down and folded the blanket over
him. Then he heard voices and walked toward them. In the
mist he found some worried looking men standing at the far
side of a pile of bundled sticks. They stopped when they saw
him.

"This is good. Half of you continue bundling, the others
move this pile out to where Robyn the Miller is standing."
Redwyn pointed, "Out there in front of the hedge."

The men began picking up the bundles and moving slowly
through the fog as if they might collide with obstacles hidden
by it.

"Move faster," Redwyn said gently. "You can see ten feet
in the mist."

One of them, a thin man, stumbled and fell, scrambling to
get up.

"Wait, you," Redwyn said. "Deliver your bundle of faggots, then come back here."

The man paused a moment, looking concerned, then picked
up his bundle and walked off. When he returned Redwyn
led him back to the tree. The man had almost no chin,
looking very concerned, and Redwyn smiled at him.

"What is your name?"

"Jeremy, Master. Jeremy Ross."

"Well, Jeremy Ross, can you climb this tree?"

"I think so, sir."

Redwyn pointed upward to the branches which rose into
the fog. "Get as high as you can into those limbs. When the
sun starts shining on this cloud, the top will disappear first.
You may be able to see over it to the castle."

The man looked concerned but came forward and clasped

the tree trunk. He stopped and looked below to Donny who was still asleep on the blanket. "We'd better move the boy, sir," he said, his expression unchanged.

"Why?" asked Redwyn.

"I wouldn't want to fall and squash him, sir."

Redwyn grinned. "You won't fall. And by the looks of you, you couldn't squash a tulip."

"Yes, sir," said the man seriously, and he jumped onto the tree trunk nimbly.

"And, Jeremy," Redwyn called. "Keep your eyes in that direction." He pointed toward the castle and Jeremy nodded.

Redwyn watched him until he had climbed out of sight, then said into the mist, "Can you see anything?"

The voice came back with a note of concern, "Not yet, sir!" Then after a pause, "But it is much lighter up here. I can almost see the sun– sometimes!"

"Good. Yell when you can see the castle."

"Yes sir," came the voice.

The Miller was standing in front of the growing pile of stick-bundles, staring intently at the fog. Redwyn came up behind him.

"Have you heard yet, Robyn?"

"I would have told you, sir," he said shortly. He turned around after having said it, and his face looked hurt. "I'm awfully sorry, sir. This mouth of mine ought to be stopped-up."

"I am not offended," Redwyn told him.

The Miller turned and stared into the mist again. "Bloody bones in hell," he said.

"Easy," Redwyn told him, and he patted the big man's shoulder. Just then it occurred to him that he was wrong about the placement of the tinder pile; for the plan to work, it would have to be moved much closer. The realization made him nauseous and sent a wave of sweaty nervousness over his skin. "I've made a mistake, men," he shouted, walking toward the half-dozen who were working on the tinder. "This pile must be closer. There is plenty here now. Tell the others to stop bundling and help to move it about forty paces forward." Redwyn turned in the direction of the castle, "Yes, forty paces ought to be about right. Then tell the riders to get their horses and come here." The Miller had been listening. He turned, barely visible in the thinning mist, and spoke.

"I am sorry, sir. I never should have said that, Master Redwyn. Here you are, standing with yourself all soaked in your own blood, and thinking for us and fighting to save our pest-ridden hides. I'm sorry I said it. You're the greatest man any of us has ever seen, let alone been with. And we're in a bloody state of hell, that's all."

Redwyn looked at the Miller through the mist. He couldn't think of anything to say, so he just turned and walked back to the tree. The men were leading the horses over, and Donny had been awakened by the hoofbeats.

"Anything yet, Jeremy?"

"I can see the castle now, sir. Just sometimes. The sun is coming out up here."

Redwyn felt a wave of prickly nausea, and he glanced down at the boy.

"You had better go now, Donny."

Donny pulled the blanket off and stood.

"Go back to Josh's inn and stay there."

Donny watched the horses for a moment, then moved off quietly into the mist.

"Redwyn!" came the Miller's voice.

He took a few steps toward it and shouted, "Go on!"

The Miller said, "The fog is lifting at the castle!"

"Tell the scouts to pull back twenty paces."

"Aye, sir."

He heard the Miller bellow out the message, faintly heard the relays repeating it.

"Jeremy, what can you see now?"

"I can see the castle plain as day now."

"Sentinels?" Redwyn called, feeling it hurt his side to yell.

"Three in the gate rook, sir! The mist is creeping off the walls now and it's starting to move down the hill. It looks like a wall of smoke coming down... I'll bet those guards can see me in this tree!"

"It's all right," shouted Redwyn, "It's better if they see you." And he thought to himself, "Then, a surprise attack would seem pointless to them."

He walked through the hedge break and up to the Miller. Almost the entire pile of sticks had been moved. The fog was separating, and rays of sunlight were starting to filter through.

"Tell them to mount the horses, Robyn."

The Miller yelled, "Mount up now! Mount up!"

The horses seemed unused to being ridden and some reared skittishly at the rider's sudden weight. Redwyn spoke through the Miller again, saving strength. "I want fifty men to stand ready with bundles of sticks, Robyn."

The big man said, "Aye," then shouted, "Men, come over two at a time and pick a bunch of faggots from the pile. Stand ready next to the horses!" He counted nervously under his breath until he reached fifty, then shouted, "Enough!" and turned to Redwyn, "Now, Master?"

"We need some fresh torches up here, and a flame to light them."

Jeremy's voice yelled something out. Redwyn walked toward the tree.

"Say it again, Jeremy."

"I say the mist has gone clear from the walls, and it's making its way toward us."

"How far down?"

"About twenty yards, sir."

"Jeremy, listen to me."

"Yes, sir?"

"Every time you think the fog has receded another five yards, shout it out."

"I will, sir. It's very broken now."

Redwyn walked back quickly to the Miller.

"Tell the scouts to pull back twenty paces."

Robyn shouted the message then turned back, his blue eyes set deep in his red face.

"Do you think they can hear us shouting, sir?"

"I hope so," Redwyn said.

"Aye," said the Miller, with a faint, embarrassed grin.

The men were waiting on the horses and looking on. Redwyn knew what they were facing and he tried to speak confidently but gently to them.

"Men, we may have to build a fire in front of the drawgate. It's to keep those devils inside."

"Aye, sir!" they returned enthusiastically.

"This fog has already cleared the castle walls. It's moving downhill toward us. Now, Morcar expects us to attack. He thinks we have an army camped at the hedge. He might suspect our trick if we wait too long, because he knows the fog will give us the advantage. So we mustn't wait. We are about mid-way here, fifty yards from the hedge and the castle—"

One of the men on horseback blurted nervously, "We do have an army, don't we, sir?"

"Aye, we do," said Redwyn. "But we cannot match Morcar's— not in force of arms. But, lads, if we can hold him until the Duke arrives, we'll have succeeded."

The same man spoke again.

"The Duke is coming, isn't he, sir?"

"He's coming," said Redwyn.

"What if something happened to old Percy?" said another.

Redwyn felt weak inside. He had already thought of that. "Listen, men, our task is to hold Morcar—"

And Jeremy's voice came faintly, "Twenty-five yards."

"Heard you!" the Miller called back.

"Right," said Redwyn. "Now we're fifty yards from the gate. When the fog is ten yards from us, that is, when

Jeremy calls forty yards, we move in. Each of you on horseback will carry a bundle to the drawgate and drop it. You must move swiftly, men; Morcar's archers won't take long to find you. If we move in swiftly, we've a chance to build the fire before they counter-attack."

"What then?" said the Miller.

Redwyn glanced about at them. "Each time you deliver a bundle, go back into the mist as soon as you can. The men here will be waiting to hand you more. You men holding the bundles, keep them high and space out evenly so the riders can reach you."

"It will be hard to see in this mist, sir," said an old farmer.

"I know it, lads, but it will be hard for them to shoot you here, as well."

"Aye," the men agreed in a chorus.

"Thirty yards!" came Jeremy's voice.

"What of me?" the Miller asked.

Redwyn picked up a fresh, unlit torch and looked at him.

"Once the pile is dropped, I am going to ride in and light it. I need a second torch and rider behind me."

"I'm the rider," the Miller said confidently.

"The archers will be alerted by then."

"I'm for it," said the Miller.

"Better get the horses then, Robyn."

The big man nodded and walked off.

A shepherd held up a bundle of sticks. "Couldn't you light the pile sooner, without waiting?" he asked.

"No. If a bundle should land on a torch, it might put it out."

"Aye," said the man.

"Thirty-five yards!" came Jeremy's voice.

"Load up now," said Redwyn. The men on the ground began handing up stick-bundles to the riders.

The Miller returned on foot leading two horses.

"Are you up to it, sir?" he asked.

"Aye. Light the torches," said Redwyn, "Get ready." He

put his foot into the stirrup and pulled up slowly onto the horse. The Miller handed him the reins, then mounted also.

"Bring the scouts back, Robyn."

And the Miller bellowed for the scouts to return.

Redwyn's brow was creased. He had forgotten something, feeling it like an empty space inside. Then a man handed him a lighted torch, and he remembered what the lost thought was.

"Men!" he shouted, "Do any of you have longbows?"

"Aye!" came a voice. "Here!" said another.

Three men came forward. Redwyn frowned and spoke hurriedly. "Back at the hedgerow, by the tree, you'll find a cask of liquor. Take some cloth strips from the bundles and tie them around your arrowheads. Soak the cloths with liquor and stand ready, here, to light them. If we fail, move up and shoot into the tinder."

Jeremy called out. "It's forty yards now, sir!"

A scout arrived, panting. He blurted out his message with short gasps of breath in between:

"Just as you called us, there were archers coming up along the parapets– they must be getting set to come out!"

Redwyn tensed and shouted stridently, "Now, men! Ride!"

He started out first across the meadow, and as the mist flew away the castle stood before him, pink in the clear morning air with sunlight shining on its walls and towers. He turned and beckoned, "Come on, Lads! Speed!" and saw the riders just emerging from the mist. He drew reins, and the others coursed around him, thundering toward the drawgate. The Robe sentinels were shouting an alarm, some archers who had been standing further down on the castle's parapet began running toward the gate rook to get into firing range.

Two riders reached the moat edge and simultaneously threw their bundles– both bundles landing too far forward and rolling into the moat.

"Turn sooner!" Redwyn shouted. "Drop them farther

from the moat!"

A horse screamed as it was hit, and Redwyn saw the animal stumble forward and the rider going off. The rider fell face down and started to get up, but an arrow pinned his ankle to the ground. Swearing, he loosened it, but two more arrows sunk into his back, and his head lowered slowly onto his arms.

There were eight bundles near the moat now. Redwyn waved his torch and shouted. "Faster men! Faster!" He handed the torch to the Miller and pulled the crossbow from his back. He scanned the parapet, then sighted on an archer in the gate rook. The second wave of riders broke from the mist and charged out toward the gate. Redwyn waited until the Robed archer had raised his bow before firing at him, then his arrow snapped into the center of the archer's chest and the man doubled over and fell forward into the moat.

"Nice one!" said the Miller.

Redwyn reloaded the crossbow and slung it over his back again. The Miller handed him the torch.

"Maybe our archers should be firing just outside the mist," the Miller said.

"It wouldn't help much," Redwyn told him. "We have to save them."

The riders had been fast moving targets which the Robes' archers, so far, had been missing. Then three riders galloping close together and returning from the drawbridge were hit in the back almost simultaneously. Two of them fell from their horses. The third slumped forward and clutched his horse's neck and hung on long enough to reach the mist.

"One more load, Robyn, then it's our task to light it."

"I'm with you," said the Miller.

The pile was nearly three feet high now, ten feet across. Another horse was hit, and it and the rider fell into the moat. Redwyn tensed convulsively in his saddle, "That is enough! We light it!"

"Aye!" said the Miller.

As they charged across the meadow, the drawgate started down. Redwyn reached the pile, dropped his torch into it, wheeled the horse around and started back toward the mist. An arrow struck the chain mail on his back like a good punch; he heard more arrows zizzing by and then saw the Miller riding toward him, his big face red and his eyes blue and fevered, Redwyn only now noticing the lumbering pace of the draft horse the Miller rode. He turned around to watch. As the Miller leaned forward to release, the clumsy horse was hit and it turned around and reared sluggishly. Then Redwyn saw an arrow bite into the big man's neck– his eyes bulge and his teeth bare– he turned and dropped his torch onto the pile, and fell off sideways at the moat's edge.

The mist had receded enough that the men were growing visible inside the thinning veil.

"Longbows!" Redwyn yelled. "The rest of you, back!" The drawgate was already halfway down and only a small fire had risen at the pile's edge. The longbowmen came from the mist with their arrows lighted, one of them hit even as they emerged. Redwyn was shaking his head and screaming, "Shoot! Shoot!"

They fired. One missed. The other struck the center of the tow. Redwyn dismounted, picked up the fallen bow, and sent another arrow into the pile's center.

"Back!" he shouted.

The drawgate was nearly down and now the fire was four feet high and crackling briskly. Horsehooves pounded on the bridge. Redwyn pulled the crossbow from his back and raised it. As the first rider moved up to attempt jumping the tow pile, Redwyn fired and the man fell back behind the flames with a stunned look on his face.

No other riders came. The loud clanging of the drawchains stopped. For a moment there was silence, then a voice rang, "Get out! Out! Out! Out!"

A Robe led a horse onto the bridge, but the animal reared at the flames and launched itself, squealing, into the moat.

Morcar was in the gate rook, still giving commands, peering from between the shoulders of two guards. Redwyn bent down slowly to pick up a longbow, but the Head Robe saw him, ducked, and disappeared.

Then Redwyn and the other longbowman who had hit the tow pile were the only two left standing in the field. They had retreated out of crossbow range. The others were already back at the hedge. The Miller's legs were lying outside the fire, the rest of him was in it. The arrow in his neck was burning brightly. The flames of the tow pile were seven feet high.

"Will it hold them?" asked the bowman.

Redwyn smiled at him faintly. "That was good shooting," he said. "Yes, it will hold them. Not very long. They know who we are now." Both of them watched for a moment as the chains receded back into the wall, clanging, and the drawbridge started to rise.

Back at the hedgerow, the men were very quiet and anxious looking. The only sounds were the moans of the wounded, and Redwyn assigned four men to take the wounded back to town. Then he called the rest of them together, and they were all sitting around him in a circle. He was about to speak when a voice said seemingly out of nowhere: "Hallo, sir! Can I come down now?"

Redwyn looked up at Jeremy in the tree branches. The men broke into laughter.

He waved assentingly, and Jeremy climbed down. As the laughter faded the peasants' faces again turned grave.

"The fire is burning quickly, men. I don't think we have much time. You, with axes, chop out places in the bottom of the hedge so that those with crossbows can lie under it and shoot from cover. Now we have three longbows, and I want longbow archers in the two places where the hedge breaks. You have the most range so you will be shooting first.

"The rest should get behind the hedge. You men with

scythes, stand aside from the breaks where the horses must come through. Chop at the horses' legs. And when a rider falls, get on him with your clubs and axes."

"Aye, we'll chop him!" "Aye!" said others.

They went immediately to work, the axemen hacking and tearing frantically at the hedge-roots. In a short time the crossbowmen were lying beneath the cover in the fresh dirt.

Redwyn had been watching from the break. There was movement in the gate rook– Robes running along the parapets. Then the clang of chains carried faintly across the field and he saw the drawbridge coming down.

"Here it comes, men. Take hold."

The drawbridge landed, and several Robes walked onto it. They came in twos, carrying bushels of dirt to smother out the greatly diminished fire. The flames gradually lowered and went out. The bridge was cleared and then the first riders started through.

Redwyn heard the men shouting to each other along the hedge: cries of, "Here they come!" and, "Ready now!" He took the longbow from the ground beside him and notched an arrow. Even from halfway across the meadow he could feel the shock of the approaching horses conducting through the ground he lay upon. Someone tapped his shoulder. Redwyn jerked around and Jeremy was there, smiling strangely without much chin.

"I think they're coming, sir," he said.

"I can see them!" Redwyn snapped. "Get back now!"

About fifty riders had cleared the gate. When the leader of the charge was halfway to the hedgerow, Redwyn rose upon his knees, drew the bone-spined, ancient looking longbow back and shot him.

"Longbows fire!" he yelled. Then an instant later, "Crossbows hold... now fire!"

But of the two-dozen arrows volleyed only three had found their marks. The farmers made ready with their scythes as the force crashed furiously through the hedge breaks, the first few horses tumbling as the scythe-blades slashed their legs—others falling into them, the horses screaming shrilly and several of the townsmen being pulled underneath them. A Robe lay sprawled out on the ground and as he lifted himself a townsman rushed forward and sank an axe into his back.

"Now it is hopeless," Redwyn thought. The robed riders were jumping the fallen horses through the breaks and nearly twenty had gotten through. They were working the hedgerow with morning stars and axes, and the townsmen were backed desperately against the impasse of the hedge, some of them even attempting to crawl under it. But the Robes were on both sides now, and Redwyn picked up an axe to meet a sword attack. He ducked and buried the axe into the swordsman's thigh, then pulled the crossbow from his back and fired into another rider who was leaning toward him with a mace.

Then, it seemed just as suddenly, the attack was over. Half of the Robes' cavalry were thundering back toward the castle; the others outside the hedge were fighting each other in a screaming maelstrom of leaping horses and flailing arms, all trying at once to enter the narrow break. Two trumpets blared, alternating their different notes. And for the first time Redwyn saw what was happening.

The red and silver clad riders charged from the highland road and stormed between the pillars. The peasants were standing again. He heard shouts of, "They're here!" "The Duke's legions have saved us!"

Then Percy rode up, his old face grimy from the road, sporting a strange and satisfied grin.

Chapter 32
The Prisoners

The Duke's legion had pushed Morcar's army from the hedgerow and now pursued them across the field. Redwyn and Percy stayed back and watched as the Duke chased, his cavalry advancing toward the castle, flanks forward, to prevent the Robes' escape. Of the forty or so that remained of Morcar's expedition, about thirty had crossed the bridge into the castle. But now as the legion closed in, the drawgate was being raised and the remaining Robes were trapped outside the moat.

"Take prisoners!" screamed the Duke.

His captain heard and was advancing through the hail of arrows being fired from the parapet, shouting, "Prisoners! The Duke wants hostages!"

But the Legion was crushing in, forcing the Robes into the dry moat, their horses screaming horribly as they fell. As the Captain shouted his command repeatedly the Duke's men started to back away from the moat's edge. They put their red and silver shields above their heads to cover against the steady rain of arrows.

Suddenly there was a brief lull in the shooting while a command was issued to the archers on the parapet. Then as the order was obeyed the arrows began hitting the stranded Robes.

"They're shooting their own men!" shouted the Duke, then annunciating each word sharply, "Get– me– prisoners!"

Finally the captain took it upon himself and rode in with his shield covering his head. He got close enough to a Robe to grab his horse's bridle, then he rode alongside, his shield over the prisoner's head and a sword against his ribs. Other soldier's went in to try in a similar fashion, but only one other prisoner was taken and with great difficulty.

Redwyn and Percy watched as the legion started back across the field. "It's over for now," said Percy. Redwyn put his arm around him and they walked back toward the wounded.

The Duke sent soldiers to get a blacksmith from the fair. They returned and chained the prisoners to a large oak tree. Other soldiers had been sent into the fairgrounds to commandeer food or whatever else they needed, and a procession of merchants followed them back to watch the siege. Josh had sent up ale, and now Redwyn, Percy, and the Duke of Cumberland sat on three upended ale casks. The Duke filled their heavy metal tankards from a cask in the center that they all used as a table top. He finished drawing the ale then handed the mugs to Redwyn and Percy, took his own from the cask and lifted it in a gesture toward the spectators.

The Duke brought the mug to his lips and took big gulps, shut his eyes and tipped it steadily higher. The metal mug was sweating and the droplets trickled down and streamed onto his cheeks. Then he paused, took a deep breath, looked at Redwyn and Percy, and gestured to the spectators again.

"*They* think it's a bloody feast day, or tournament, or some bloody thing like that!" A squire stepped up and offered to take the Duke's tankard, but he waved him off, leaned over to the cask and put it under the bung-stop, watching it fill.

"It's all too damned fantastic," he said, then sat up and

guzzled about half the ale he had just poured. Then he looked at Redwyn and spoke directly to him for the first time.

"I don't know who you are, Redwyn, but Sir Perceville has told me of the things you've done– your troubles with this Morcar. I am grateful to you."

Redwyn said quietly, "It is I who should be grateful to Your Grace, for saving my life."

The Duke reached for the others' ale mugs and filled them from the cask. Then he handed them back, and the men were silent as the Duke sipped and stared into the ground.

"What does this Morcar think he's doing?" he asked.

"You can bet it's evil," said Percy.

"It's treason!" said the Duke. Then he was quiet again, his jaw muscles working nervously as he stared into the ground. He took another sip then raised his hand for the squire. The Captain, who was talking with some soldiers, saw him motioning and came up from behind.

"Yes, Your Grace?"

The Duke recognized the voice and turned his neck to look out of politeness.

"Oh, it's you, Robert."

"Does Your Grace require something?"

"Have one of the prisoners brought to me." He glanced over to the tree where they were chained, about sixty feet away. "Bring the little one first, the one who tried to throw himself into the dry moat. Bring *that* little pig turd here!"

"Yes, Your Grace."

The Duke looked sullenly toward the ground again. They all three waited quietly for the prisoner to be brought.

The guards were holding him by his arms and the man's feet were barely touching as they half-carried him. The Duke heard them coming. He stood and walked clear of the ale casks. The man looked nervous; but when he neared the Duke his face grew tight with hatred and he spat viciously.

"Ptwah!"

The Duke was expressionless. The man tried it two more times, annunciating, "Ptwah, ptwah!" but his mouth had gone dry and no saliva was discharged.

The Duke's jaw muscles began working again. He pursed his lips then threw the mug of ale onto the man's chest. Percy leaned toward Redwyn, "Good idea to hit his chest," he said. "If he'd gotten some in his face, the bugger might have spat it back at him!"

The Duke gripped his ale tankard and cocked his arm across his chest so that the back of his hand was turned to the man and his fist was clenched tightly around the tankard's handle. The man looked at the heavy mug and the hatred drained out of him momentarily and he was nervous again.

The Duke dropped his right shoulder slightly and the man thought it was coming, then, and flinched. But the Duke said, "Right then. You're going to answer some questions."

The man was still nervous, but there was hatred in his voice.

"What questions?"

"I want to know just what this Morcar is planning. Why he would attack Solway."

The man stalled for a moment, then Redwyn saw it coming as the prisoner's face tightened and the hatred came back into it. He threw his head forward and spat viciously, "Ptwah!"

There was an instant of hesitation, then as the prisoner stretched his neck forward to spit again, the Duke swung upward and smashed the tankard into the right side of the man's face. The man's head was knocked sideways, and he howled with pain and fear. His lip and mouth began to bleed, and for a moment he just stared. Then his eyes began to roll wildly in his head and the hatred miraculously returned.

"Ptwah! Ptwah! Ptwah! Ptwah!" he spat.

He was discharging blood now, and the Duke stepped back from the man as he spat and twisted in the guards' grasp. Then the prisoner began to pant, drawing his breath in loud growls, and gasped:

"My Lord Morcar– destroy you– Satan's engines! Flames from his engines!" He went on repeating himself and working into hysteria. "Destroy you! Satan! Engines!..."

And after listening intently for a time the Duke made a gesture toward the tree and said, "Hang him!"

The soldiers nodded, and the man continued to growl as they carried him off.

The Duke sat down on his cask again, flushed with anger, his bright hair cropped pointedly like a crown upon his livid head.

The man to be hanged was standing beneath the tall oak now. The spectators grew noisy as a rope was slung over a high branch. A loop was tied crudely around the man's neck; but the Captain came over and told the soldiers to untie the bad knots and showed him how to tie a proper noose. The soldiers nodded appreciatively, and the man had begun to look nervous again. As they put the second noose over him he tried feebly to raise his bound arms. The crowd made a rising, "Aaaaahhhhh!" sound that crescendoed into cheers. Redwyn turned and saw the prisoner being hoisted into the air.

"They're entertained," said the Duke bitterly, keeping his back to the scene.

The other prisoner had slumped against the tree, sobbing. The spectators began jeering and throwing things at him.

The Duke looked to Redwyn and Percy and said, "What the devil did he mean by 'Satan's engines'?"

Percy frowned, "A cannon, perhaps. They used them in Crecy not ten years ago."

"Yes, a cannon," said the Duke.

Redwyn felt an emptiness again, the vacancy of a thought which eluded him.

"A cannon, Redwyn?" asked the Duke.

"I think not, Your Grace."

"Why not?"

"I feel it is... something else."

Then after they had just sat for a time, silently drinking ale, the Captain came up behind them with the second prisoner.

"This one wants to talk, Your Grace."

The Duke stood up again. The Captain had brought the man over without assistance and was holding him by one arm.

"So, he's ready, is he?"

"There is more rope, Your Grace."

The man tried to drop onto his knees, then, but the Captain held him up a moment and lowered him down slowly.

"I'll tell you if we need some, Robert."

"Yes, Your Grace."

Looking down at the man, the Duke said almost gently, "Now, what of these engines your friend was ranting about?"

The man kept his eyes fixed on the ground and shook his head. "He wasn't my friend. I heard him and some others talking, Your Grace, in the great hall. They were told to build something by Master Brech. They called it the 'Devil's engine,' Your Grace. He used to be a glassblower– that one." The prisoner gestured to the gently pendulating corpse. "That's all I know. They've been building things." He was sobbing now.

"What else?"

The prisoner sniffed with a thread of mucous distending from his nose. "A gallows and some wagons," he said. "And they were getting the rats in the plague-cell all ready–" He looked up after having said it and his realization stunned him to speechlessness.

The Duke's eyes went wild, white rimmed like a wild horse's. He drew his sword and quickly put it to the man's throat. Redwyn stood and touched the nobleman's shoulder. "Easy, Your Grace," he said. The Duke glanced back at him feverishly, but he was almost beyond understanding words now and grabbed the man by the hair and clenched it.

"Speak!" he gasped.

The prisoner was frozen with fear. The Duke swung the man's head back and forth by his hair, jerked it steady again and put the sword hard against his neck. "Speak, or I'll cut your head off and throw it on a dungheap!" The man was moving his mouth twitchingly, but was unable to dislodge the words.

"My brother!" said the Duke with his teeth clenched, seething. "How did Morcar kill my brother!"

"The soldiers," whispered Redwyn.

The man burst out, "Oh God I pledged my mortal soul!"

The Duke wrenched him by his hair again, and the man cried, "He uses rats to spread the plague! They put people in the dungeon and give them plague! Yes, yes, they killed Thragonparke of Galway! Oh God!"

Redwyn had risen to his feet. Some soldiers had been listening and looking on. He glanced at them nervously then shouted so they heard:

"This man is insane, Your Grace! Captain, come take this madman away!"

Then he stood close to the Duke and gripped the hand that held the sword to the man's throat. "Your Grace, what would your men do if they knew the Black Death were against them?"

Reason slowly returned to the Noble's crimson face. He relaxed his hold on the man and looked at Redwyn searchingly. Then he motioned to the Captain, "Yes, this man's gone mad. He'll be of no use to us."

Two guards stepped forward and pulled the sobbing Robe from his knees. The Duke's face had become vacuous.

"Your Grace?"

"What is it, Robert?"

"Shall I hang him?"

"No. Hold him for now."

The Captain took the man from the ground and led him back to the tree. Percy followed and helped to chain him.

The Duke was staring toward the ground, his forehead creased, and he spoke quietly with Redwyn standing near.

"During the ride to come here I nearly turned back a dozen times. Just too fantastic, just rambling, some old man's delusions, I thought. But how, I asked myself, could an old man like Perceville have got my brother's seal? And now, this. It is all true, isn't it? This madman controls the plague and he killed my brother with it. And you, Redwyn..." The Duke paused and studied him. "Do you really possess the ancient sword Excalibur?"

Redwyn looked up slowly.

"It is all true, Your Grace."

Their eyes met briefly then the Duke's eyes shifted in the deep set of his brow. He straightened, and cleared his throat nervously, and said, "Then you shall be *Lord* Redwyn from now on."

"Your Grace needn't."

"No, you shall be that." The Duke looked at Redwyn's empty scabbard gleaming brightly in the late-morning sun.

"Why don't you wear it?"

"I left the sword in the castle last night, Your Grace. With the Lady Lynn."

"You mean, you saw her!"

"Yes."

The Duke swallowed, then squinted toward the castle. "Well," he said slowly, "It would be nice if she lopped off this Morcar's head! Then we could all go home– Heh?" He laughed boisterously and slapped Redwyn's back. Redwyn smiled but the thought of Lynn was heavy inside of him. The Duke's laughter softened to a chuckle. He glanced back to the ale cask.

Redwyn picked up the mug from the ground, wiped it carefully and handed it to him. "I have a plan, which, if successful, Your Grace, would take Morcar's chief weapon away from him."

"The plague."

"Yes."

"And what is the plan?"

Percy overheard as he approached, "What plan?"

"Lord Redwyn was about to tell it," said the Duke.

"Percy and I had attempted it last night," Redwyn explained. "To destroy the rats in the plague cell. But the Robes were at the dungeon already."

"Dungeon?"

"The dungeon that lies beneath the ruined walls of Camelot is where Morcar keeps the rats. An old tunnel that hasn't been used in centuries would get a squad of archers into the castle grounds– *if* we can slip by unseen."

"And then?"

"We would burn them."

"We'll wait until nightfall," said the Duke.

"We mustn't wait, Your Grace. I stopped Morcar from spreading the plague last night. It is only a matter of a day before he infects new plague rats. I know it takes that long to do this. It must be what he is waiting for."

"I don't understand," the Duke said.

Percy interjected, "A wise man instructed us on these matters. I trust him, Your Grace."

"Damned magic!" said the Duke. He put his sword into his scabbard and rested his hands on his hips. "What shall we do, Redwyn?"

"The tunnel lies just beyond the end of the hedge, but well into the meadow. If Your Grace could launch a frontal attack, as a diversion, we could possibly get across the open grounds unseen."

"Yes, it's a good plan." The Duke's eyes fixed rigidly as he considered it, then he quickly glanced to the sun to note its position. "It will be risky to take my men so close to those archers– I don't like weak-hearted attempts. My infantry was a half-day behind us. I'd pledge them here by eventide. Can we wait that long?"

"Every moment draws us into peril," Redwyn told him.

"Consider the Lady Lynn as well," said Percy.

Redwyn's face darkened. He had already considered that.

The Duke sighed, "Very well. Assemble the men you need– my Captain will help you. Robert!"

Chapter 33
Battle II

The Captain came over. The Duke instructed him to choose twelve of his best archers and send them to Redwyn. As these men prepared themselves, the Duke marshalled a force of cavalry for the frontal attack. When both teams were ready, Redwyn and the Duke met behind the hedge. Redwyn looked over and saw the battalion of about fifty riders, about half of the Duke's force, Percy among them. The Duke gestured toward the men.

"No sense in exposing my whole cavalry to those archers. I'm letting half of them rest."

"We are almost ready, Your Grace."

The Duke nodded gravely and walked off. Redwyn turned to his small band.

"Hello, lads."

"Hello!" they answered.

He began cocking his heavy crossbow, winding it as he spoke. "Lads, it is my ambition to reach that dungeon without being shot."

"Aye!" said the men. Some of them were smiling at the remark.

"We shall wait until the cavalry is halfway across the

meadow and the Robes are sure to be looking at them." He slung the crossbow across his back, and said, "Then we run like the devil's mistresses!" The men laughed softly. "Have you brought the liquor?"

Three of them held up swollen animal skins.

"Good. Be sure to keep the torches burning, too. Move down the hedgerow now, and await the charge."

Redwyn's band reached the far break and waited. The Duke rode to the front of his battalion and looked searchingly down the hedge. Redwyn stepped out and waved. The Duke nodded then threw his arm forward and started the advance.

As the riders moved across the field, Redwyn saw the line of archers stiffen along the castle's parapet.

"Now!" he said.

His party ran into the meadow, single file coming through the break, Redwyn limping in front of them. They reached the tunnel entrance quickly and Redwyn pulled the hatch open, stood aside and hurried the men down into it. He had seen no sentinels on the facing flank battlement, and as the last man went into the tunnel he left the door open and climbed down after him.

It was dark but the torches gave them enough light to tell direction by. Redwyn said, "Hurry," his voice washing out into the shuffle of their boots.

The tunnel was about seventy-five yards long, and when daylight appeared at the other end Redwyn was surprised the men had reached it so quickly. Then he saw two figures drop into the light, heard a crossbow's unmistakable "crack!"–another fired. "Get out!," he shouted. "Out!" Two more figures dropped down and two more bows went, "Crack!" Redwyn heard his men returning fire; then groans. Everything echoing. Then two of the figures climbed back out and he heard the loud "Splash!" of liquid being dumped in.

"Retreat!" he cried frantically. "Out men! Out!"

He was already running back toward the entrance himself

and could hear others running just behind. He pulled himself out and turned, kneeling, and yanked the next man from the doorway. He and the other man pulled two more soldiers out quickly. Then all four of them were pushed backward, feeling the violent "thump!" of the hot air as it exploded from the tunnel, a column of fire roaring out behind it, then black smoke issuing thickly with the reek of burning hair and flesh.

He struggled to his feet and saw Percy galloping toward him leading another horse by its reins. Redwyn suddenly knew what Morcar's mysterious weapon was. He could not see around the castle where the Duke's men were, but he was certain of it.

As if out of a nightmare, Percy reached him and said, "The plan's gone bad. We know what the 'Devil's Engines' are."

Redwyn was filling with rage, for his own stupidity. He took the reins from Percy, climbed onto the spare horse and kicked it into a gallop toward the moat. Turning the castle wall, the battle was there raging before him, his worst fears made real.

Spread out in front of the drawgate, there were five flame throwing devices, each one worked by a pair of Robes. The front man of each pair had a goatskin of hot oil on his back; he held a tube out to discharge the oil and ignited it with a torch; the bellows was being pumped by a second Robe who walked behind the first. The flames were blazing thirty feet into the Duke's lines. His horses had been spooked, and Morcar's archers were between the phalanges of fire and shooting with deadly accuracy.

Redwyn could see the Duke, his horse rearing and him trying desperately to control it. Half his force was dead and burning.

Redwyn shouted, "Your Grace! Fall back! Fall back!"

The Duke looked up and saw him, turned his horse away from the flames and repeated the cry, bellowing, "Fall back!

Fall back!"

The Captain had been shot in the leg, and he rode along the line of frenzied horses and relayed the command to pull away. The Duke was searching for Redwyn again. Redwyn shouted and waved.

"Dismount, Your Grace! Off the horses!"

Redwyn jumped off his own horse, pulled the crossbow up and ran toward a burning body. He held the tip of his arrow over the flames on the corpse's back until the arrow ignited, then stood and ran along the left flank, behind an advancing flame thrower. "Your Grace!" he shouted. The Duke looked over. "The skins!" And Redwyn sighted on the jiggling goatskin and squeezed the trigger, the arrow striking almost before he had finished shouting– the oil sack exploding– flames mushrooming flatly across the ground and re-shaping into a ball, a dozen Robes burning as it lifted.

The Duke's men gave a rallying cheer. The Captain quickly formed a party of archers and was leading them toward the flanks where the line of fire to the flame throwers' goatskins was clear.

Redwyn saw a dead Robe lying in front of him, an unfired crossbow still in hand. He ran over, picked the weapon up, and as he stood up straight something struck him in the middle of his back and threw him forward onto the corpse.

He tried again to get up and managed to move off the dead body, but his strength was gone, his head swam, and his shoulders eased forward into the grass. His last thought was that Percy was trying to tell him something. And it seemed like hours later when the wave of heat rushed over him and he opened his eyes to the smoke and heard the battle still going on. A voice shouted, "Him! Him!"

Redwyn turned his head and saw a pair of men with a flame apparatus walking awkwardly toward him. They advanced a few more paces and the front man lifted the tube and a huge curl of flame unfolded from it and onto the ground. Redwyn went flat upon the earth and covered his head with his hands, the flame hissing, his hands blistering where it scorched them. When he looked up the ground in front of him was black and smoking. The men with the flame thrower were waddling closer. He pushed up on his arms but they collapsed underneath him, and then he saw Percy riding over with his shortsword drawn.

Percy came up behind the flame throwers. He hacked down the bellows operator, then plunged his sword deep into the goatskin on the other man's shoulders.

The other man wailed as the hot oil ran crackling down his back and onto his legs. He dropped his torch and flailed his arms, then disappeared into a flattened ball of fire.

Redwyn yelled, "Percy!" and saw the old man fall out of the ball of flames, burning, his burning horse bucking wildly across the field. Percy rolled slowly onto his back and the flames extinguished.

The Captain's archers had found their marks, and two more skins exploded. Morcar was screaming from the parapet, "Get the riders out! Finish them! Out!"

A column of Morcar's cavalry moved into position to cross the bridge. Redwyn struggled to stand then looked behind him to the Duke's men at the hedgerow. Taken by surprise, they were scrambling to arm themselves, utterly vulnerable to attack. Redwyn knew that if Morcar reached them, the legion would fall.

The Robes were still on the drawgate. Their horses were rearing from the fire and smoke in front of them, and the Robes were fighting to bring them under control. The oil from the four ruptured goatskins had spread across the ground and nearly the entire battlefield was in flames. There was one remaining passage where Morcar's cavalry could get through to the hedgerow, and the men working the undetonated flame device were standing in it. Redwyn began running toward the Captain, half staggering, the ground feeling like quicksand as he moved along the outside of the flames. The pair with the flame thrower had begun running too, toward the castle with their backs to the Duke's men. Redwyn saw three archers fire at the jiggling goatskin, missing it. The Captain was holding his wounded leg and swearing at his men. Redwyn at last reached him, caught him by his armor vest and turned him around.

"Get your archers outside the flames, Captain. Shoot through the flames."

The Captain looked up, immediately saw the strategy and began yelling the order. The Robes were advancing from the drawbridge, covering their horses' eyes with their hands. But the horses were skittish of the heat, and the Captain's men were running in front of them, winning the race to the outside of the flames. Redwyn muttered something about Percy, and collapsed.

The next that he knew, he felt himself being carried, raised his head and saw the drawgate, closed again. The Duke was walking alongside. Morcar's voice was distant, screaming. The Duke turned around and shouted back:

"He's alive, you bloody filth! And he'll see you hang for treason!"

Redwyn heard Morcar's voice very faintly shout, "You are going to die, Magician!" And then the blackness came again.

Chapter 34
Threshold

He opened his eyes. His head cleared slowly and his shoulders, neck, and head all hurt together in throbs. His side hurt, too, but was no longer bleeding.

He raised up onto his elbows and saw the Duke in front of him, eating from the top of a cask. The Duke had a mug of ale on the ground by his foot and he had not seen Redwyn lift himself, but his squire pointed and whispered, "Your Grace—"

The Duke said, "What?" looked, and picked up the ale mug hurriedly, brought it over and knelt at Redwyn's side. "Here, drink this," he said.

Redwyn sipped the ale and, focusing the strength into his voice, said, "What came of it?"

"We nearly lost everything," the Duke told him.

Redwyn shut his eyes.

"Here, drink some more." The Duke held the mug up again and said, "I'll not underestimate this Morcar a second time. The infantry will be here after the noon; then we'll storm that castle the *right* way."

Redwyn took some more ale.

The Duke said, "Aye. It's a good thing you came back

when you did. We were taken off guard and I was a damned fool to use only half the force."

"It was my plan, Your Grace."

"Christ, it was a good plan. Who would have thought the devil would have flame engines."

"I should have," Redwyn said. "I gave him the idea for them."

"What!" The Duke frowned in disbelief.

"I used a flame shooting engine in my magic show. Morcar tricked me into telling him how it worked."

The Noble wagged his sweaty, crimson cropped head and said, "Ah, now don't start blaming yourself! I should have listened to Lynn St. Du Lac months ago. The filthy snake had tricked me, too."

The Duke set the ale mug down. "You fought more bravely than any man I've seen, lad. How do you feel?"

Redwyn said, "Something hit me..." And as the images from the battle came back he tried to lift himself, to stand.

"Aye!" said the Duke, helping him. "I saw it. One of those rat herders pummelled you in the back with a chain ball."

"Where is Percy?" Redwyn asked, now standing.

The Duke looked into his eyes and said, "Over there. But he's not well, lad."

Without even a nod to the Duke, Redwyn began walking toward the wounded. There was a large group of bleeding and badly burned, and he looked over their faces and saw Percy set apart on a blanket. He approached slowly, his legs feeling weak and uncontrolled. Percy was lying on his back, staring upward with his arms down at his sides. He turned his head, saw Redwyn, and said, "Thank God!"

Redwyn moved up to him quickly and knelt beside him on both knees.

"How are you, Percy?"

"Bad a moment ago. I don't feel bad now."

"Where are you burned?"

"My backside mostly. I wasn't quick enough."

Redwyn looked down and saw the blood soaking into the blanket and he went hollow inside, groping for words. "You mean your damned horse wasn't fast enough– you'd have gotten out."

"No, this horse wasn't fast enough. Not nearly as good as my last one."

"You shouldn't have done it, Percy."

The old brown face was pale.

"Am I not your Knight?"

After an infinitesimal pause, "You are my Knight."

"And are you not my King?"

"Yes. I am your King, Sir Percy."

"Good. That's enough of the nonsense, then."

Redwyn was fighting it. "You are brave," he said.

"Nonsense."

Redwyn fought it back and said, "You're an old fool then."

Percy's eyes began to drift into the cloudless and ice blue sky as if searching it for something, and he said very tiredly, "All the brave are fools, or dead, Redwyn; but they are the only men worth knowing."

Then Redwyn said something else, but Percy's gaze had fixed on something distant, it remained fixed, so Redwyn just brushed his hand over the Old Knight's eyes and closed them.

When he stood and turned around the Duke was there, holding three tankards of ale. He saw the look in Redwyn's eyes, then saw Percy, and handed the mugs awkwardly to the squire attending him.

"He was a brave knight– your friend Perceville."

"He was," said Redwyn, looking away.

"He must have loved you," said the Duke.

Redwyn looked up to the sky. "He loved honor. He was the last of an old and dying breed, and he was surely a man worth knowing." Then he had to walk away. The Duke understood and watched him descending on the town road toward the sea. He took a mug of ale from his squire and drank a little and turned back and looked silently at Percy's face. The Duke wanted to remember it.

As Redwyn had walked through the spectators, he had not heard the whispering or the scattered applause, nor even seen their faces. He walked down the long hill road and through the fairgrounds then turned past the boats and walked on the scorched yellow grass along the sea.

He climbed over the white rocks and around the huge, sun bleached boulders until he stood at the edge of the water where the beach was of smooth, disc-shaped pebbles about the size of peach stones that made a loud "shhhhh" sound as they rolled in the big surf. The surf was five feet high and crashed with the dark stones churning in the white rollers, each time some of them flying free and landing wet upon the sun-dried pebble drifts.

He watched the swells coming in at angles, crashing, following the line of a swell as it travelled down the shoreline and turned white against the beach. Now, if he closed his eyes, the rushing of the sea came into the emptiness inside him and brought its rhythm like a pulse that he could use. He kept his eyes closed and felt it, while he shed his blood soaked blouse and jacket and let them drop onto the rocks. The wind blew cool and fresh against his chest, and he felt more sleepy as he pulled off his boots, rolled down his breeches, then felt the cool breeze wash over his entire naked body with the sun warming briefly when the breezes ebbed. His eyes were open as he moved into the surf and felt the little stones hitting him as the white rollers broke against his legs. The water was cold, and already his feet were growing numb to the larger stones on the bottom that were the size of fists and round but uncomfortable to walk on. He turned his uninjured side to the surf and moved outward until he was past the breakers. Then with the water chest high and numbing-cold, he plunged forward as a swell came and felt the icy freshness on his face and shoulders, rolled onto his back and pushed his arms down and kicked with a scissors kick and began swimming steadily out to sea.

The cold numbed the physical pain of the wounds, and he kept his eyes shut except to check his course by looking briefly at the shore. The sound of the surf was growing fainter and the swells shallower and now he could keep his eyes closed entirely and hold his course by feeling his body's angle to the waves. The water was very cold, only his forehead was not numb but rather ached as he swam further, steadily, and grew more tired, groggy, then very, very sleepy from the cold.

Finally he stopped swimming and stayed on his back and his legs sank down in front of him. He opened his eyes and was a half mile from the shore. The castle had a bluish look through the haze. The road going up to it was yellow and meandering. Redwyn tried not to think of anything as he let the air out and sank, legs first, descending beneath the swells, opening his eyes and the water blurry green where the sun shot down in a circular pattern of distinct rays. Below, the sea was dark green and slanted down into blackness. His chest began feeling constricted, his throat tight; and he looked above and saw the surface rising away, stroked once, twice, three times, four times upward and broke through finally and gasped and gasped for air.

He turned on his back again and felt a sense of relief. And though he swam sluggishly, the swells and incoming tide brought him in quickly to the beach. The waves were breaking around and sometimes over him then, and he stood with his back to shore. When he turned around Donny Gwaith was standing there with the barmaid.

Redwyn walked slowly through the breakers and onto the beach and did not care that the barmaid could see him naked, nor did he look at either of them, but walked to a flat, wedge-shaped boulder and lay face down on it in the sun-shine with his arms hanging down against its sides. His body was still numb from the cold as the barmaid stood over him and said, "I am going to wash your clothes, Master Redwyn." But he still said nothing, nor felt nor cared for anything. And a cloth of some kind was pulled up lightly along his backside. He felt a soft pressure on his left arm and opened his eyes and saw that Donny Gwaith had rested his head there. He saw one sleeve of the Merchant's embroidered coat hanging from where Donny had draped it, and then it was all coming back. It came in images of Lynn and Percy, and images from the battles, and of Nelrum and of Percy until he wept, the sound of the sea filling in between the waves of hurt.

And in the calm fatigue that followed, his body felt like it was floating, still moving with the undulating motion of the waves. He slept. When he awoke much later and opened his eyes there were dark green leaves over his face and he could feel leaves touching the full length of his body.

Pushing the branches aside, Redwyn saw Donny leaning against a boulder with a branch propped up to shade him from the sun. Nearby, he saw the spindly body of the sapling that Donny had stripped.

Redwyn took the Merchant's coat off and folded it, then sat up on the rock with the sleep still leaving him.

"Thank you, Donny."

The boy looked up, and Redwyn said, "The sun would have burned me pretty badly by now." He was holding the coat over his lap, and Donny stood and walked up higher on the shore to take the clothing from the rocks where it had dried. He came back and draped it over the boulder, and Redwyn handed him the coat and said, "Thank you for the use of your coat."

Donny pointed to the coat, then to Redwyn, then to himself.

"What? I gave you the coat?"

Donny nodded.

"No," said Redwyn. "It was that nice man with the funny

shoes."

Donny laughed out loud, then realizing he had made sounds looked frightened. Redwyn pretended not to notice his fear and glanced out at the sea.

The surf was higher and the waves surged up foaming and soaked into the drifts of stones.

"There is a wind rising, Donny."

The boy turned to look and the wind tousled his long brown hair wildly.

"See the color of the water now?" said Redwyn. "Look at the waves curling with green tops on them. Even way out. And look at how the water streaks, in lines, with the foam in-between. The whole sea is green."

Donny looked at him and smiled.

"It is green now. But when the storm comes it will turn black."

Donny looked at him again then side-stepped closer.

"Sometimes our world isn't as we want it to be, Donny. It hurts us. And it cheats us and scares us. There are terrible people and terrible situations that we find ourselves with. But courage makes you a man, Donny. You can fight anything with it." The boy folded his arms and Redwyn saw goose pimples on them.

They watched the small, white clouds come rapidly, flying low over the sea with their shadows moving as dark spots on the green water. The line of storm clouds was black at the horizon and they could see lightning flashing there with the wind blowing strong and cool from the incoming storm. But the storm was still far away and there was, yet, no thunder.

Redwyn turned his head against the wind and looked off toward the cliffs and saw the dark patches from the clouds moving steadily over the cliff face. He followed the shadows as they bent and dipped along the jagged wall. Then far off on the cliff the first of the Legion infantry came around the far turn into view.

The line of soldiers grew from around the cliff, with frequent bright flashes from what Redwyn said was probably armor or the polished heads of spears, the line growing longer, and finally the last soldiers coming around the turn and the whole infantry moving like an undulating ribbon, growing brighter as it neared, until the crimson of the uniforms was visible, and the red and silver shields.

As the soldiers descended below the bluff Redwyn and Donny turned around to watch them come back into view and ascend the twisting yellow road up to the castle. Then Redwyn said, "It's time to go." And together they moved slowly and carefully over the large rocks, with Donny looking toward the ground and frowning as they left the sea behind them.

Chapter 35
Inside the Castle

The castle's great hall had been built so that it would capture the sunlight at the end of the day and the Baron's guard could eat their dinners there. At ease from the lack of danger in their duties, they were usually friendly men, and it was a custom for them to drink ale moderately after dining until the sunlight failed and then to post their watches for the night. Now all that had changed, but it was late afternoon and the sun came through the tall windows as it was meant to, falling in long slanting rays upon the tables and scattering off their bright worn surfaces to make light patterns on the stone walls. The Robes had not been allowed a meal since the siege began, and as the two servants came in they looked about the giant emptiness of the hall until one of them gestured with his platter.

"There it is," he said. "Under the stairs."

They walked between the furniture into an alcove where a table had been prepared with eating utensils, bread, and a pitcher of ale. They set their platters down and the servant who had spotted the table first stepped back into the sunlight. He was small, standing uneasily amid the giant vacancy, and his eyes continued to search for something as he waited for his companion. He finally said, "Come out here and help me get the rest of it!"

The other man stepped out of the alcove chewing, turned halfway back and pointed to the nook. "Look at this! The hall is empty, but they want to eat beneath a stairway."

"It doesn't matter where they eat."

"But look here—"

"No I won't, you're chewing! Now help me with the rest of it."

The roundish man swallowed the evidence and went on good naturedly, "But look. This is a nice hall, and with all these tables they want one under the stairs. It's dark in there. But I suppose that Morcar likes it dark."

"Shut up, damn you! Brech will hang you by that fat tongue of yours! A fat man like you would be good sport for him!"

The heavy man blushed. "Yes? And you must be awfully afraid of him, too." He was irritated now, and turned back toward the table.

"I'm going to *eat* some more."

"No you're not! I'm not going to die because you filled your fuming guts!"

The short servant drew a cutlass halfway out of it's scabbard, and the fat man heard it coming out and looked back from the nook and smiled falsely with his big red face. "You *must* be afraid," he said, watching the sword as he turned. "I was only jesting, Philip. I only wanted my tray. You see, I left it on the table."

The short servant waited, angry and taut-faced, and kept the sword drawn until his partner had picked up the tray and stepped in front of him. Then without speaking again they both walked stiffly from the room.

A few moments later Brech pulled the tapestry aside and he and Morcar came in together and stood for a moment looking carefully over the tables, and under them, and into the shadows of the sunlit hall. When Morcar was satisfied, he gestured to the meal made ready beneath the stairs. They walked over and sat down opposite each other in the semi-darkness.

Morcar positioned himself rigidly in his chair and made one more self-assuring sweep of the surroundings. Then he picked up a lamb shank from the platter and began to eat it, turning the bone nimbly with his thin fingers, tearing strips of meat loose with his bared front teeth. Brech began carving a roasted goose. And while they ate, they both sat quietly, separate in the darkness, the only sounds the clinking of their eating utensils or the soft knocks that the ale mugs made when they set them on the heavy wood. They ate steadily for some time and then Morcar began to pause, setting his lamb shank down to squint at the sunlight that only glanced over the tables now and landed mostly on the pale stone walls. He pushed his plate aside, and his hand was trembling as he caught the ale mug and raised it to his lips. He did not drink from it, but held it quivering at his lips for a moment, then put it down.

"We're beating them!" he said.

Brech looked up with a leg of roast goose in hand. "My Lord?"

"I said we're beating them." Morcar grinned nervously, his crooked lips shiny from the mutton fat, his hand still trembling as it rested on the mug.

"We would have had it," he said. By conquest I would be the ruler of this dukedom now. These lands and vassals, wealth, properties, would be mine. I would *have* them, were it not for the Magician. I should have killed him when he was standing in my chamber. When I had the opportunity. I should have killed him, then!"

Brech said, "But it was wise not to kill him here– to preserve our secrecy."

Morcar squinted against the sunlight, then shut his eyes and turned away and rubbed them. "No, Brech. Secrecy has imperiled us. Hiding and secrecy have made us timid when we should have been bold. We should have displayed our weapons so the enemy could see them. We shall now."

"But the whole kingdom will know what has happened here," Brech said.

"And they can choose," Morcar told him. "Death, or my terms for their surrender."

Just then the two servants came back. Morcar saw them from the corner of his eye and turned in his chair. He watched their movements closely, as they came up and set the trays of fresh fruit and wine down on the table then went back to stand against the wall.

Brech reached out to the goose carcass and put his big hand over it and crushed it, the brittle rib bones snapping beneath his grip. He dug into the body cavity and pulled the liver out, brought it steaming and dark up to his mouth and held it there. He said, "Get out." And the two men started awkwardly, nearly stepping into each other as they left the confinement of the alcove and hurried across the room.

"They wanted to listen," Morcar said.

Brech's eyes shifted toward the tapestry that partitioned the corridor and great hall. He scanned the space where it hung above the floor and answered, "No one is listening now, Lord."

"You cannot be sure of that," Morcar warned him.

And Brech nodded in deference and continued to eat.

Morcar poured some wine into a silver goblet that was inscribed, TO THE BARON OF SOLWAY FROM FIVE DEVOTED SONS, leaned forward and stared sullenly into its purple depth. "Hiding and secrecy have made us timid. I could have killed him once. Be certain, there will be no second mistake..." His voice trailed off as the rays of sunlight suddenly vanished and the room fell into darkness. But a moment later the beams of light restored themselves in sequence from the long row of tall windows. Morcar settled back in his seat and said, "It was only a passing cloud."

Just then a soldier pulled the tapestry aside and came in

from the corridor, breathing hard. He said, "My Lord, one of the guards at the Lady's chamber has been killed."

They stood up from the table.

"What do you mean! Who killed him!"

"I cannot say, Lord. I was sent to tell you that he was killed inside the Lady's chamber. That is all I know."

Brech stepped around the table and shoved the guard toward the tapestry. The young man stumbled, then recovered and pulled the drape aside so that Morcar could pass. Brech took it from him and shoved him again, out into the antechamber. All three of them began walking toward Lynn's quarters.

As they neared, the light from the open chamber door was falling into the dark corridor. Morcar slowed his steps. Brech went into the chamber first. The dead guard was lying over the end of the bed, face down, with Redwyn's sword stuck vertically between his shoulder blades. His feet drooped onto the floor and blood was dripping to the floor from the fingers of his left hand. His right hand was up by his head where it had locked into a clutch hold on the bedding.

Brech put both hands around the handle of the sword, jerked it powerfully upward and pulled it free. The corpse's weight shifted and it folded into an awkward sitting position on the floor.

Morcar came in slowly and stared at the half-squatting, half-kneeling cadaver, then fixed his gaze on Lynn. She had been there all the while, but he had just now noticed her.

"Clean this up," he said. "Then come with me, Brech. I want an escort to the study."

Brech went into the corridor and brought back two guards for the removal of the corpse. As they lifted the dead man by his arms, his legs swung underneath him as if trying to walk. Morcar backed away in revulsion as the legs swayed reciprocatingly through the door.

Returning down the long, curved corridor, they remained close together until, when nearing the antechamber, Morcar went ahead into the darkness. He began to scratch upon the lock plate with his key, and Brech stepped over and pulled the tapestry aside to give him light. In the great hall Brech could see a rat rustling over the floor reeds, moving erratically toward the unfinished meal.

The study door swung open. Morcar waited for Brech to enter first, then he went in himself and closed the door and locked it with his key. The lone ray of sunlight glistened through the small window and struck Lynn's portrait. Morcar glanced at it and said, "So, Redwyn was here again. He may be somewhere in the castle."

Brech said nothing. He was looking at the sword inside his belt.

"How long before the gallows will be finished?"

"It is done, Lord."

"And the other?"

"Soon now. Very soon."

"Then all is well. I will feel better when the Noble Wench is hanged."

Chapter 36
The Architect
of Fate

When Redwyn and Donny returned, the infantry was sitting behind the hedgerow and resting from their long march. Some townsmen were carrying water buckets and sacks of bread to the soldiers to refresh them. Donny walked off. Redwyn saw the Duke coming toward him in full armor, a chain mail coat and pants, and a breastplate with his crest, and plated gauntlets. He walked heavily in the metal clothes, and Redwyn walked forward and met him.

"As soon as the men have had a rest– we are going in."

"Yes, it is best. Time gives them an advantage."

"It will not be much longer. Do you need a horse?"

"Yes," said Redwyn.

"I'll get you a good one. Is there anything else?"

"I could use another bow and sword."

"I will send them over."

"Thank you, your Grace."

The Duke nodded and walked away toward the Captain. In a few moments a squire came over with a crossbow and belted sword. He had pale blue eyes like Percy's.

"I've brought these for you, sir."

Redwyn took them and said thank you, and the squire

smiled nervously and walked back into the ranks.

The officers had begun shouting to marshal the troops. Redwyn buckled the new sword around his waist but kept the empty scabbard strapped around him too. He slung the loaded bow across his back, and the Duke came toward him on horseback leading another horse by the reins.

"This one ought to do," he said, and leaned down and handed the reins to Redwyn. It was a fine dark stallion with black hooves and a mossy iridescence in its hide.

"He's beautiful," Redwyn said, moving over to the horse's left side to mount it.

"The mare was from Alexandria, and my best stallion was his sire."

"He's strong," said Redwyn settling onto and patting the animal's withers.

"Aye, he's strong," said the Duke. "He'll last through it all. But I don't have armor for you."

"Thank you, Your Grace. This is better, I think."

"Lighter," the Duke muttered, and he gripped the reins in his metal gloves. "I have told the men to watch for those flame engines; and we'll have archers on the flanks with lighted arrows." He looked darkly at the castle. "It is still possible they have some sort of cannon, so we'll watch for that, too. How do you feel, lad?"

"I've slept, thank you, Your Grace. I feel better now."

"God save you, then, Redwyn."

The Duke turned his horse around and walked it slowly toward the Captain. The Captain was on horseback too, giving orders. The Duke and Captain talked for a moment, then both of them rode up to Redwyn and the Captain gestured forward and said, "We'll lead the charge to the drawgate. If we get close enough, perhaps our troops can raise some ladders over the moat and onto those walls. It would help if we can clear around the gate rook first; so with Your Grace's permission we shall try that before the ram goes in."

"Of course, Robert, whatever you think."

The cavalry had begun forming attack lines, and the infantry was falling into ranks behind them. There were over four-hundred, Redwyn thought, and he looked back and saw catapults being wheeled toward the flanks, men with flame pots following ready to load them. A team of soldiers manned a battering ram that was on a tall covered platform with wheels and arrow shields.

"Captain," said Redwyn. "There are oil kettles hoisted on both sides of the drawgate. I saw them there last night."

The Captain looked at him and nodded. "I suspected it. This makes it even more necessary to clear that section of wall before we move the ram in."

"Yes," said the Duke, "We get in first to stave off any surprise moves by their cavalry– then our archers can go to work on those walls. Are you ready, Robert?"

"In a moment, Your Grace. I just want to tell the sergeants about the oil."

The Duke nodded assentingly and the Captain rode off along the lines. The Duke was red-faced and sweaty and his neck looked red and tense. He whispered, "It's so damned, damned fantastic." But Redwyn heard him.

As the Captain was riding back the Duke saw him coming and wound the reins tightly around his metal gloves. "God save you, lad," he said.

"And you, Your Grace."

"God save us all," said the Duke.

The Captain aligned his horse with Redwyn's, glanced back, and lifted up his arm. The ranks made ready for the charge, the Captain waiting for them to poise themselves. Then he dropped his arm and shouted,

"Legion– forward!"

The three of them took the lead: the Captain, Redwyn, and the Duke of Cumberland. And Redwyn was pulling the crossbow from his back when he saw the drawbridge starting down. He heard the Duke shout, "Flame engines!" The

Captain nodded and then slowed up the center of the charge by raising his hand.

As the bridge landed two box-like enclosed wagons being pulled by single horses were driven across it.

"Cannons!" shouted the Duke.

The Captain slowed the center cavalry to a trot while the flanks coursed outward. There were no archers or sentinels along the castle walls, and Redwyn felt deeply sick down through his bones and into his bowels and insides.

As the wagons cleared the bridge they were pulled forward and turned so their rear doors faced the charge. Then a tall gallows on a wheeled platform was towed onto the bridge by men. Lynn was on it, tied with her arms around a heavy log that was set over what Redwyn knew must be a trap door. The noose was tight around her neck. Her face was as white as her linen dress and Brech stood beside her with his hand on a lever. Redwyn had seen them use a log in hangings before. The extra weight pulled the head off the victim and was horrible to see. The entire Duke's entire cavalry had stopped. The infantry were walking up quietly behind them, and the men had uncomprehending looks on their faces.

A moment passed in silence, then Morcar appeared, climbing over the top of one of the wagons. His face was smeared freshly orange with tannin and the hood of his robe was down. He walked on top of the wagon to the rear of it, looking hideous, then he picked up a rope that was tied to something.

The Duke advanced into the clearing in front of him, and with his horse snorting and champing skittishly shouted, "I order you to yield this castle!"

Morcar said nothing, but kicked a latch on the top of the wagon. The rear planks fell down with a loud "crack!" and the screeching of a thousand rats carried over the silent field. The Duke's horse reared. The rats were piled five feet deep in the wagon, writhing and screeching shrilly, and those against the mesh door were gnawing to get out. It was clear that Morcar held the rope that would raise the door and release them. A deep tremor of laughter travelled through the ranks.

The wind had been calm, but suddenly dust swirled up over the heads of the soldiers. And as Morcar rattled the door he cried, "I shall yield? No, Your Grace, it is *you* who will!"

The clouds were coming fast and dark across the sky, bringing the storm nearer. Faint rumblings of thunder quaked in the distance.

The Duke shouted, "Traitorous eel! I'll have your hide stretched on a dung heap for this!" A sudden gust lashed against Morcar and pressed his robe against his sickly thin legs.

"If you move against me– if even one man moves against me– I shall pull this rope and set the Black Plague loose upon your dukedom!"

Laughter broke through the ranks again, but it was short lived. Morcar waved violently, and the Robe standing on top of the other wagon kicked its door down. Inside this second wagon two men and a woman had been hung upon vertical posts. They were naked, all three grotesquely disfigured by the plague that had killed them. The soldiers shuffled back in a unified reflex of revulsion. Redwyn thought that Morcar must have selected these from all the hideous gallery of the dungeon for the unmistakable panic that their blue and frozen faces portrayed.

Thunder had stopped rumbling for a moment, and the low sky boiled with a tint of green.

"Yield!" Morcar's voice echoed along the walls of the parapet. The Captain's face had turned pale and almost expressionless. Morcar pulled the rope– as the mesh door rose slightly the screeching of the rats increased.

"It is the only course," the Captain whispered.

The Duke, sitting rigidly, working his jaw and metal fists,

suddenly grunted and threw his sword to the ground. "Treasonous filth," he bellowed. "Damn your rotting hide!"

The Captain immediately dropped his sword, and Redwyn heard the sound of other weapons hitting the ground behind him.

Morcar stood up straighter atop the wagon as the legion disarmed. The Duke of Cumberland dismounted. The Captain and the rest of his cavalry followed. Then Redwyn alone was conspicuously higher, still sitting on his horse.

"Now you, Magician. Or the noble slut dies."

Just then there was a motion in the ranks and Redwyn twisted around and saw Donny Gwaith moving toward him through a labyrinth of the Duke's men. Redwyn frowned and turned back. The Duke had been watching Redwyn, the green eyes in The Duke's crimson face searching for the faintest prospect of hope.

"Throw down your sword!" came Morcar's shriek.

Redwyn took the sword from its scabbard and displayed it across his hands. "This is not my sword," he said, turning aside and dropping it. "There!" He pointed to Brech. "Mine is in that awful fellow's belt. I think he has a habit of taking my things, and I would like that weapon returned to me."

Morcar panted, "Would you?"

Redwyn said, "Yes. My sword has no place tied to a sack of bloated guts. Look at him! I am sure the swine would not know which end to hold."

Brech's hand flinched on the gallows' lever, and the Duke whispered, "Christ, lad!"

"Watch yourself," uttered the Captain.

Morcar stared icily with the taut rope in his hand. His gaunt face twitched into a grin, and then he laughed, a wheezy high pitched rale. The Duke muttered something in relief.

"You are a fool, Magician. Your Lady is on a gallows with a rope around her neck; this swaggering Duke stands defeated; and you, dull lad, are left with death. So choose. Will you destroy the dukedom and your Lady as well? Or do you yield to me your life?"

Redwyn looked across the space that separated them. He said, "After knowing you, Morcar, the worms that rot a man's flesh would seem good company."

"Aye, lad!" the Duke shouted out, "no worm would suffer his unnatural hide!"

Then Redwyn dismounted. And the Duke's squire came forward and led his horse away.

"Kill him, Brech. Return the Magician's wondrous sword."

And at the command the huge man began climbing sloth-like down the gallows. He set one foot upon the earth, then the other, then turned around slowly and straightened his clothes.

"Quickly! Quickly!" Morcar squealed, glancing back. "What are you waiting for!"

Redwyn lowered himself onto one knee and bowed his head.

Thunder rumbled in and growled along the castle walls. Brech was not eight feet away when Redwyn looked up and saw the fear, unexpected, like an odd misshapen mask that hung upon the giant's face. But Redwyn bowed his head again, and Brech moved over him with the sword.

Morcar's voice came through the quiet and said:

"You die well, Magician."

And as Brech looked down at the back of his victim's neck, pale and contoured, with long tresses of blonde hair parting over it, he felt the sword-handle heating in his grasp. He brought it up slowly and looked at it, turning its blade, as the fear drained out of him and a sudden strength coursed into his arms. Morcar was laughing. Donny moved into the clearing, tried in vain to cry out, then started searching desperately over the array of abandoned weapons. Soft thunder rumbled over. Brech stepped to one side. He covered the sword handle with both hands and raised it above his head.

A bolt of lightning flashed and he paused, the sword raised, as if waiting for the blast of thunder with which to deliver his fatal blow. And in that pause of death Donny Gwaith had found what he was looking for. Almost unnoticed now he stepped in front of the ranks, raised the crossbow awkwardly to his chest, and put an arrow into the poised executioner's huge and murderous heart.

Chapter 37
The Silence
of God

For a moment there was no motion at all except for Morcar's wagon pulling away, Brech falling over, and then Redwyn prying the sword loose from the goliath's clenched hand. The long awaited thunder clap arrived, shocking the still air asunder. The Duke, as if awakened from disbelief, shook his fist and yelled, "Burn those bloody carcasses! Now!"

And the legion clamored forward.

Redwyn was already up on a horse, and he turned it in time to see Morcar's wagon going out of sight behind the wall. He looked to Lynn, saw the Captain beside her with a sword in his hand, saw the Captain cutting the rope above her head– the loose end falling limp across her breast. Then Redwyn wheeled the horse around and kicked it into a gallup along the moat.

The horse's gait was smooth, and he went forward and caught its mane and brought his knees up and leaned into the right turn. As the outer wall cleared he could see the wagon Morcar was driving on the little stretch of road beside the ruins, the wheel dust flying sideways in the wind. Redwyn cut diagonally across the field and came up behind him, the wagon rocking over the road and Morcar looking back with the mesh door buckling as the rats flew up against it.

"Damn you– don't look back!" he muttered. And as his words escaped, the wagon leaned over sideways, up on two wheels, then came back rockingly to earth. Redwyn's heart jumped. It was then he saw that there was no place for the Head Robe to go. The little road they were on ended at a bluff that fell steeply into a field of boulders some several hundred feet below. To the right there were the ruins, and to the left there was the equally impassable hedge.

The horse pulling the wagon bucked twice as Morcar drew reins violently, to stop about twenty yards short of the cliff edge. He threw the reins aside and came over the wagon top, fell, and crawled forward until he had the latch rope in his hand.

"I've still won, Magician!" he screamed.

Redwyn countered, "No!" trotting his horse up within ten yards and stopping. "If you loose the rats you haven't won!"

Morcar rose upon his knees and said, "What victory could be greater! The rats will carry the seeds of plague over roads and fields, onto ships and even across the seas, until the stench of death reeks!– reeks in every nostril!"

Redwyn said, "Victory is always measured by the strength of the enemy. How much greater your triumph, if only you knew who I am."

"You're nothing!" Morcar spat in contempt.

Redwyn dismounted, clawing desperately for words. All else failing he raised his right hand in a flourish and cried, "I am a Magician! My skills were taught me by a sorcerer, a wizard all powerful and known to all!" Morcar blinked at him in disbelief. "It was in Edinburgh we met. I was an infant. He found me in a basket beneath a burning wall. There was plague in the city. Think, Morcar! There was plague! The sorcerer found me in a basket– covered in a bloody red stain."

There was a long silence. Then as the Head Robe stood

from his knees, transfixed, the latch rope dropped onto the wagon's roof.

Without moving his body Redwyn reached the crossbow hung by a leather strap upon the saddle horn. He held it out of Morcar's view behind the horse.

"You remember, Morcar! My name is Redwyn– I want you to remember– Redwyn!"

As if in a trance, the Head Robe pointed and his lips moved silently to form three words. Redwyn jerked up the crossbow and rested it on the saddle. It was as if Morcar had not even seen him. He stood there, frozen in the certainty of his own death. And for the rest of his life Redwyn would ask himself whether, at that moment, he had hesitated. He would remember seeing Morcar's body divided by the vertical quill of the arrow he sighted over– remember the trigger's polished bone smoothness against his fingertip– And then the brilliant flash, and a thunder clap that felt like a tremor in the ground, his horse pulling away, the crossbow jerking loose from his hand and still dangling by it's strap from the saddle horn, flopping unfired as the horse ran.

Morcar rocked unsteadily on the wagon top then slipped onto his back. Another blast of thunder and the wagon's horse jumped again and started running toward the bluff– Redwyn limping after it– Morcar on his back with his arms spread, flopping, and the wagon bumping steadily away.

At the bluff's edge the wagon's horse started to buck. The harness tongue snapped and the horse pulled the straps loose and bolted, bucking all along the cliff edge. Redwyn took another step and halted. He watched the wagon roll a few more feet down the grassy incline, dip forward and then vanish over the cliff, a thin scream lingering behind.

Chapter 38
Among the Ruins

He walked to the bluff's edge and looked below to the smashed planks and the Head Robe's lifeless body spread almost angelically upon the ground. The rats were strewn downward from the first large boulder the wagon had struck, and they lay in black streaks upon the hillside. He could see no motion among them but he thought it was possible that some of them had survived.

It started to rain as he walked back up the road along the ruins. Then with sudden hail falling he climbed over the tumbled blocks of granite and sought shelter beneath an ancient arch, that stood, yet as a passage to nowhere.

From the vantage of the hill he could see down into the castle's courtyard. The Duke's men had encircled the large black mass of the Robes. The fighting was over.

Redwyn took the sword from its scabbard and pushed its point absently into a crack in a granite block. He felt hollowed out inside, as if there were not enough left of him to create even tears. But his face was still wet from the rain, and for that he felt in some way grateful.

"Redwyn," the voice from behind him said.

He turned and, half expecting it, saw Nelrum standing on

the rubble above him, his grey robe only spattered from the rain. The old man descended over the blocks of a fallen wall and stepped in to stand under the arch.

"You are scarcely wet," Redwyn said.

"There is still a portion of roof left in the old castle. I was under it."

"Watching?"

"Yes."

"Then you saw." Redwyn leaned the sword against the inside of the arch and turned away. Down at the castle small parties of Robes were being ushered from the towers and brought to stand out in the courtyard in the rain.

"How are your wounds, my son?"

"Those to my body will heal, old man. But I have others."

"Tell me."

"Tell you!" Redwyn turned and saw, as he had anticipated, that the sword was now in the cloth belt of Nelrum's robe. "You knew it before I did. Treason you called it– to tear at a man's innocence with horror and put outrage where innocence belonged. You knew I wouldn't listen."

"I told you something else. That man is past the time when he could live as a moral race. That there are no victories in this world. Only–"

"Yes," said Redwyn, interrupting. "Only the truths we live by– and what are these truths without the fundamental one, the truth of the Druids. The Plombe Hortre. The thing you have taken from me."

"Have I taken something?"

"It is gone and I am desolation inside, Nelrum. The voice of my childhood is mute forever in my mind."

"So I have taken your innocence."

"You have shown me the horror and today I learned of the utter uselessness of fighting it. You knew I would. You have taken the only refuge that any man has."

"Then innocence is the truth you would live by?"

"It is the absence of evil."

"Then perhaps, Redwyn, I have given you the one chance you otherwise would not have had. That night in Grinmere I never told you what the third and most absolute truth is: That in order to achieve innocence you must first lose it. The ignorance of the child cannot last. And true innocence is a choice– to live, in spite of the painful costs, in a state of personal salvation."

Redwyn stared at him numbly; for all his gratitude and regrets there was not a thing he could say. He just unbuckled the scabbard, and Nelrum took it and stepped into the rain.

"Merlin!" he shouted after him.

And the old man turned and regarded him with his sad blue eyes.

"Will I see you again?"

"Perhaps," he answered patiently from the rain.

"There is one other thing I would ask: How does one find it again– once it has been lost?"

"My young companion. The only road to innocence is courage."

Then Nelrum nodded goodbye. Redwyn watched him go down the hill, watched him grow distant on the highland road and then begin his descent into Grinmere. And with the rain falling harder his grey robes vanished into dusk.

The End.

Epilogue

Lynn was sleeping, breathing lightly. The chamber was dark except for the faint blue cast of moonlight that entered through the open doorway. A breeze came through and made the big door sway. He rose carefully from the bed and walked toward the moonlight and through the open door and onto the balcony that overlooked the Grand Canal of Venice. Beneath the moon, the canal looked like a river of blue light.

A falling star streaked across the September sky, arced in its trajectory, then steeply arced and fell into the darkness beyond. He felt Lynn's breath caressingly upon his back, her bare nipples, and her whole body warm and moist from the bed. Her arms came around his sides and her hands locked just below his chest. She whispered, "Why are you here, My Love?"

Redwyn put one hand on her arm and was silent for a long time as he studied the sky.

"I was just saying good-bye," he said, "To an old friend."

Child,
You who even the restless ages could not still
though time has edged you from the precipice of life
and cast thy frailty into the timeless sea
the tide will surge and then recede
and you will emerge,
a new and greater man.